The SUMMER of BROKEN RULES

ALSO BY K. L. WALTHER

If We Were Us

The SUMMER *of* BROKEN RULES

K. L. WALTHER

sourcebooks
fire

Published by Sourcebooks Fire, an imprint of Sourcebooks
P.O. Box 4410, Naperville, Illinois 60567-4410
(630) 961-3900
sourcebooks.com

Library of Congress Cataloging-in-Publication data is on file with the publisher.

Printed and bound in the United States of America.
SB 26

Always, for Dad. Thank you for the Dave Matthews–fueled drives, cups of chowder, and introducing us to the most wondrous place on the planet.

And to Trip, for the twilight tractor rides, tubing wipeouts, nine o'clock steak dinners, and for being his best friend.

THE FOX FAMILY

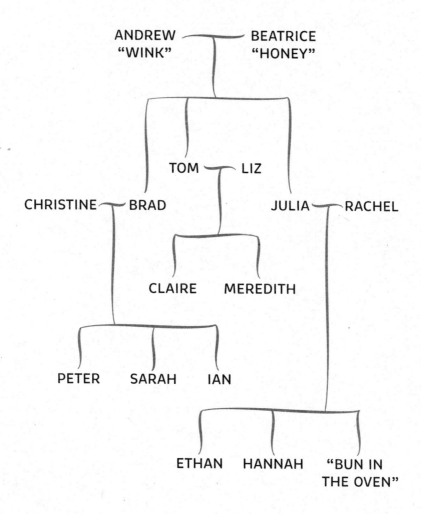

SUNDAY

ONE

Nobody ordered the fries. Three cups of creamy clam chowder, but no basket of the most addictive fries on Cape Cod. "Anything else?" our server asked, as if he knew something was missing. Maybe he did. Maybe he somehow recognized us—it was tradition for our family to grab lunch at Quicks Hole before boarding the ferry to celebrate the last leg of our journey. Only one more hour, and then we'd finally be on Martha's Vineyard.

I caught my parents exchanging a glance. *Anything else?* After so many summers, everything was second nature—we didn't need menus. Our orders were ingrained in the deep depths of our minds, and none of them included fries for the table.

Because it was Claire who always took care of them for us. *In the biggest basket you have*, she'd say. *We're starving!*

Now I realized it was my responsibility to take over the duty. "Actually, yeah," I said, swallowing the lump in my throat. "Some fries, please. Truffle fries."

"Great choice." Our server nodded and turned toward the

kitchen. My parents and I sat at our high-top in silence, all trying not to stare at the table's fourth chair. Consciously or unconsciously, my mom had slung her purse over the back so it would look less empty. Like the person sitting there had gotten up to go to the bathroom and would be right back.

Quicks Hole Tavern was aptly named. It only took fifteen minutes for us to get our food: three steaming cups of New England's magical concoction and a seemingly bottomless bowl of French fries dusted with parmesan cheese and parsley. Dad raised his beer as I shook the requisite five dashes of Tabasco into my soup. "To Sarah and Michael," he said. "May this week be one to remember."

"To Sarah and Michael," Mom and I echoed, raising our own glasses.

We clinked.

"And to our grand return," he added, kissing Mom on the cheek. "It's been too long."

Two years to be exact. My family had been vacationing on the Vineyard since before I was born—over eighteen years—but we'd spent last summer hidden away at home in upstate New York. I stole a glance at the empty chair again.

Yes, I thought. *It's been too long.*

And then I stirred my spoon around in my soup, watching the red hot sauce swirl until it disappeared, and wondered if anything had changed while we'd been gone.

One thing that definitely hadn't changed was Falmouth's Steamship Authority. As the sun shone high in the blue July sky, it was like people were waiting in line for the biggest concert of the century. Cars, cars, and even *more* cars had their tickets confirmed and parked in numbered lanes to wait for their respective boats. I pulled my honey-colored hair into a loose braid as my parents and I weaved our way through them. There were a colorful assortment of Jeep Wranglers, mostly roofless and a few also doorless, with music pulsing through their speakers. Then we had the Volvos with kayaks strapped on top and the sleek silver Range Rovers. Bike racks made the giant SUVs look even more massive. I overheard one toddler having a meltdown. "No, Jeffrey, you cannot have more chips!" his exasperated mother said. The walk-on line was a motley mix of college students, families, dogs, bikes, rolling luggage, and well-traveled older couples calmly absorbing all the chaos.

Loki was panting heavily with his head out the window when we made it back to our Ford Raptor truck. "You want to give him some water, Meredith?" Mom asked after we'd settled in our seats. I didn't answer, grabbing my water bottle and squeezing it so our Jack Russell terrier could drink. He gulped it down like a human, a trick Claire had taught him when he was a puppy. "It'll be useful," she'd said. "We won't have to bring a water bowl when we take him on walks."

It wasn't much longer before the Steamship Authority began loading the hulking 2:00 p.m. ferry, *The Island Home*. "Wait, open the sunroof!" I blurted as the attendant waved our car onto the boat and Dad eased on the gas. My pulse pounded. It was another one of Claire's and my traditions, one I wanted to keep alive: popping up through the sunroof and cheering like we were riding around in a limo. Most years, people cheered back, especially the guys in the Wranglers. "You're so hot!" a few of them had shouted on our last trip. Claire seventeen, me sixteen.

"Too bad she's taken!" my sister had shouted back, assuming he meant me and not her. She subtly put herself down a lot, and I'd never understood why. Claire was beautiful, tall and athletic with auburn curls, not to mention the coolest collection of eyeglasses. She couldn't wear contacts, so she had amassed an eclectic array of specs, everything from retro to modern. She'd been wearing the square-shaped ones with the clear frames that day.

The only thing that made us look like sisters was our green eyes, since I had light hair and dark eyebrows ("striking," according to most people) and was a good five inches shorter than Claire. "Monkey Meredith," she'd called me after catching me scaling our pantry shelves when we were younger.

Now, as we drove up the ferry ramp, I didn't cheer (the Jeep guys still did). Instead, I closed my eyes and took a deep breath. The sea air—I loved that smell. I'd *missed* that smell. It was everything. My family used to joke that we should bottle the scent to give us hope during New York's bitter-cold winters.

My parents unbuckled their seat belts once Dad put the car in park. Loki barked and sprang over the center console onto

Mom's lap. She laughed and clipped his leash onto his green collar. "Well, that's the signal," she said. "Let's head up."

"Up" meant the ferry's top deck. Of course you could stay in your car, and there was also plenty of indoor seating. But just like the sea air, there was nothing like the wind whipping through your hair as the island came into view.

"Sounds good..." I trailed off when something caught my eye. My phone, suddenly beaming and buzzing obnoxiously in the back seat's cup holder. The name on the screen was obnoxious too: Ben Fletcher.

My stomach twisted into knots. Ben had texted me.

"Um, you go ahead," I heard myself say, staring at his name. It blurred a little, my eyes pooling. "I'll be there in a minute."

I didn't read Ben's message until Dad handed me the keys and he, Mom, and Loki disappeared into the stairwell. Then I swiped into my phone to see: How's the drive going?

That was it. Not a hello or an apology or a change of heart. Not that I wanted one, but still.

How's the drive going?

Really? Just that?

Don't respond, the voice in the back of my head said, but I ignored it, typing back: The drive's over. We're on the ferry now.

Ah, gotcha, he wrote. How long is the ride?

"An hour," I mumbled to myself. I'd mentioned it a hundred times, so excited after receiving the invitation back in April. MISS MEREDITH FOX written in silver script on a light blue envelope. "The RSVP card asks if I'm bringing a date," I'd told Ben later, cocooned in his arms while we watched Netflix. "Will you be my plus-one?"

"Your plus-one?" he'd asked, breaking into a grin. "Of course!" We kissed.

I didn't blink away my tears when they fell. If only months-ago Meredith could see me now—on my way to Sarah's wedding not only *dateless* but more generally *boyfriendless*. Because after four years together, Ben and I had broken up.

Well, *he* had broken up with *me*. Last month, out of nowhere at his graduation party. One second, we were dancing to his dad's hilarious Woodstock playlist, and the next, he tugged me off the floor and started saying stuff like, "It's been a good run... but being friends might be better...from what they say about long distance..."

"But we agreed," I cut him off. "We talked about it, remember?" I latched on to his strong arm, suddenly dizzy. "And we said that we're going to *try*." Ben was going to the University of South Carolina in the fall, while I was staying in town, only moving up Clinton's big hill to Hamilton College. My dad was their soccer coach, and I wanted to be close to home. "Remember?"

Ben didn't say anything.

My grip tightened. "Don't, Ben." I couldn't keep my voice from wavering. "Please, I need you. You know how much I need you. After everything..."

"I know, I know." Ben pulled me into a hug, headfirst

into his chest. Which was usually comforting, but now it felt like he was trying to shush me. "Look, I do love you, Mer," he whispered, letting me collapse against him and cry. His heartbeat muffled most of his words and made me dissolve into more sobs. It was only the last part that gave me the strength to stand. "I'll still come to the wedding, though," he said. "If you want."

"What?" I stepped back, shivering in the chilly night air. "As my date?"

"Yeah." He reached out to squeeze my shoulder. "This doesn't change anything." He half smiled and recited the old-fashioned-sounding line he knew I loved: "You're still my favorite girl to have on my arm."

Now, I couldn't remember how I'd responded, but it definitely had ended with me making a run for it in my sky-high wedges. And okay, maybe it had also involved me getting stopped by the police on the way home. For speeding? Or swerving? I'd barely been able to talk through my tears, so Officer Woodley had let me off with a warning (and followed me home).

A beeping noise came over the ferry's intercom. *Time to go,* I thought, but I felt another buzz in my hand—a third text from Ben: Mer, I really would've come with you this week.

Before I knew it, my cheeks had flared and I'd dialed his number.

He answered on the first ring. "Hey—"

"I didn't *want* you to come," I cut in, on the verge of

crying. "I wanted my boyfriend—my *boyfriend*—to come, not my shithead ex!"

Silence.

Ben sighed. "Mer..."

I hung up and wiped away my tears, needing to get out of the car and into the fresh air. The ferry horn sounded as I reached for my door handle, but by now, the boat's huge hold was completely full, cars packed so tightly together that it was impossible to open the door without slamming it into the car next to me. *The sunroof*, I realized. It was still open; I tried not to think about how many people had overheard me yelling at Ben. My face was blotchy from crying, so I dug around in my backpack for my sunglasses and slipped them on along with one of my dad's baseball caps before shimmying up and out of the truck. I smiled a little.

No problem.

Then disaster struck.

Instead of jumping to the ground, I grabbed for one of the roof rack's rungs...but didn't double-check the narrow aisle between the cars to make sure it was clear. I just swung myself down jungle-style, shock waves going through me when my foot collided with something.

And by *something*, I meant *someone*.

"Oh, whoa," the guy said, caught off guard. His shoulders hunched, and I watched him press a hand to where I'd kicked him. His face, somewhere near his nose. "Ouch!"

"Sorry!" I blurted. "I'm so sorry. Really, really sorry!"

"No," he replied. "It's, uh, fine."

But before he could straighten up and properly look at the person who'd assaulted him, I was gone. Sprinting away toward the stairs and taking them two at a time to the top deck.

My mom put her arm around me when the island came into view. It truly was a beautiful day, not a cloud in the sky. No fog surrounded the East Chop lighthouse or the boats bobbing along in Vineyard Haven's harbor. "What a welcome!" Dad remarked, and suddenly I was misty-eyed, thinking of Claire. Half of me was so happy to be back, but the other half wanted the ferry to turn around and take me home. It didn't feel right being on the Vineyard without my sister. She'd loved it most of all. *It's been too long*, my dad had said at lunch, but now I also couldn't help asking myself, *Has it been long* enough?

"I wish Claire were here," I whispered to my mom.

"She is," Mom whispered back, giving my shoulders a warm squeeze. Then she gestured to the sky. "She's making the sun shine."

"For Sarah," I said.

"No." She shook her head. "For everyone."

TWO

My cousin was getting married. Sarah Jane Fox and Michael Phillipe Dupré, set to wed on Saturday, the sixteenth of July, at four o'clock in the afternoon at St. Andrew's Church in Edgartown. Dinner and dancing to follow at Paqua Farm.

Paqua Farm, or The Farm, as we called it, had been in the Fox family since before World War I. It was no longer a working farm but a sprawling six-hundred acres between Edgartown and Tisbury with a mile of private beach. For hours, we would get bounced around by the ocean waves and then blissfully float in the Vineyard's famous lakes and ponds. Claire's and my favorite had always been the secluded Paqua Pond.

I hugged a wriggling Loki close as Dad sped up Paqua's three-mile sandy dirt road, leaving dust in our wake. "Dad, slower," I said from the back seat, but he was too busy laughing. The road's unofficial speed limit was twenty-five miles per hour, but everyone loved bending that rule. "We raced back in the day," Uncle Brad would sometimes say, clapping my dad on the shoulder. "Oh, how we *flew*."

It used to be fun, breaking the rules. But now my gut was twisting, and I leaned forward to see the speedometer: a little under fifty. "Please, Dad!" I repeated, shrilly this time. My heart pounded. "Slow down!"

Mom put a hand on my dad's arm. "Tom," she said quietly.

My stomach settled when he hit the brakes, the speedometer immediately dropping to twenty. Soon we reached the fork in the road, where a tall wooden sign steadfastly stood year after year. It finally had a fresh white paint job—definitely Aunt Christine's doing—and pointed out the direction of each summer house. There were eight of them scattered across The Farm, no two alike. Some were bigger, some smaller, all rustic with their own names and character. Most of the wedding guests were staying out here, so I knew every house would be filled to capacity—maybe more, as Uncle Brad had told my dad about some people pitching tents.

Dad veered left, and a few minutes later, the Raptor's wheels crunched onto the Annex's gravel driveway. Well, parking spot. The rest of the houses had driveways, but the Annex just had a parking spot. It was a cottage, only one story and cedar-sided with a pitched roof, and it was considered ours whenever we were on the Vineyard. We usually rented it for three weeks, and the rest of the summer it saw a series of extended family and friends. Two green Adirondack chairs sat on the tiny weathered deck, overlooking the big green field speckled with yellow flowers. The tall grass and scrub trees swayed in the breeze, and in the distance, I could hear the ocean washing up on the beach.

We're here, I thought, suddenly wanting to break into a dance. *We're here, we're here, we're here!*

Through the screen door was the sitting room with a braided rug covering the worn oak floor and a faded green-and-white-striped love seat facing the small TV positioned in between the two front windows. Books upon books had been crammed into both bookcases, and photographs covered the beadboard walls, including some really old black-and-white ones. Decades and decades of Foxes and our friends.

The tight hallway was flanked by the galley kitchen on one end and my parents' room on the other. Straight ahead was Claire's and my room, the bunk room that was roughly the size of a ship's sleeping quarters. So many nights, Claire had accidentally woken me by rolling over and bronco-kicking the wall. *Sorry, Mer*, she'd say in a sleep-slurred voice.

I bit my lip and pushed open our bedroom door to see that nothing was out of place, that nothing had changed. There was the light blue dresser with the sea glass-and-wampum framed mirror above it, along with the Paqua map my sister and I had drawn when we were younger. After so many scavenger hunts and games of manhunt, the two of us had learned every inch of The Farm.

A white wicker nightstand stood next to the bunk beds, matching their white coverlets. Claire was afraid of heights, so she always slept on the bottom with me on top. The ladder had broken long ago and was never replaced, but I had a special talent for scrambling up the side.

After unpacking my duffel and hanging up my dress for the wedding, safe in a garment bag, I heard the Annex's door swing open and shut. "Anyone home?"

Mom and Dad were outside, unloading the last of our stuff from the car, but I called back a hello and bounded into the sitting room...only to trip over the rug once I got there. My heart stopped when I saw Claire standing there and smiling at me.

But no—no, it wasn't Claire.

The corners of my eyes started to sting as my cousin said my name. Because while Claire and I looked nothing alike, she and Sarah were nearly identical twins. The same cascading auburn hair and slenderness, the same love of being barefoot, even the same tilt of the head when they smiled. It was only when I noticed the pink-and-green Lilly Pulitzer shift dress and pearl earrings that I really relaxed. Sarah—this was *Sarah*.

"Hi," I said, my voice wavering a little. But I surged forward and let the bride hug me tight. It had been so long since I'd seen her, months and months. Uncle Brad, Aunt Christine, Sarah, and her brothers were from Maryland and spent every summer on the Vineyard, living in Lantern House. If you looked up "preppy" in an encyclopedia, their family Christmas card would be right beside it.

Now Sarah was twenty-six, and after graduating from Tulane a few years ago, she worked for New Orleans's preservation society. "How're things?" she asked after pulling away, giving me a look through her horn-rimmed glasses. Like Claire, Sarah loved interesting glasses. But this pair was a little too big.

I watched her push them up her nose, which drew attention to the sharp scar across her forehead, running from her hairline all the way down past her right temple. Straight and thin for the most part, but with one jagged zigzag above her left eyebrow. From the shattered glass, from that awful night two winters ago.

I blinked. "How are you doing?" she asked again.

Ben. I knew she was talking about Ben. Because without Claire's shoulder to cry on, I'd called Sarah the morning after his grad party. "He—said—he—would—still—come," I hiccuped over the line. "If—I—wanted—him—to."

"Wait, what?" she said. "He said *what* now? That he was ending things but still wanted to *come*?"

"Uh-huh."

"Oh, jeez, Mer," Sarah sighed. "I'm sorry. What a dick. Please tell me you said no."

"But I said I was bringing a date," I blubbered. "On your invitation. I told you I had a plus-one. I need a plus-one."

"No, you don't," Sarah said. "You absolutely don't. One uneaten fillet—or whatever he requested—isn't going to make or break the wedding."

Now, I gave my cousin a smirk. "Well, he texted me earlier," I said, folding my arms over my chest. "And I straight-up called him a shithead."

Sarah gasped. "You didn't."

I grinned. "I did."

I'd been crying at the time, but technically I had.

"Yes!" She grinned back. "Go, Mer! Assert yourself!"

My smile slipped.

Assert yourself.

Claire had loved that phrase. "I know I'm on the sidelines here," I remembered her once saying, "but it seems like you need to stand up to Ben more." She shrugged. "If you don't want to go to the party, tell him that. Assert yourself."

It was always about Ben, I was beginning to realize. Our relationship was uneven—never about me. Everything revolved around him.

Claire had seen it, but I hadn't listened. *She doesn't have a boyfriend; she's never had a boyfriend,* I'd tell myself as I pulled on jeans and cute tops and curled my hair and applied eyeliner. *She doesn't get it. She's wrong.*

"Sarah!" My parents appeared in the sitting room. The cozy space was now even cozier with four of us in it. The most people we'd ever squeezed in here was ten. "We thought we heard your voice!"

"Aunt Liz!" Sarah gave them both hugs. "Uncle Tom! Welcome!"

"You look beautiful," my mom said as I noticed her eyes land on Sarah's scar. My heart dipped. Part of me suspected she couldn't really tell how well it had healed, instead still seeing all the stitches. Neat and clean but also grisly and brutal. I hadn't seen them in person like my parents, only in pictures...but there had been so many. I worried my mom would always be haunted by them. "You're radiating that bride-to-be glow!"

Sarah smiled. "I just came by to say hello," she said, then

turned to my dad. "And to tell you that the outhouse is *fully* stocked."

"Charmin?" my dad asked.

She nodded seriously. "Of course."

Everyone chuckled. Another one of the Annex's quirks was that it had no bathroom. All the houses on The Farm had outdoor showers—heavenly after a long day on the beach—but our cottage had no bathroom, *period*. You had to follow a well-worn dirt trail several yards into the woods, where a tall wooden structure waited at the end. A quest that was especially daunting in the middle of the night.

"Well!" I jokingly clapped my hands together and started backing toward the screen door. I wanted to hear my mom laugh again. "On that note, if you'll excuse me a moment..."

Sarah told us there was a cookout planned for that night to officially welcome everyone, but once she left, I dug one of the beach cruisers out of the Annex's storage shed, pumped air into its tires, and pedaled off to do some casual recon. Just down the road was the Cabin, covered in rust-colored wooden siding and built like an old motel: T-shaped, with each bedroom door leading out onto the front porch. I slowed a little when I saw a few cars parked haphazardly at the side of the house, their trunks still popped open, along with a handful of guys sitting around the front yard's huge firepit. Michael's groomsmen.

I spotted the groom among them, a can of beer resting on his knee as he used his arms to reenact some story for everyone. Even from afar, it was impossible to ignore how handsome Michael was: built like a quarterback with deep bronze skin, dark hair that Sarah was always running her hands through, and the smoothest Southern accent. He and my cousin had met at Tulane, but Michael had lived in New Orleans his whole life. His family had Creole roots, French and African ancestry. A die-hard football fan, Michael now worked in the Saints' front office.

Michael spotted me, too, and raised his hand in a wave, but right then, a guy burst out the Cabin's main door. "Why isn't there more ice in the freezer?" he asked as everyone turned. "His face is getting worse—seriously a *mess*. Looks like he went a couple rounds in the ring..."

Well, good luck with that, I thought, whatever it was. I'd talk to Michael tonight. I gripped my handlebars and resumed pedaling, upping my speed and then coasting until I turned onto the road that led straight to the Big House.

The Big House was not Paqua's largest house, but it was the oldest. A Victorian farmhouse with cedar shingles and faded green shutters, it was the only house that wasn't rented each summer, since Wink and Honey—my grandparents— lived there full-time.

Now they were on the Big House's slightly sagging front porch, Honey serenely swinging in the hammock and Wink leaning against one of the columns, tracking me through his ancient binoculars. "For bird-watching," he always said, but I knew my grandfather liked keeping an eye on Farm activity. The Big House's porch was the perfect spy base. It wrapped around the entire house, so you could see *everything*.

"Anything good happening?" I asked after hitting my kickstand.

"Julia and Rachel just arrived at the Camp," Wink replied, still scanning the horizon. "It appears Ethan is having a tantrum, and Hannah must really be enjoying her ballet class. She's wearing a pink tutu."

I laughed. Aunt Julia was my dad's younger sister. She and her wife, Rachel, had two kids: six-year-old Ethan and four-year-old Hannah. Aunt Rachel was very pregnant with their third child, a boy. She was due sometime next month.

"Come sit by me, sweetie," Honey said and patted the spot next to her in the hammock. She put her arm around me once I was all settled in, her lavender scent so familiar. I thought my grandmother was one of the most beautiful women in the world with her long white hair, blue eyes, light linen tunics, and chunky necklaces to add "pops of color." She designed and beaded them herself, and they were always in high demand at jewelry stores around the island.

"It seems like everyone's here," I commented. "I passed Michael and his groomsmen outside the Cabin."

Wink put down his binoculars. "Yes, he stopped by earlier to promise they wouldn't trash the place."

Honey laughed. "I do so adore that boy."

I smiled. My grandmother's crush on Michael was no secret. "Where's his family staying?"

"Christine assigned them Moor House," Wink said, gesturing to the hill in the distance. "It's on the Excel spreadsheet." He grumbled a little. "Honestly, you'd think this was *her* wedding."

"Oh, now, now." Honey rolled her eyes. "That's not fair, Andrew. Sarah's her only daughter, and we know how Christine is."

I nodded, picturing the wedding invitation, right down to the little lighthouse embossed on the envelope flap. That detail was unmistakably Aunt Christine's touch. "She might be wound a little too tightly," my mom had admitted, "but she has impeccable taste."

"At least Sarah put her foot down about it being black-tie," Wink said. "Black-tie outside in July?" He shook his head. "I've done it too many times, and it's not fun."

"Though I'm sure Michael looks gorgeous in a tux," Honey said dreamily.

"Then why don't you marry him, Bea?" Wink asked, and when he winked at me, I giggled. That's why he was "Wink" to us grandchildren.

"Sarah did say she had a surprise, though," I said. "Back at the Annex, she said she and Michael were announcing something tonight."

My grandparents exchanged a look.

"You already know," I guessed. "You already know what it is."

"Perhaps." The corner of Wink's mouth tugged up slyly. "Perhaps we do."

"Tell me!"

His smile widened.

I groaned and buried my face in Honey's shoulder, and a second later, I felt her kiss the top of my head.

"We're so happy to see you, Meredith," she whispered. "So, so happy."

I had plenty of cousins on The Farm, but there were also close family friends in the mix. Eli, Jake, Luli, and Pravika were practically family. They were already at Lantern House when my parents and I arrived for the cookout, sitting together at the picnic table under the big oak tree. "There's the crew," Mom said as my heart hesitated, giving me a little push toward them. Two years—I hadn't seen my friends in almost two years, and it would be different now without Claire. She'd been the oldest, our unspoken captain.

"Meredith!" Pravika called. "Meredith!"

Okay, here we go, I thought, seeing the others' heads turn and their eyes find me. A shiver of shyness ran up my spine. I'd been terrible about keeping in touch, barely reaching out or responding to their texts, calls, Snapchats, or FaceTime requests.

Pravika pulled me into her arms first, squeezing me so tightly that I worried my lungs would collapse. "I'm sorry, I'm sorry, I'm sorry," she whispered. "I love you, I love you, I love you."

The corners of my eyes instantly stung. "I love you, too," I whispered back.

"Jeez, Pravika, let her breathe," Eli said, and after Pravika and I broke apart, he moved in for his hug. "Missed you."

"You too," I said. "I really like the hair." Eli had grown out his light brown curls since I'd last seen him, down to his shoulders. Right now, he had half pulled up in kind of a man bun.

He stepped back and grinned at me, touching a strand. "Thanks."

"Ugh, no." Jake shook his head. "Dude, it *has* to go."

"You're just jealous," Luli said to her brother. "Since you're following in Prince William's footsteps."

We all assessed Jake's fair hair. There was still enough to ruffle, but it had thinned since I'd last seen him. Baldness ran in his family. "Okay, Jake," I said to change the subject. "Where's my welcome-back hug?"

Then only Luli was left. While Jake burned within an hour of being on the beach (even after liberally applying sunscreen), his sister had been adopted from Central America and tanned like she was born to live by the sea. She did not move forward to hug me. All she said was, "It's good to see you, Meredith."

"It's good to see you, too," I said back, swallowing hard. Those ignored texts came to mind again. What were the odds she was thinking of them, too?

My stomach knotted.

Pretty damn high, I thought.

There was a moment of awkwardness before Pravika suggested we get food. Neither Sarah nor Michael had arrived yet, but a conga line of family members, bridesmaids, grooms-men, and other guests was forming, so we headed over to the house and fell into place. Even from the back, I could tell Uncle Brad and my dad were joking together behind the grill while my mom stood with Aunt Julia and Aunt Rachel a few people ahead of us. "Oh, I feel it!" she exclaimed, a hand on Aunt Rachel's swollen stomach. "What a kick!"

As we waited, I glanced back at Lantern House. It was undeniably gorgeous: white clapboard with big bay windows and a tiny top-floor study that looked like a lantern when lit up at night. The side deck's door kept swinging open and shut, Aunt Christine constantly going in and out with another big bowl of potato salad or more juice boxes for the kids.

"Would you like some help, Christine?" Honey asked from her Adirondack chair. Every house had a cluster of them; Lantern House's were yellow.

"No, no," Aunt Christine told my grandmother. "Don't worry. I've got it." She sighed. "Now if only Sarah and Michael would show up."

Cheers suddenly erupted. Because finally, there were the bride and groom, walking hand in hand. Still barefoot, Sarah had changed into a blue cocktail dress, and even though she wore no makeup, her cheeks were sun-kissed pink. Her hair was wet and tangled, as was Michael's. They'd probably been at the beach and lost track of time—Sarah had never been known for being punctual.

"Hi, everyone!" she shouted before her mother could march up to her and say, "You're late." She smiled and waved. "How'd y'all feel if we crashed your party?"

⁓

It felt really good to be back with my friends. After filling our plates, we reclaimed the picnic table and stayed there long after finishing our burgers. "So guess what," Eli said once Pravika had admitted that working at Murdick's Fudge this summer had made her a total addict.

"What?" we said.

"I saw him," Eli replied, unable to contain his excitement. "Today, in town."

Everyone but me groaned.

"Wait, huh?" I said, turning to Eli. "Who's *him*? You have a *him*?"

"No, he doesn't," Luli said before Eli could. She shook her head. "It's just this guy he's seen around Edgartown a few times, and now he thinks they're meant to be, so he's stalking him."

"Haha." Eli rolled his eyes. "I am *not* stalking him."

"Then how do you know he teaches sailing at the yacht club?"

"Ooh, the yacht club?" I said. "Swanky!"

"Look," Eli said, "he was wearing a windbreaker! It's not like I hung out on the docks and watched him lead a whole session."

"Funny," Jake said dryly, "because if I'm remembering correctly, those kids had some solid skills."

Eli hid his head in his hands as we laughed.

I nudged him. "Okay, where'd you see him today?"

"Walking into the bookstore." He sighed. "Which means he's a reader, and whoever I date has to be a reader."

"Why didn't you go inside?"

"Because..." He hesitated, then sighed again and looked at his empty plate. "Because you know I'd have no idea what to say."

"Oh, come on," Luli said, pulling her hair up into a not-so-subtle imitation of Eli's man bun. "Hi, my name is Eli. I saw you at the yacht club the other day, and I think you're really hot, so I've been tailing you ever since—"

"All right, all right." Eli's cheeks were so red that I swore I saw flames flickering. "Quit it."

Luli gave his arm a loving squeeze before her attention shifted to me. "What about you, Meredith?" she asked.

"What about me?" I asked back, able to feel the tension between us.

"Well, we heard Ben dumped you," she said, just like that, so matter-of-factly that my cheeks started burning like Eli's. "Which means you're here alone." She cocked her head. "Are you gonna find someone to stalk?"

"I'm *not* stalking him!" Eli shouted.

The table snickered while I did my best to keep my voice level. "No," I said. "I don't think so."

"Why not?" Pravika asked. "Everyone hooks up at weddings." She gestured to the front lawn where some guys had started up a game of cornhole. "They're perfect for a fling."

"Maybe," I said. "But I'm not looking for a rebound." I shrugged all thoughts of Ben off my shoulders. "I'm here to celebrate Sarah and Michael and spend time with my family." My voice quieted, and I wished for the millionth time that Claire were sitting next to me. "And you," I added. "I'm here to hang out with you guys, friends and family." I waggled my finger like Aunt Christine to get a laugh. "Forget about any flings!"

Even after a lot of joking and laughter, I still felt the divide between Luli and me once the table disbanded. Eli and Jake left to join the cornhole game, and Pravika wanted to see Sarah's engagement ring up close while Luli walked off to talk to another friend and her boyfriend, the two of them arm in arm. *That would've been Ben and me*, I thought before telling myself to stop sulking. It was Sarah's wedding, and I was here to have fun!

But first I felt like I needed to apologize to Luli. Her name had popped up on my phone the most over the last eighteen months, and I'd ignored her again and again. Why? Because when I wasn't working at Clinton's bagel shop, I'd spent all my time with Ben, and after the accident, I'd held on to him even more tightly, eating only the occasional lunch with my school friends. I found myself turning down invitations to get ready and pregame before parties together. "Wow, Meredith," a friend had said at one party as I held her hair back. She was drunk and hunched over the toilet but had somehow still managed to laugh so hard. "This is, like, the most time we've spent together in *forever*."

Tomorrow, I thought now, seeing Luli smile as she shook the boyfriend's hand. *You'll apologize tomorrow—apologize for shutting her out, apologize for going off the grid.*

My stomach rumbled, so I slid off my bench in pursuit of the buffet, deciding it was time for dessert. Which wasn't an easy mission—there were people *everywhere*. Sarah and Michael had wanted to keep their wedding small, but it seemed like there were a hundred guests here.

"Meredith!" Aunt Julia swept me into a hug, and then I met Michael's mom and older sister, whose toddler had the cutest chubby cheeks. Then Ethan, Hannah, and a couple other children tackled me to the ground. I wrestled with them for a minute, not really caring about getting covered in grass stains or messing up my hair.

"Kids!" Aunt Rachel called from the deck. "Enough!"

After brushing myself off, I tried to edge around a circle of bridesmaids, but a hand on my arm stopped me. "Wait, are you Meredith?" an African American girl with the whitest and

brightest smile asked. Danielle, Sarah's maid of honor. I recognized her from my cousin's Instagram. "Claire's sister?"

Claire's sister.

"Yes," I said. "That's me." I felt myself smile. It was nice
being called that. Even though I was a year younger, Claire was
always "Meredith's sister" at Clinton High School. She was
quiet and shy and hid behind homework while I went to games
and parties and could put a name to every face. "You should
run for student body president," Claire had encouraged me,
but when the time came, I didn't. The possibility of winning
haunted me, knowing I wouldn't be able to call her afterward.

Danielle squeezed my arm. "Claire was the coolest," she
said gently. "A bunch of us met her when she came to visit New
Orleans." She shook her head. "So vibrant."

"Yeah." I nodded, my smile growing but my eyes also
watering. "She was." I blinked away some tears, because that
was the true Claire: vibrant, full of life...especially out on the
Vineyard. "My happy place," she called it. Three weeks was
never enough. "I'm going to live here," I remembered her
saying. "After my freshman year of college, I'll get a job and be
able to spend the whole summer out here."

I liked to think she would've worked at Edgartown Books
or Bunch of Grapes Bookstore in Vineyard Haven. Claire
never went anywhere without a book, and she'd taught me to
do the same.

Someone behind us called Danielle's name, and I took the
opportunity to slip away, my stomach *really* demanding dessert.

Aunt Christine's famous ice cream sandwiches were waiting in one of the big Yeti coolers by the buffet table. I sighed at the sight of them: chocolate chip cookies the size of your hand with a huge scoop of ice cream in the middle. Chocolate, vanilla, mint chip, banana cream pie—anything and everything. The various flavors were arranged in boxes lined with wax paper, of course labeled in Aunt Christine's beautiful penmanship.

I grabbed one mint chip sandwich, a salted caramel, and a honey lavender before spotting my grandparents still holding court by the Adirondack chairs. Wink had his arm casually around Honey's waist, and after taking a brain freeze–worthy bite of ice cream, I weaved my way toward them to see if they'd spill the beans about Sarah's secret announcement.

By the time I made it over, they'd struck up a conversation with someone new—a mystery man, his back to me. "You can call me Wink," my grandfather was saying. "And this is my bride, Honey."

I smiled as I took another bite of my sandwich. Wink and Honey had been married for over half a century, but that was always how he introduced her. "And that's what I'm going to call *him* someday," I suddenly remembered telling Claire years and years ago. We'd been here on The Farm, squashed into an Adirondack chair together. "It'll be 'This is my groom' instead of 'This is my husband.'"

My sister snorted. "What's his name? This *groom* of yours?"

"How am I supposed to know?" I said. "I haven't met him yet."

"Stephen!" Claire had giggled. "His name will be Stephen!"

"Stephen?"

"Stephen."

I'd pretended to consider before launching a tickle attack.

Sarah had introduced us to Taylor Swift's early albums that summer, and there was this one song I played from dawn till dusk and even sang in the shower. I just couldn't get enough of it. Now I hummed the tune softly as if I still listened to it daily.

Honey's face lit up when she noticed me. She beckoned me over, melting ice cream sandwiches and all. "Sweetie!"

"Hi!" I called, and when the mystery man turned, it took everything to force my feet forward and put on a pleasant smile, not to spin around and make a run for it like I had this afternoon on the ferry. My insides churned upon seeing the purple bruise that had since bloomed on his cheekbone, spreading up under his eye and across the bridge of his nose. "Oh, whoa," he'd said after I kicked him. "Ouch!"

Yeah, whoa, I thought. *Ouch.*

THREE

I told myself he didn't recognize me, that he *couldn't* recognize me. It was impossible—I'd been disguised, wearing a hat and sunglasses. "This is Wit," Honey told me. "He's one of the groomsmen, Michael's brother."

Brother? I thought, because this guy looked nothing like Michael. Wit was wiry, no taller than five foot ten, and had a mop of sandy blond hair that needed a little smoothing back right now.

"Technically stepbrother," Wit said without a hint of a Southern accent. "He's my stepbrother."

"Oh." I nodded. "Gotcha."

"His mom and my dad got married when I was sixteen," he explained. "I'm from Vermont."

"Sounds freezing," I commented, suddenly aware that I was double-fisting ice cream sandwiches like a little kid. How awkward. I hid my hands behind my back to drop them, hoping I could be subtle about it.

"Freezing?" Wit tilted his head to give me a look. "Aren't you from upstate New York?"

My spine straightened. "How do you know that?"

He gestured at my grandparents, who had silently disappeared and now were heading toward the deck, where Sarah and Michael were whispering to each other. *Their announcement*, I wondered again. *When is it?*

"What else did they tell you?" I asked Wit in a harsher voice than I'd intended. It just sounded like he'd been briefed or something, and though I loved her, I wouldn't put it past Honey to spill the whole story about Ben.

"Relax, Officer," he said, putting up his hands. "Not much. You're Meredith Fox, you're eighteen, you'll be a freshman at Hamilton College this fall. Just the bare bones basics." He smiled. "That okay?"

I didn't respond, instead turning away so that my body wasn't angled directly toward his. My stomach swooped, a feeling so unfamiliar and uneasy. Because his grin was the type of imperfect crooked grin that made you want to grin back, and his eyes...if you looked past the dark bruise, they were straight out of one of the fantasy novels that Claire and I loved so much. The eye color of an alluring stranger you weren't sure you should trust but soon had to share a bed with for whatever reason on the quest you were on, then eventually fell so irrevocably in love with that you would die for each other. Basically, an eye color that wasn't supposed to exist in real life: deep turquoise with gold rings around them.

I'm not kidding, Claire, I thought. *Turquoise!*

"How old are you?" I asked, crossing my arms over my chest.

"Ninotoon," Wit answered, crossing his, too. Like we were in a standoff or something.

Was he mimicking me?

"So you're in college?"

A nod. "I just finished my first year at Tulane."

"God, what is with that school?" I mumbled to myself. Sarah, Michael, Wit, and if everything hadn't happened, my sister.

"Repeat that?" Wit said.

"No, um, nothing." The back of my neck prickled. "It seems like everyone loves that place."

Wit was quiet for a moment. "Most people think it's great." He scrubbed a hand through his hair. "But it all depends—"

"Hey, everyone!" Sarah's voice cut him off, light and lively. We turned to see her standing on one of the deck's wood benches, Michael at her side. "If you'd all gather around..."

The party migrated over, surrounding Sarah and her fiancé like they were onstage. I didn't try to stick with Wit, and he didn't try to stick with me, so I wedged myself between Eli and Pravika. Luli and Jake were there, too. "Who was that guy you were talking to?" Pravika asked.

"No one," I answered. "A groomsman."

"Michael's stepbrother," Eli said at the same time, of course having all the information. "The one who basically got his ass kicked on the ferry." He chuckled. "You saw the bruise, right? Half his face is blue!" He elbowed me. "Did he tell you who did it?"

"He doesn't know," I said quickly, praying that was true. My neck flamed. "Apparently the person was wearing sunglasses."

The other two nodded, and we refocused on Sarah. "Michael and I are so happy you could join us this week," she was saying, "to celebrate family, friends, and our marriage." She laughed when everyone clapped, and then her expression fell a little. "But there is someone very special who wasn't able to make it. My cousin Claire." Her voice quavered, and Michael took her hand.

Just like someone took mine.

"It's okay," Eli whispered. "It's all right."

I nodded and squeezed back as hard as I could.

"This week is not only about us," Sarah said. "It's also about honoring Claire's memory." She smiled—or tried her best to smile. "And I believe I speak for the entire Fox family when I say there is only one way to pay tribute to her."

Wait, I thought, heart speeding up. *What is she talking about?*

"Do y'all remember filling out your RSVPs?" Michael asked after exchanging an almost-imperceptible nod with Sarah. "Checking those boring boxes?"

"Well, the last one wasn't boring," Sarah said, playfully slapping his chest. "I thought it was intriguing!" She was now genuinely grinning. "Do you guys remember that one?"

Having RSVP'd months ago, no one offered up even a nod, but I nearly gasped, the riddle suddenly solved. Do you want to play? the silver-edged card had asked, and I checked yes without thinking twice. Neither my parents nor I knew what it meant, but I didn't want to find myself left out of anything. I wanted to be all in at this wedding.

"Assassin," I murmured to myself just as Sarah voiced the word to everyone else. We had unknowingly signed up to play Assassin. *I* had unknowingly signed up to play Assassin.

My heart sank at the thought. It was a Paqua Farm tradition. Every summer, we played a Farm-wide game of Assassin, where players used water guns to eliminate one another and become the last active killer. Each person was assigned an initial target, and when they successfully "took care of" said target, they inherited their victim's. For the couple of weeks we played, the paranoia on The Farm was unparalleled. People hesitated before going on kayak rides together, spied on their targets from the dunes, and even formed secret alliances. It was a ton of fun, and Assassin lore lived on forever.

"Michael and I will not be playing," Sarah said as Michael good-humoredly pouted. "We have too many other obligations." She poked him in the cheek. "But we can't wait to see you guys battle it out to make Claire proud!"

My sister had been the undisputed Assassin queen, our most decorated champion. She had taken Assassin so seriously that she had multiple weapons: a water handgun, a Super Soaker, and some jetpack-looking high-pressure soaker with pump action and multiple nozzles.

As I shifted from one foot to the other, Sarah and Michael handed off the torch to our "Assassin Commissioners," Wink

Condo Complex, Eli had dubbed it. Thankfully, no one had mentioned anything about sleeping in Claire's bed.

I wandered along the well-worn sandy roads, keeping my flashlight pointed at the ground so I didn't come across any night critters. Nothing had ever happened to me, but *everyone* had heard Sarah scream bloody murder the time she got skunked on her way back from a beach bonfire with her brothers.

A few minutes later, though, I heard a rustling noise. *Tree branches swaying*, I assumed, until the rustling turned into clear footsteps crunching over bits of broken seashells. I picked up my pace but was unable to tell which direction the person was coming from. All I knew was he or she was walking *toward* me.

Blood pulsed in my ears. I'd never been *scared* on The Farm before; I didn't know how to react. My first impulse was to scream, but it was like my mouth had been sewn shut. Then I considered running off into the night, skunks be damned, but my body had gone rigid.

So what I settled on was stopping in my tracks, swallowing hard, and saying in what I hoped was a threatening tone, "I have a knife."

"Really?" a male voice called back. Familiar, but one I couldn't place after meeting so many people today. "You have a knife?"

"Yeah," I lied. "I do."

"What kind?"

"Swiss Army," I said, thinking of a Netflix documentary

I'd watched with Ben once, all about the history of the knife company. It was random and far from romantic, but I'd found the intricate design and construction process interesting.

"Hmm, a Swiss Army knife." A low whistle. "Impressive."

I didn't say anything. The voice sounded closer now, and it was almost unnerving how melodious it was. My toes curled in my flip-flops. Who was I talking to?

"So I suppose this afternoon wasn't enough," the guy continued. "You gotta maul my face even *more?*"

My breath caught in my throat.

Crap.

Wit appeared in front of me like magic, the starlight shining on his wicked bruise. I couldn't tell if it looked better or worse. "Oh, um," I fumbled. "You, uh, know it was, mmm, me?"

"Yes."

I winced. "How?"

"The hat-and-sunglasses routine only works on TV, Killer."

"I'm sorry," I blurted. "It was an accident. I wasn't paying attention." I sighed. "And I'd just been on the phone with—"

"Your shithead ex," Wit finished for me, grinning his crooked grin. "If I'm quoting correctly."

"You heard that, too?"

No response.

"Well, that's great," I mumbled, feeling my neck prickle—partially out of embarrassment but also because he was still smiling. Smiling with his blond hair mussed and falling across his forehead, and wearing a fraying sweatshirt like mine. My stomach did that strange swooping thing. "What are you doing out here?" I asked, hoping it would stop.

Wit shrugged. "Exploring."

"At night?"

"Yeah, I wanted to see the stars. There's no light pollution like in the city." He paused. "I also wanted to escape the best man and maid of honor banging in the next room."

"Ugh," I said. "Really?"

"Yep." Wit nodded. "I mean, you know how people get at weddings."

"Yeah." I nodded, too, Pravika's words from earlier coming to mind: *They're perfect for a fling.*

But not for me, I thought. *Family and friends. It's all about family and friends.*

The ocean drowned out whatever Wit said next, waves crashing hard on the beach. I hadn't noticed how close to the dunes we were, so I shined my flashlight and motioned for him to follow me so we could find a nook away from the noise. My flip-flops slapped against the sand, and Wit's half-tied sneakers scuffed like he had a habit of not picking up his feet when he walked.

"So what are *you* doing out here?" he asked once we sat down, tall grass swishing around us but safe from the wind.

"Oh," I said, hiding my hands in my sweatshirt pocket. "Just thinking."

Wit was silent for a second, pulling up the hood of his own sweatshirt. I thought it was more than obvious what I was thinking about, but he didn't say Claire's name, and I was grateful for it. "Assassin, right?" he eventually guessed. "Gearing up for tomorrow?"

"Perhaps," I replied, an attempt at coyness. Wit didn't need to know how hesitant I was to play. That I hadn't even opened my envelope yet to find out my first target—they'd been left in each house's mailbox earlier. MEREDITH FOX, one was labeled, and inside would be a laminated slip of paper with a single name on it.

"The rules seem simple enough," Wit commented, and I nodded. "But strategy...there must be a ton of strategy involved. Type of water weapon, if you want to play offense or defense, that kind of thing." He shifted so that his leg brushed mine, his striped pajama bottoms against my floral-patterned ones. Was it on purpose? "Also alliances," he added as goose bumps blossomed under the thin fabric. "I bet a ton of alliances form."

I stayed silent, realizing where he was going with this. Almost immediately after the announcement had been made, Luli had created a group chat that included Eli, Pravika, Jake, and me. Tubing on the Oyster Pond tomorrow, she'd texted. Noon. Tell no one, invite no one. Business to discuss.

Whether I liked it or not, it appeared that I was part of an alliance.

Wit let a beat pass. "I'm assuming you have one already," he said. "Being a skilled veteran and all—"

"I wouldn't call myself 'skilled,'" I cut in, turning toward him. Our knees knocked again. "The best I've ever done is five days, and most of that was spent in hiding. My cousin Peter followed me to the old tractor yard one day and shot me before I made it through the barn door." I shrugged. "I always take a defensive stance."

"Seriously?" Wit said. "I would've thought the opposite."

I snorted. "Why's that?"

He laughed, lyrical like his voice. "Because you threatened to pull a knife on me?"

"Well, you shouldn't have snuck up on me like that!" I said, flustered. My cheeks heated. "You should've announced yourself!"

"Okay, yes, I should've said something," he conceded, "but swinging back to alliances—"

"I can't betray mine," I told him, because focusing on my friends this week involved staying loyal to them. If Luli needed me to lead her target into a trap, I would do it. I'd been MIA for over a year, blown off my friends' concerned texts and calls, and the fact that they seemed willing to forgive and forget...I couldn't mess with that.

"I wasn't asking you to," Wit replied. "But I was wondering..." He casually flicked some sand at me, and I flicked some back. "...if you'd be interested in forming a pact."

My ears pricked up.

A pact?

"Think about it," Wit said. "We could really help each other. You're on the bride's side, and I'm on the groom's—there are so many people I don't know that you do and vice versa."

A lump formed in my throat. It was dawning on me that Wit was approaching Assassin exactly like Claire—offensively and astutely, already planning and plotting. He wouldn't be searching The Farm for a good hiding spot anytime soon.

"So instead of you sniffing around and asking everyone and their mother who Michael's uncle's daughter is," he continued, "I'd be your go-to source."

"And instead of solving the mystery of Honey's brother's third wife," I said, liking this more and more, "I'd lay out her entire schedule for you, tell you her favorite Pilates studio in Vineyard Haven."

"Exactly," Wit said. "We'd keep the information between us, so no rumors about betrayals would flare up—we wouldn't tip anyone off." He released a deep breath. "What do you say?"

My stomach stirred with excitement. "I think it's brilliant."

"Excellent." He smiled and held out his hand. "Now we shake on it."

"Wait," I said before we did, hands hovering inches apart. I could feel the warmth radiating off Wit's skin. "One more thing."

"Go."

"If we hear each other's names going around, we'll let the other person know."

Wit considered for a moment, then nodded. "Deal."

I nodded back. "Deal."

And so we shook.

Before sneaking back into the Annex that night, I visited the ancient oak tree on the edge of the lawn and ran my fingers over the notches carved into the trunk. Summer after summer, Claire used an ax to keep track of her victories. "I'm going to win," I whispered once I'd reached the final mark. "I'm going to win this thing."

MONDAY

FOUR

I woke up on the Annex's couch at sunrise, my face smashed into an old needlepoint throw pillow and legs bent at an odd, almost painful angle. *I can't go back to the bunk room*, I'd decided once Wit and I had parted ways last night. *I can't sleep there without her.*

Across the sitting room, Loki stared at me from his dog bed. It was so early, but the Jack Russell was ready for the day. "All right, all right," I said after rubbing my eyes and stretching my arms above my head. "Breakfast time."

He leapt up and followed me into the kitchen, where I scooped a cup of kibble into his bowl, and he gobbled it up as I grabbed a banana for myself. Loki finished his food before I finished peeling the fruit, so I paused to open the back door and watched the dog shoot outside and vanish into the woods. It was like that with all the dogs on The Farm—they'd eat breakfast, then disappear until dinner. Sometimes even later.

Any other early morning, I would've gone back to bed, but today was not any other early morning. It was day one of

Assassin. Mom and Dad were still asleep, so I tiptoed into my room and changed out of my pajamas and into Claire's and my standard Vineyard outfit: a bikini with jean cutoffs and a light-weight fishing shirt on top. Instead of flip-flops, I grabbed my sneakers and laced them up on the back stoop, just in case I needed to run for my life.

After a quick visit to the outhouse, I cracked open the storage shed. Because along with the bikes, crabbing nets, boogie boards, toolboxes, and other randomness, it was where Claire kept her arsenal. The water handgun, the Super Soaker, and my sister's big kahuna: the high-pressure soaker contrap-tion. Everyone had a weapon of choice, and thank goodness Claire kept hers on The Farm. Since no one had known about Assassin ahead of time, each house had been gifted a basket of tiny squirt guns, compliments of the bride and groom. Last night, Wit had told me that his was pink and wouldn't cut it. "I mean, Amazon's fast," I'd replied, thinking he meant to order something online, "but out here, it's not *that* fast."

"Oh, no." He shook his head. "I don't need Jeff Bezos's help on this one! I already have an idea."

Of course he'd already opened his envelope, and I'd crossed my fingers when ripping into mine when I had gotten home— crossed my fingers that I hadn't made a mistake in waiting, that I hadn't wasted an opportunity for a dossier. Wit and I hadn't exchanged numbers, so I couldn't text him.

But it turned out I'd gotten lucky. My first target was not only someone I knew but also someone whose *routine* I knew.

RACHEL EPSTEIN-FOX, my slip of paper read, and I'd smiled to myself. Aunt Rachel, who was known for rising at the crack of dawn to meditate in the Camp's front yard. Assassin wasn't the bride's side versus the groom's; it was everyone for themselves.

I scanned Claire's weapons once more before selecting the water handgun. The Super Soaker had been her favorite—she liked to intimidate, to send people's paranoia through the roof by walking around with that flashy water gun slung over her shoulder twenty-four-seven. Its neon-orange and electric-green color combination warned everyone to watch their backs.

Nope, I thought, unable to imagine myself being that badass. *Not for me.*

After shutting the shed door, I loaded the gun with water in the Annex's shower, tucked it into the back of my shorts, and set off as if taking a casual morning walk. The Camp was a ways down the road on the other side of the Cabin. I wondered if I would see Danielle, Sarah's maid of honor, embark on a walk of shame from the best man's room. Or was it too early for that? The sun was getting higher in the sky—I had to hurry so I wouldn't miss catching Aunt Rachel midmeditation.

But as soon as I picked up my pace, someone shouted my name. "Meredith!" Michael called, and I turned to see him running toward me. Sweaty, shirtless, six-pack on full display. He shone so brightly that it took a beat for me to notice there was someone at his side. The two slowed in front of me. "Bit early for you, isn't it?" Michael asked, smiling with his head half-cocked. Everyone on The Farm knew I liked sleeping late.

"Well, excuse me," I said, a joking hand on my hip, "but people *change*, Michael."

Sarah's fiancé chuckled. "This is my stepbrother, by the way," he said, motioning for the Gatorade bottle full of water his running partner held. He squirted it in his face. "I don't know if you got the chance to meet yesterday."

"Oh, we've met," Wit said before I could. He wore a white T-shirt and looked so slight standing next to six-foot-four Michael. But I noticed the sinewy muscle cording his arms when he took the water back. He, too, was strong, just in a different way. I thought I remembered him mentioning something about skiing and rock climbing on our 2:00 a.m. walk back to the houses. "Meredith made quite the first impression," he added now and motioned to his bruise. "The next Picasso."

Michael's jaw dropped, horrified.

I shot Wit a glare.

He smirked.

"Why, Mer?" Michael asked. "Just why? Sarah's mom is talking about leaving him out of the wedding photos!"

"Listen, it wasn't on purpose," I said, then glanced over my shoulder—I really had to move it. "And I'm sure he'll heal by then..."

I trailed off, Wit suddenly at my back. "Hold on a sec," he whispered, breath swirling warm against my ear. "Conceal your weapon." He pulled up the back of my shirt to cover my water gun. Slow shivers rippled up my spine. "You'll lose the element of surprise."

"Thanks," I whispered back. "I only have limited time, too. I gotta go."

Michael had an eyebrow raised when we both straightened up, like he'd caught us making out or something. His eyes went from me to Wit and back to me.

Pulse pounding, I chose not to explain. "Enjoy your run, Duprés. I'll see you later!"

Wit responded by spraying me with his water bottle. I dodged him, but the bottle's stream did have a nice range to it. *Forget the tiny squirt gun*, I thought, deciphering his silent message. The Gatorade bottle was Wit's weapon. Shrewd, sly, something no one would suspect.

He was clever.

"Wait," Michael said as I started speed walking away, and I thought he was talking to me, but before pivoting back around, I heard, "She thinks your last name is Dupré?"

———

The Camp had been built a few years before World War I, and back then, it was George Fox's duck hunting camp. It resembled the Annex from the outside—a simple one-story shingled structure plus a pine front porch—but it was deceptively big inside, able to sleep twelve people and with space for two full bathrooms. "Aunt Julia's kids will never know the terror of sneaking out to an outhouse in the dead of night," Claire and I once joked. "How cruel!"

Sure enough, decked out in Lululemon, Aunt Rachel with her big belly had unrolled a yoga mat by the flagpole and sat cross-legged with a perfectly erect spine. Her palms rested on her lap faceup, and her eyes were calmly closed. I remembered her mentioning that it was counterproductive to squeeze them shut. It didn't let the rest of your body relax.

I crept as quietly as I could across the grass, wincing every time my sneakers squeaked from the morning dew. "Hello?" Aunt Rachel said once I was only a few feet away, keeping her eyes closed. "Julia?"

My shoulders sagged. "No," I felt like I had to say. "It's, um, Meredith."

"Oh, Meredith." Eyes still shut, she didn't shift her position, but she did smile. "Isn't it a little early for you to be out and about?"

I didn't reply, unable to breathe. My heart was beating so fast.

"Feel free to join me," she said as I pulled my water gun from the back of my shorts. I aimed it at her head, hand shaking. "Your mom and I were talking yesterday, and we agreed meditation might be good for you—"

I pulled the trigger, a fatal blow to her temple.

My aunt laughed. Her eyes popped open, she fell back against her yoga mat, and she *laughed*.

It wasn't nearly as dramatic a takedown as I wanted. Far from it.

"Oh, come on!" I whined like one of her young children.

"You think this is funny?" I stamped my foot for emphasis. "Really?"

"Yep." She sat up and nodded. "I'm pregnant, silly." She rubbed her stomach. "I was hoping someone would shoot me today. There's no way I can play this game. I almost texted Wink to drop out, but I didn't want to mess up the assignments."

I sighed an especially melodramatic sigh. "Well, I *guess* that's understandable."

Aunt Rachel gave me a lopsided grin. "I'm sorry for not being more pissed." Then she patted her mat. "Join me."

My stomach churned. Claire used to get up early on the weekends for yoga and would always demonstrate the difficult poses when we hung out in her room. I failed miserably whenever I attempted them. "That's okay," I said softly. "I'm not flexible."

"This isn't yoga," Aunt Rachel replied just as softly. "It's simple meditation." She gestured to the mat again. "Please sit."

I fled the Camp once Aunt Rachel passed on her target after about twenty minutes of meditation exercises. "Do you feel that?" she asked during one deep-breathing sequence. "Do you feel the flow?"

"I do," I whispered, even though it was a half truth. I felt more calm but not *fully* calm, squeezing my eyes shut to hold back tears. Meditation might not be the exact same thing as yoga, but it was still *Claire*. "I actually do."

Michael was doing crunches when I got to the Cabin. *Good*, I thought; I was hoping he and Wit would be back from their run. Because the name on my new slip of paper?

It did not ring a single wedding bell.

"Hey," I said to him. "Is Wit around?"

This time, no eyebrows were raised; Michael kept doing his crunches but avoided my question. "Who'd you off?" he asked instead.

"I don't know what you're talking about," I replied. "I went to the Camp to meditate."

"So Aunt Rachel?"

"Fuck," I mumbled.

"Don't worry," Michael said. "Sarah and I are impartial. Wink and Honey made us swear we wouldn't help with any eliminations."

"And you're confident Sarah's gonna abide by that?" My cousin was the worst secret keeper. Claire always used that to her advantage, feeding Sarah incorrect intel to spread around The Farm.

Michael laughed. "She's going to do her best."

"So..." I ventured after a beat. "Wit?"

"Ah." He nodded. "What's up with you and Witty, anyway?"

"Nothing," I said quickly.

The corners of Michael's mouth turned up, bemused.

"Impartial," he reminded me. "I'm impartial." He mimed zipping his lips, then pointed to the far end of the Cabin, to the last room in the row. "He's in the shower right now, but that's his."

"Thanks," I squeaked and dashed over to Wit's door before Michael could say anything else, taking a seat on the ancient wood bench outside his room. While waiting, I unlocked my phone and texted Wink that I'd eliminated Aunt Rachel.

He responded: Roger that.

Along with: What are you doing awake, Meredith?

I rolled my eyes and started to type something back, but then I heard a surprised, "Oh."

Wit was standing there with only a red beach towel around his waist. I didn't even blink, used to seeing people walking around in only towels that was how it was with outdoor showers. Much to Aunt Christine's chagrin, Uncle Brad was infamous for enjoying a beer in his towel while listening to James Taylor on Lantern House's deck.

"Hi," I said to Wit, rising from the bench. "Mission accomplished." I patted my water gun. "Not as dramatic as I wanted, but..."

"But you got the job done," he said. "Awesome." Then he adjusted his towel around his waist, and it wasn't like I *meant* to check him out, but it happened anyway. The beads of water dripping down his chest and his tanned, taut, washboard abs.

"I need your help, though," I said, clearing my throat. "I don't know who"—I pulled my new mark out of my pocket and waved it around—"this is."

"Sure, of course." Wit nodded, and when he swung his screen door open, I started to follow him right into his room. He turned and blocked the doorway, that crooked grin on his face. "Nice try, baby." He motioned to his half-naked body. "Give me a sec?"

"Oh, yeah, sorry." My cheeks blazed, both with embarrassment and irritation. I didn't like being called baby. Ben used to call me babe.

Hey, babe.

Love you, babe.

Bye, babe.

When we first started dating, he called me his "girl" in an endearing and old-fashioned way, and it seemed so special... but then somewhere along the way, I became an impersonal "babe." Babe in public, babe in private, babe always.

"All right!" Wit called from inside his room. "All good!"

He was pulling on a T-shirt when the door shut behind me, and I had to bite back a laugh.

The shirt was a transformed version of Sarah and Michael's wedding invitation—pastel blue with a lighthouse sketched on the front, and in the reflection in Wit's mirror, I made out #HurrayShesADupré on the back.

"Hurray, she's a Dupré?" I said.

"Yeah." He glanced over his shoulder. "It's the hashtag for the wedding. You know, for Instagram and stuff."

I smirked. "I know what it's for, *baby.*"

Wit blushed through his bruise.

Good, I thought. *Payback.*

"I don't really do Instagram." He shrugged. "But all the groomsmen and bridesmaids have been instructed to wear these whenever we do something together."

"By my aunt Christine," I guessed.

"By your aunt Christine, yes, but fully backed by Jeannie." He flopped down on his bed, full-sized with a plaid patchwork quilt on top. "Michael's mom."

I nodded and perched at the edge of his bed, looking around—it had been a while since I'd been in the Cabin, which had the most masculine décor of the houses. Wit's walls were wood paneled and his dresser dark green. I remembered there was a hilariously obnoxious painting of a tiger bearing its teeth hanging over the massive stone fireplace in the main room.

In short, it was the perfect house for a groom and his six buds to spend the week.

"What're you guys doing today?" I asked. "Going into town?" My heart sort of sped up, secretly hoping he'd say no. Sarah and Michael would be excellent tour guides for their wedding party, but I didn't want Wit to sit down for lunch at Atlantic in Edgartown and squeeze lemon and shake Tabasco onto his oysters (as delicious as they were). I wanted him to cram into the local dive, Dock Street Coffee Shop, and devour a messy breakfast sandwich with me.

That was the Vineyard.

"No." Wit shook his head, and my pulse spiked before slowing in relief. "Not today. We're taking a big group photo and then heading to the beach, I think." He yawned. "Which is cool, because I want to get going." He gestured lazily to the Gatorade bottle on his dresser, correctly assuming I'd decoded why he'd sprayed me. I watched him snuggle up with his pillow, wince slightly because of his bruise, then yawn again and close his eyes. "Tell me who you have," he said as I moved a little farther onto the mattress. "I'm listening."

I told him, and then he told me what I needed to know.

"And you can lie down if you want," he said afterward. "I hear you yawning."

"Oh, no," I said, even though I *had* yawned more than a handful of times. Because believe it or not, it wasn't even 9:00 a.m. I'd need a nap before tubing at noon. "That's okay. I'll go back to the Annex."

"Nah, stay," Wit said, his eyes fluttering open. His impossibly turquoise eyes. "I promise I won't call you baby again."

I felt pinpricks on my neck. Had it really been that obvious? How much it had bothered me?

"That's what Shithead called you," Wit said. "Isn't it?"

"Shithead's name is Ben," I replied, sighing. "And it was more *babe* than baby."

"Ben? I like Shithead better."

"Me too, actually." I laughed and stretched out next to him. Not close enough for us to touch but more than comfortable enough to fall asleep. The sheets and pillows smelled like the sea and citrus. "Oranges," I murmured.

"My shampoo," Wit murmured back.

"I love oranges."

"So you love *me*."

I giggled. He hadn't phrased it as a question, and for some reason—lack of sleep, probably—that made me giggle. *Really* giggle.

"You have a nice laugh," Wit commented.

"A nice laugh?" I asked, giggles gone. Nobody had ever told me that, at least not in a long time. The last time someone had mentioned my laugh, it was my dad saying he missed it.

"Mm-hmm," he replied and rolled over so that our toes touched. I curled mine, tingles going through them, but didn't move away. "I like it."

So you like me, I thought about saying but didn't. A little casual flirting with Wit was fine, but a lot was not. He was my new partner in crime, my new pal, my new *friend*. I wanted him to *stay* my friend. It had been so long since I'd made one.

"Wit?" I whispered.

"Yes?" he whispered back.

"What's your last name? It's not Dupré, right?"

"No," he said. "My dad's married to Michael's mom. Our last name is Witry."

"How alliterative," I said. "Wit Witry."

"Mmm, that's..." Wit started but drifted away to dreamland before he could finish his thought, breathing now slow and steady. I suddenly wanted to reach over and feel his heartbeat.

But instead I burrowed deeper into his pillow and closed my eyes.

FIVE

Part of me wanted to invite Wit tubing when we woke up, but then I remembered it was actually an Assassin alliance meeting and that Wit had groomsman obligations.

#HurrayShesADupré.

Will it be like that all week? I wondered as he mentioned that their rendezvous point for the group picture was the Pond House, since it had the most breathtaking view of the Oyster Pond. *Will he just hang out with the wedding party?*

"Let's do something later," I blurted before leaving his room. "I want to take you somewhere."

Wit raised an eyebrow. "You want to take me somewhere?"

I raised an eyebrow back. "Any objections?"

"No." He shook his head. "But do you think it's a good idea? I mean, shouldn't we keep stuff on the down-low? So people don't suspect anything?"

"Um, I hate to break it to you, *sweetheart*," I said, "but Michael saw us earlier, and he definitely told Sarah, so I'd wager the whole Farm knows we're friends by now."

Wit wrinkled his nose. "I don't like 'sweetheart.'"

"Fine, cross it off the list." I smirked, my heart racing. I had no idea where this was coming from, who this person inside me was, but it felt good. *I* felt good—confident and a little daring. "No *baby*," I told Wit. "And no *sweetheart*."

"Sounds good, darling." Wit winked. "Now, where're we going today?"

"It's a surprise, dearest," I said. "Just meet me at the Annex at 1:15."

He nodded. "Okay."

I nodded back. "Okay."

"So..." we then said at the same time, unsure how to say goodbye. An awkward handshake? An even more awkward hug? Where was the non-awkward middle ground?

"Good luck out there," I said a minute later to break the silence.

"With my target?" he asked. "Or your aunt Christine and the photo shoot?"

"Both."

"Thanks." He smiled, and I was so busy smiling back that I didn't register him grabbing his Gatorade bottle from his dresser. "Have a productive strategy session."

And when he raised the bottle to spray me, I made a break for outside—so gracefully that I banged my knee on the door frame. It would bruise for sure.

"Now we're even, peaches!" Wit called after me.

By 11:50 a.m., there were plenty of Foxes sneaking around The Farm. My dad and Uncle Brad were like overgrown teenagers, sporting camouflage hats, hiding behind scrub trees, and army crawling through the tall grass with their identical water guns. I looked up the road to see who they were tailing: an older couple walking toward the beach.

Meanwhile, Aunt Julia wasn't taking the same subtle approach as her brothers; she was stationed outside Lantern House, gun aimed at the door. "I know you're in there, Peter Fox!" she said. "I know you're chugging your third cup of coffee, but you better hurry up, because I *also* know you have someplace to be soon."

Peter, Sarah's thirty-year-old brother and another grooms-man. Instead of the Cabin, he was staying in Lantern House with his wife and their new baby. *Third cup of coffee?* I thought. *Nell must not be sleeping through the night yet.*

"You get him, Aunt Julia!" I said as I passed by but then picked up my pace—it suddenly hit me that *my* assassin could be out on the hunt.

I felt a few imaginary creepy-crawlies scuttle up my spine.

Who had me?

To be on the safe side, I veered off the sandy road and onto one of the worn trails—the labyrinthine way to the beach. It was almost out of a fairy tale, a wooded pathway with sunlight stream-ing through the tree branches. Birds chirped as I walked along.

Eventually, the path opened out onto the shore of the Oyster Pond, blue-green water glittering. When I squinted, I saw that a group had already gathered across the water on what we all considered the *true* beach, a stretch of sand halfway between the placid pond and rolling ocean so you could swim in either. It offered the best of both worlds. Claire and I used to challenge each other to flip into the ocean's waves and avoid getting stuck in "washing machines" (whenever a wave broke overtop one that was retreating back out to sea). Then we'd go to the pond and float on our backs for a while. "This is heaven," my sister once said. "I love this so much, Mer."

Now, I waded in the opposite direction of the ocean, freshwater soaking my sneakers, until I reached the small dock nestled in between dunes. A rickety old set of stairs led up the hill to the Pond House. "Aunt Christine is taking this *way* too seriously," Eli said to me from Wink's Boston Whaler. I was the last one to arrive. Pravika and Jake were already sorting the life vests while Luli tied the oversize tube to the back of the boat with a complicated knot. Eli pointed up the hill, where the wedding party photo was being taken. *Listen*, he mouthed.

"No, no, everyone," my aunt was saying. "Sarah and Michael will be in the middle, then bridesmaids on one side and groomsmen on the other."

"But don't you think alternating might be cool?" someone asked, a confident voice I now immediately recognized.

Wit.

"Yeah, Mom," Sarah agreed. "Michael and I will still be

in the middle, and we can mix it up with bridesmaid, grooms-man, bridesmaid, et cetera. It'll be less formal and more fun. We should save the traditional poses for the wedding day."

A moment of silence, then, "I suppose so."

"Yes!" Sarah exclaimed at the same time Wit went, "I'll stand next to Isabel!"

No, I thought, stifling a snort. *No way, not here.*

Isabel Davies, Sarah's college roommate and Wit's first target. "She's been to The Farm before," I'd briefed him, "so she knows it pretty well. She's not just going to be lying around on the beach all day. She likes playing tennis in the mornings, paddleboarding after lunch, and then she usually reads a book near Job's Neck Pond before dinner."

"That's fine, Wit," Aunt Christine replied as Jake helped me into the boat. Luli finished securing the tube. "Just get rid of the water bottle, please."

"Oh my god," I whispered to myself. *Yes way, yes here.*

But I didn't get to overhear Wit's first takedown, because Eli powered up the Whaler, its engine drowning out everything. "Let's go!" Luli called over the droning.

Eli steered us out to more or less the middle of Oyster, yards and yards away from shore, avoiding kayakers, paddleboard-ers, sailboats, and swimmers. The four of us shouted "Hi!" and "Hello!" to everyone, even if we didn't know them. There was a scattering of houses surrounding the pond, ranging from cute cottages to grand mansions. My favorite one always threw a huge Fourth of July party, and during our last summer together,

I'd convinced Claire to crash it with me. "They won't notice," I told her. "There are so many people already there!"

Now I stared at the sprawling cedar-shingled house, at its stretch of private beach, and remembered Claire having her first kiss that night. During a silly game of spin the bottle by the bonfire, with a handsome blue-eyed boy.

"All right," Luli said once life vests had been buckled; no one made a move for the tube yet. "First thing's first: Who do you have?"

With no hesitation, we revealed our targets. Everyone had chosen to play Assassin except Eli. "I can't, guys," he said as we groaned. "You know this game spikes my anxiety. Even the 'Will you play?' question made me nauseous!"

I kept my mouth shut about eliminating Aunt Rachel earlier and trusted her to stay quiet, too. For some reason, I didn't want people to know how hard I was playing this year. Well, anyone but Wit.

"So now I have Great-Uncle Richard," Pravika said a couple minutes later, after we'd "shuffled the deck." One of our alliance's standard strategies was to leak our targets, or our *alleged* targets. Naturally, this had been Claire's idea. Great-Uncle Richard was really Jake's target, but we'd make sure word would spread that Pravika had him in her sights. "That's genius, Claire," Luli had said when my sister first presented the plan a few years ago. "*Genius.*"

And I'd agreed, because when you didn't know who had you in Assassin, you were ultraparanoid and suspicious of everyone. But if you found out so-and-so was gunning for you, you automatically trusted other people again.

"Good luck with yours, though, Meredith," Jake said now. "Daniel Robinson?" He shook his head. "Whoever that is?"

"Oh yeah, tell me about it." I fake-laughed, my stomach stirring. "Total John Doe!"

Thanks to Wit, Daniel was no mystery to me, but I'd never been the best liar. My laugh was too high-pitched, and I felt Luli's eyes on me. Before she asked any questions, I volunteered to brave the tube first. Pravika joined me, and she and I lay on our stomachs with our arms, life vests, and legs pressed up against each other, waiting for Eli to zoom off across the pond. We gripped the handles as tightly as we could, since Eli was famous on The Farm for really whipping you around.

Pravika sighed and nudged my hip with hers. Our bikini bottoms were double-knotted but would still come off once we hit the water. They always did. "Why do we do this?" she asked.

I smiled. "Because we're bonkers."

She laughed, and right on cue, the rumbling Whaler lurched forward, our tube splashing and swirling. Eli's idea of a "warm-up."

But *barely* a warm-up. He soon revved the engine and gunned it full speed. The wind picked up, hungry to blow us backward, and we were skimming the boat's wake like a stone skipping across the water, bouncing up and down.

"Oh my god!" Pravika shouted after Eli's first abrupt turn, sending us spinning in the opposite direction. She screamed her head off no matter how many times she tubed, and somehow it never got old. "Meredith!"

"Hold on!" I shouted back. Everything was now slippery, the water spritzing up in our faces. I shut my eyes for a second, then cracked one open to see our audience in the distance. Jake was giving us a thumbs-up, but his sister had her arms folded across her chest and was grinning villainously. She always loved a good wipeout.

I gulped, knowing I still owed her that apology.

Soon Eli struck again, slowing up so Pravika and I jostled over the wake waves.

Aye-yai-yai-yai-yai!

"Ahhh, I'm falling!" Pravika said after another quick turn and zigzag combination. Her voice was almost lost to the wind. "I think I have to—"

She couldn't finish the sentence, suddenly just *gone*. I was alone on the tube, and up ahead, I saw Luli cover her mouth. It must've been a complete catastrophe.

Eli didn't stop there; he never did until both tubers had been obliterated. Pravika would bob like a buoy until I lost control. Which didn't seem far off—my body had slid down the tube, toes dipping into the water. I tried to pull myself up to get a better grasp on the handles.

But I, too, was soon flying through the air, clenching my teeth and bracing myself for impact. I catapulted into the water with a loud *smack*. The Oyster Pond swallowed me up before my life vest tugged me back to the surface. *Everything* hurt.

And then unexpectedly, I was crying, sobbing uncontrollably by the time Eli pulled up beside me. I was in a haze as Jake and Luli helped me into the boat, asking if I was okay when my legs wobbled underneath me. I hardly heard them, tears still falling.

Is this what it felt like? I didn't want to wonder, but did. It was impossible not to now. *Is this what it felt like when she was hit?*

I chalked up the crying to being out of practice. "Really, I'm fine," I told my friends, hugging my beach towel around my body. Every limb was still in shock. "I just need to get back into the swing of things."

"But look," Pravika said, pointing to my knee, "you have a bruise." She turned to Eli. "You're a monster!"

Eli immediately apologized, but I shook my head, my arm jittering too much to wave him off like usual. Then it was Jake and Luli's turn to hop on the tube. I didn't watch, bundling myself in another towel and lying low on the Whaler's deck to hide from the wind.

"So we're all set?" Luli asked once we'd anchored the boat near the beach. Wink and a few parents were walking toward us, kids streaming ahead of them. It was their turn to tube now. "Time for the leak?"

Pravika, Jake, and I nodded. The beach was the perfect

place to begin spreading lies; the sun was high in the sky, and most of The Farm had set up camp for the day. My parents waved to me from a circle of beach chairs that included Uncle Brad and Aunt Christine, along with Michael's mom and a silver-streaked blond man who must've been Wit's father. Honey and Aunt Julia supervised little Ethan and Hannah playing with some younger Duprés at the pond's edge. A tiny green squirt gun was tucked into Aunt Julia's swimsuit, and she kept glancing over her shoulder to scan the beach. "Aunt Julia!" Pravika called. "Did you get Peter this morning?"

My aunt smiled.

Yes.

Several yards away, Aunt Rachel looked as carefree as could be, sipping seltzer and swapping *People* and *Us Weekly* magazines with Michael's older sister, Kasi.

And then there were Sarah, Michael, and their posse. They were lounging in the pond's shallows on top of gigantic pool floats. One was a hot pink flamingo, another a swan, and the third a rainbow unicorn, so big that the groom and three of his groomsmen had climbed aboard and were now floating along comfortably. "Over here, guys!" Danielle, the maid of honor, shouted from ashore. She raised her phone. "For the 'gram!"

Everyone laughed.

The five of us dispersed among different groups to plant seeds of deception, but after chatting with my parents for a few minutes, I asked my dad what time it was. He grinned and told me I'd better get going. It was 1:00, and everyone on the

Vineyard knew Morning Glory's famous pies were set out at 2:00. Time was ticking.

I quickly glanced around for my wingman but didn't see Wit. He was probably at the Annex already. "See you tonight, Meredith!" Honey called after me as I tried to sprint through the sand—an impossible feat—slowing down once I was up and over the dune and passing the dusty cars in the beach's parking lot. *Home free*, I thought, since nobody was around. The lot appeared safely deserted.

Then I heard a voice.

"Hey, Meredith," Luli said, and I turned to see her trailing me. "Not in the mood for the beach?"

"Oh, yeah, no," I said while reminding myself that her target was someone else in the Fox family, *not* me. "I actually have to run an errand, so..." I gestured at the houses ahead of us.

"For Wink and Honey's dinner?"

I nodded. Tonight, my grandparents were hosting a potluck meal at the Big House, but only for their immediate family: children, grandchildren, and spouses or significant others. I guess it seemed exclusive from the outside, but it was one of the few times we were all together during the year. "No ifs, ands, or buts," Honey always said. "You're there in a chair!"

Luli and I kept walking together, and as we got closer and closer to the houses, I knew I couldn't put it off any longer. It was time.

"I'm sorry, Luli," I told her. "I'm sorry for everything I did last year." I paused to exhale a long breath so my voice wouldn't shake. "Or *didn't* do, really. I was terrible—not answering your texts or calls or Snaps."

Luli was silent. My heart hammered, but it steadied some when I spotted Wit standing by the Annex. His T-shirt was now green, the light blue wedding one gone.

"Thanks, Meredith," Luli finally said. "That means a lot. It does." She kicked up some dust and added in a smaller voice, "But why? *Why* didn't you answer them? You know how much I loved her." Her voice dropped even more. "We both needed—"

"Hey!" Wit called out, cutting her off. "Angel!"

Luli stopped in her tracks. "Uh, excuse me?"

"Don't worry," I said. "It's only a joke. He's harmless." Then I shouted back to Wit, "Shut it, you devil!"

Wit broke into his crooked grin.

Luli sighed. "So that's him, huh?"

I nodded. "Yeah, that's Michael's stepbrother, Wit. We met last night. He's—"

"The new Ben," she finished dryly and gestured to Wit. He was now jogging over to us. "From the looks of it."

The new Ben? I tightened my grip on my towel. *What's that supposed to mean?*

"I heard you went on a run with him and Michael this morning. At, like, the crack of dawn. When have you ever gotten up that early?"

Thanks a lot, bride and groom, I thought. Michael had indeed told Sarah about this morning, and she'd spread the word that

Wit and I were hanging out. Which didn't bother me...but why was Luli on my back about it? Why was she bringing up Ben?

I mumbled something like "I couldn't sleep" as Wit slowed next to me, a smirk still on his face. The sight made me want to smirk back. Even if I *had* agreed to keep our friendship a secret, it never would've lasted. Wit was too smiley around me, and I found myself too smiley around him.

"Hi," Wit said to Luli, offering her a hand to shake. "You're Luli, right?"

"Yes." She nodded. "And you're the groomsman who got clocked in the face on the ferry."

Wit bumped his elbow against mine, setting off this strange sensation—spirals under my skin. "Courtesy of this one, yes."

Luli gave me a look.

"It's a long story," I said, then tugged Wit's sleeve in the direction of the storage shed. We needed bikes. "I'll tell you later."

"Right," she said slowly. "Your errand."

"Wait, errand?" Wit said. "I thought you were taking me someplace special."

"Morning Glory Farm *is* special," I said.

That made Luli laugh. "It is, buddy," she told Wit. "Morning Glory Farm is *really* special."

She and I exchanged a smile.

And I hoped that meant we were okay, even though I had an inkling that Claire would've said Luli's smile was strained.

SIX

Morning Glory Farm was only a short bike ride from Paqua, but first Wit and I had to make it the three miles down The Farm's sandy dirt driveway. "Give me five seconds!" I'd said to him after Luli had circled back to the beach, pulling my hair into a messy bun and racing into the Annex to change out of my swimsuit. My sneakers were still wet from the pond, so I switched to my spare pair.

Now we were riding our beach cruisers, the sun beating down on us but a smooth breeze also blowing. My guess was that it was about seventy-five degrees, the perfect Vineyard temperature. I wanted to ask Wit about eliminating Isabel, but his head was on a swivel, taking everything in—the magic of it all. The tall oak trees and short scrub trees with their spider-leg-like branches, the sweet grass and patches of violet flowers, not a streetlamp in sight. "When we were younger," I said at one point, "it was a dare."

"What was a dare?" Wit asked.

"This." I nodded at the road ahead. "When Claire and I

were in middle school, Sarah's brothers would dare us to walk to the top of the road and back alone."

Wit wasn't fazed. "That seems pretty doable."

"At *night*," I added. "Pure darkness, no flashlights, with all the animals lurking."

"Okay, yeah," he said after a beat. "I see it now."

"Claire and I did it, though," I said, a small lump forming in my throat. "We danced the entire time and belted out Taylor Swift songs."

The *Fearless* album flashed through my mind. We'd sung every song so loud and off-key to scare away any skunks, raccoons, or foxes. *Real* foxes.

Wit chuckled. "Did you win anything?"

"Not really," I replied. "Bragging rights, I guess, even though Peter and Ian never believed us." I rolled my eyes. "According my mom, it also gave us a boost of self-confidence."

He nodded. "Well, I'm game," he said. "Should we do it sometime this week?"

"Sure..." I said slowly, already able to picture us strolling together. Like we had last night around The Farm, talking and joking and laughing.

"*Sure...*" Wit echoed. "That didn't sound very convincing."

"No, we'll do it." I blinked a few times, then turned to give him a leering smile. "I officially dare you."

"Excellent," Wit said. "And hey, if you're still scared, you can always bring your *knife* for protection."

My knife—the Swiss Army pocketknife I'd threatened

him with in the darkness. "I actually do have one," I said as the two of us reached the stone obelisk at the tip of the drive. PAQUA was carved vertically down the front. "Wink gave it to me for my birthday this year, but it's at home." Hidden in my jewelry box, because Ben thought it was weird that I had one. *For Meredith*, the blade's engraving read. *May you always kick ass and take names.*

Wit and I coasted right onto West Tisbury Road's paved bike path. "Oh, trust me, I figured as much," he said. "Seems totally on-brand for you."

Totally on-brand for me?

"What's that supposed to mean?" I asked, a bit breathless. "What's my brand?"

Because maybe I wanted him to tell me. Maybe I wanted to hear what he thought of me.

But he just smirked and shrugged.

So I scowled at him and kept on pedaling, staying silent for the next ten minutes until we reached our destination. "Welcome to Morning Glory!" I said, hitting my brakes and sliding off my bike. Wit followed suit, and we leaned them against the split-rail fence.

Morning Glory Farm was one of my favorite places on the Vineyard: sixty-five acres of fields with big barns, greenhouses, and best of all, the community farm stand. It was the antithesis of every supermarket back on the mainland, a rambling house full of warmth, wood beams, fresh fruits and vegetables, and plenty of homemade treats. Morning Glory was so popular that it had published its own cookbook. Claire had gifted a copy to my parents one year for Christmas, its spine now cracked from so much use.

I watched Wit admire the farm, no doubt noticing all the people unwrapping and digging into mouthwatering sandwiches at the worn picnic tables, the children playing tag, and the dogs running around with them. But then I checked my phone to see that it was 1:55. We only had a few minutes. "Okay, okay," I said, grabbing a handful of his shirt. "Come on!"

He let me drag him down the gravel walkway, past the buckets overflowing with beautiful wildflower bouquets, up the porch steps, and through the swinging doors. Voices reverberated off the high ceiling, and bursts of every color in the rainbow greeted us. I wanted to show Wit everything, but first we had a mission to accomplish. A crowd was beginning to congregate. "Are you going to tell me what's happening?" he asked.

"The pies," I whispered, like it was some big secret and not common knowledge. "The pies come out at 2:00 but are immediately ravaged. They're picked over by 2:15."

Wit raised an eyebrow. "So they're pretty good?"

"*Pretty* good?" I gave him a look. "Try *delicious*! My dad and Uncle Brad once ate *nine* in only *five* days..." I dropped off; that was a story for another time. We could now smell the sweetness of the pies as Morning Glory's bakers brought them out of the kitchen and arranged them on the display. We needed to focus. "Here," I said, my hands going to Wit's waist and forcing him over a few steps. My fingers tingled a little as I felt his warm skin through his shirt. "Stand here, and don't move. You need to be a blockade."

"For what?"

I gestured around us at the customers closing in on the pies. Personal space did not exist at a moment like this. I also wasn't afraid of playing dirty, dropping down to the floor to crawl through the people in front of me. A perk of being petite.

When I glanced back at Wit, he was standing in place like a wiry pillar. But now his head was cocked and one side of his mouth turned up at the corner. Sandy hair flopped over his forehead.

"What?" I asked.

"Nothing," he said. "You're just—"

"Don't say cute," I cut in, neck heating. "Everyone says that."

Ben was one of them, especially when I got really enthusiastic or passionate about something. The Vineyard, for instance. "And the pies!" I remembered once saying, my voice loud and proud. "They're made daily, in the afternoons, and you don't even need to reheat them after dinner. They're still so *warm*, and with a huge scoop of ice cream..."

Afterward, he'd kissed me and told I was cute for the millionth time. It was like being called babe. Claire had known it bothered me, so whenever she was in a bad mood and wanted me to shut up or leave her alone, she'd flatly say, "Aw, you're cute, Meredith."

Wit gave me a wry look. "That wasn't exactly the word I had in mind..."

Whatever he said next was drowned out, the jockeying for a prime position now in motion. I started pushing through shuffling legs, smiling to myself. It was officially pie o'clock.

"Oh my!" a baker exclaimed when I popped up in front of the display. Now nothing stood between me and my prize. "Where did you come from?"

After successfully securing three pies (blueberry, peach, and strawberry rhubarb), I handed them to Wit and found a wicker shopping basket for us to fill. "The zucchini bread is incredible," I said, grabbing a loaf. "So are the champagne grapes." I dangled a bunch in front of Wit, the purple grapes so adorably tiny. "Especially if you freeze them. They're the perfect beach snack."

Our basket got heavier and heavier as Wit added ripe plums, raspberries, big bell peppers, tomatoes, and freshly squeezed orange juice. We soon needed another basket to hold two dozen ears of corn. Then we ordered sandwiches at the deli counter: turkey, cheddar, and sliced Granny Smith apple on sourdough bread.

"Wow," the girl at the register commented once we finally made it there. Her blond hair was pulled up in a ponytail, and she gave Wit's bruise a funny look but didn't say anything. "You guys have quite the haul here!"

I nodded, and we chatted while she scanned our groceries—well, she chatted with *Wit*. She smiled when she noticed his shirt, wrinkled from where I'd snatched it and pulled him inside the little market. SUGARBUSH, it said across his chest. "Yeah, I'm from Vermont," he explained. "My mom works there as a ski instructor."

"I love Sugarbush!" she said as I hid my hands behind my back and knotted my fingers together, resisting the urge to smooth out Wit's shirt. "That's where my family and I spend Christmas, and it's only an hour away from Middlebury. I'll be a sophomore this fall."

Wit went quiet. "That was my first choice," he said eventually. "But I'm at Tulane now."

"Cool, New Orleans!" The cashier was still expertly unloading, scanning, and bagging—a talented multitasker. SAGE, her name tag read. "My friend goes to Tulane, and I'm hoping to visit during Mardi Gras. Do you know..."

Okay, that's it, I thought, untangling my fingers and stepping closer to Wit so that our arms were pressed up against each other. *Enough!*

I reached to smooth the front of Wit's T-shirt, feeling the flutter of his heartbeat. It soon fluttered faster, and mine did, too, when he casually slipped an arm around my neck, fingertips dancing along my collarbone.

"Oh," Sage said as I held my breath. "Oh no—sorry, I didn't mean anything." She laughed and shook her head, then held up the last item to scan: a pie. "Strawberry rhubarb is my boyfriend's favorite." Her face lit up like the sun. "He says it's totally epic."

Wit's and my coupledom charade ended as quickly as it had begun, right after I swiped my dad's credit card to pay our outrageous bill. Wit was in complete shock. "Seriously?" he said once we'd walked back to our bikes and arranged our paper bags in the old fruit crates attached to the backs. "Those pies were twenty-five dollars *each*?"

"Uh-huh," I replied and recited one of Wink's favorite sayings. "It's impossible to leave Morning Glory with pies and a bill under a hundred dollars!"

Wit laughed, but I all could think about were his fingers on my collarbone, the way they had flashed against my skin—the little shocks of electricity. It had left me so light-headed that I felt myself swaying.

"Hey." Wit's voice made me blink. Somehow we were now sitting across from each other at a picnic table, chowing down on our sandwiches. "You okay?"

"Yeah," I said and forced myself to take a bite of sandwich. "I'm fine."

Wit didn't look convinced. "Are you sure?"

I evaded the question with one of my own. "You wanted to go to Middlebury?"

"Yeah." He nodded. "I was really bummed when I didn't get in."

"Then why Tulane?" I asked. "They seem like polar opposites."

Wit sighed. "Because if it couldn't be Middlebury, I wanted college to be an adventure. New Orleans sounded like the ultimate one." He shrugged. "It's where my dad lives, but I'd never spent much time down there. I've always lived with my mom." He glanced away for a second. "And my dad was obviously a fan, since the Duprés liked it so much."

"But you don't like it, do you?" I guessed. "It's not an adventure?"

"Oh, it's an adventure," Wit said. "I'm just not sure it's *my* adventure." He chuckled. "I'll shut up now. I don't want to ruin Michael and Sarah's NOLA utopia for you."

"Already ruined," I murmured, more to myself than him. "A while ago."

But Wit heard it anyway, eyes widening. "Shit," he said. "Meredith, I'm sorry." He patted the bruise-free side of his face. "Feel free to kick me."

I shook my head and tried to smile. "Let's talk about something else."

He nodded and swung his leg over the side of his bench to join me on mine—settling in close, like in the checkout line. "Have you been on Instagram lately?"

"Not since last night," I said, watching him unlock his phone and tap the app. "But I thought you said you didn't do Instagram." I searched the screen for his handle. "Apparently I was mistaken, @sowitty17."

Wit sighed. "Sarah asked me to make an effort this week."

"Ah, I see," I said. "Now, am I the only one who thinks your username's obnoxious?"

The only response I got was a grumble.

I laughed and absentmindedly touched his bruise with the back of my hand. It was still big and blue and, from the way Wit winced, extremely tender. His fingers stopped typing. "Ouch," I said, as if I were the one injured. "My bad."

Literally.

Wit glanced up, turquoise eyes bright in the sunlight, their impossibly gold rings gleaming. "You're very affectionate," he said, gaze catching mine. "You know that?"

I shook my head, unable to respond. Who said stuff like that? *Affectionate?* I couldn't imagine Ben or any of his friends ever using that word. And the *way* Wit said it—his *voice*. It was gentle, honest, intimate. How could it be that intimate? We'd just met.

My sister would've said it didn't matter. An astrology lover, Claire believed that some people had written-in-the-stars fated connections, and even though I'd always rolled my eyes, maybe now I was beginning to believe her. I got goose bumps remembering Wit's and my knees knocking while we created our pact and feeling disappointed when we'd said goodbye. *I want to see him tomorrow* was the last thing I'd thought before falling asleep in the Annex's sitting room. There was an undeniable *something* between us.

But I couldn't put my finger on it yet.

"Just an observation," Wit whispered after several silent seconds. He shifted in his seat and went back to his phone.

#HurrayShesADupré, he typed into the search bar, and I pretty much leapt when I realized what he wanted to show me.

"Oh my god!" I exclaimed. "The group photo!"

Wit laughed, that melodious sound. "Wait until you see it." He scrolled through a few pictures with the wedding hashtag—I caught a glimpse of Michael and the three groomsmen on the unicorn float—before tapping one posted by @Sarah_Jane. It had been taken in the Pond House's backyard, and Sarah and Michael had their arms around each other in the middle, with the best man on my cousin's other side and the maid of honor on Michael's. Their smiles were picture-perfect.

But at the very end of the line, there was a look of complete and utter *horror* on bridesmaid Isabel's face. Her eyes were so wide that if you zoomed in, it appeared they were about to bulge from their sockets, and her mouth had dropped open in a scream.

Because Wit, while grinning at the camera as commanded, had raised his arm high to dump his entire water bottle over Isabel's head.

"Holy crap," I breathed, awestruck. "Why didn't you spray her?" The bottle's orange cap was nowhere in sight, unscrewed and tossed away ahead of time.

"She called me *kid* earlier," he replied.

I pretended to gasp. "How dare she!"

Wit frowned. "I don't like kid," he said. "Only my mom calls me that."

"What happened afterward?" I asked, wishing Eli had waited one more minute before powering up the boat. We could've heard the whole thing!

"Well, she pretty much cursed me before going inside with your exasperated aunt to get a new shirt and blow-dry her hair, and when they came back twenty minutes later, we had to retake the photo."

"And then did she pass on her target?"

"After another series of curses, yes."

I laughed. "So who is it? Who do you have?"

Wit leaned in, and as he whispered a familiar name in my ear, a light hand landed on my knee. He didn't give it a reassuring squeeze like Ben used to; he just let it rest there...which was somehow even more calming. Warmth ignited under his palm, and I felt myself wanting to twine our fingers together.

"You're affectionate, too," I murmured, and when Wit looked at me, I smiled. "Just an observation."

SEVEN

By the time Wit and I returned to Paqua, my alliance had suffered its first casualty. "Dad, *really*?" I asked later as we headed to Wink and Honey's for dinner. My parents each carried a bag of corn, and I had the pies. "You couldn't have given Pravika more time?"

My dad sighed. "What do you want me to say, Meredith? She was *right* there. I know she's part of your crew, but her guard was down, and I couldn't waste that opportunity."

Next to him, my mom stifled a laugh. I shot her a glare.

Meredith!!! Pravika had texted our group chat while I'd been biking home. Your dad!!!

She was asleep on the beach, Jake explained, and let's just say your dad woke her up.

Luli had then sent a video—filmed by Uncle Brad—of my father sneaking over to Pravika's towel and giving the camera a thumbs-up before ending her Assassin career by splashing her with one of the little cousins' buckets. She'd jolted awake and, once oriented, screamed, "I hate you, Uncle Tom!"

The only good thing that had really come of it was that we all knew who my dad's next target was. In the video, Pravika had rifled through her beach bag and angrily flung the slip of paper at him. It was another cousin.

Uncle Brad gave my dad another high-five when we got to the Big House. He, too, had successfully killed his first target.

I set the pies far back on the kitchen counter, away from Wink and Honey's golden retriever—Clarabelle was known for counter-surfing, ruining many a meal. The dogs somehow knew something was happening tonight, because they'd abandoned whatever adventure they'd been on to congregate in the kitchen. Even Loki, whom I hadn't seen since this morning. "Behave," I told him. He was named after the god of mischief, after all.

The kitchen was crowded; nobody had abided by the traditional definition of *potluck*. Everyone had brought food, but it all still needed to be cooked. Sarah was at the sink washing lettuce for a salad while Michael stood next to her chopping cucumbers. Wink and Aunt Julia were seasoning the steaks together down the counter. My mom had thrown herself into sprinkling basil on the tomato and mozzarella platter while Aunt Rachel checked on something in the oven. Sarah's younger brother, Ian, was mixing drinks at the table. He'd just turned twenty-one and apparently fancied himself a bartender.

My stomach twisted into a knot. The kitchen was about to burst, but at the same time, it felt so *empty*. Where was she? Where was Claire, balancing plates, water glasses, and utensils so she could set the table? Where *was* she?

"Okay, okay!" Honey started shuttling the roughhousing Ethan and Hannah outdoors. "This corn isn't going to husk itself!" She turned to me, and I forced myself to push away thoughts of my sister. "Show them, Meredith?"

"Yeah, of course," I said but pointed down the hall. "I need to use the bathroom first."

"I'll keep an eye on them, Honey," Kate, Peter's wife, said before I escaped the kitchen. She handed off their babbling baby to her husband. "Pete has Nell."

Perfect, I thought, but instead of ducking into the first-floor powder room, I crept up the Big House's old oak staircase to the second floor and slipped into the bedroom where Great-Uncle Richard and Wife #3 were staying. They'd driven into Vineyard Haven for dinner, so the coast was clear. I swallowed and stared at the bay window across the room—a window that not only overlooked the ocean but was also big enough for a person to climb through onto the porch's roof. "I know helping each other with execution isn't part of our pact," Wit had said at lunch, "but since you're having dinner tonight, it seems like a prime time."

I had hesitated at first. Yes, elimination assistance wasn't what we'd agreed upon—just sharing intel, information, and potential threats. The end. Setting an actual snare together meant we'd immediately be labeled accomplices. My friends would be pissed.

But...

"I'll open the window for you," I'd told him once he'd

explained his plan. "That's it. I will open the window so you know which room it is, but that's all." I thought for a moment. "You also can't do anything until I'm hanging out with everyone again. I can't have this traced back to me."

Now I sat on the bedroom's cozy window seat and waited—waited for Wit to come sprinting into sight, pretending to be on his second run of the day. And when he did, he waved at the corn huskers and whoever else in my family had migrated out to the porch. "Witty!" I heard Michael call as I pushed the window open, praying his booming voice muffled the squeaking. Its hinges needed to be oiled. "On another tear, huh?"

Impartial, Michael! I thought. *Don't give anyone any ideas!*

Wearing headphones, Wit simply smiled and waved again. He didn't stop to chat; if anything, he picked up his pace. I took that as my cue to book it back downstairs, knowing Wit planned to race out of view but then loop around and sneak through the side door.

Which I was about to prop open with one of Honey's painted rocks so no one would hear those hinges squeak either. They needed to be oiled, too. Pretty much all the door hinges on The Farm needed to be oiled, except for Lantern House. Aunt Christine kept on top of little things like that.

Wit raised an eyebrow when he found me standing in the doorway. "I thought you said no colluding," he said, pulling out his earbuds and giving me a half smile, half smirk. "Doesn't waiting here seem like colluding?"

I chose to ignore that comment. "Where's your weapon?" I asked instead, very quietly. "Your water bottle?"

"Everyone knows I used it on Isabel," he replied, even more quietly. "I couldn't exactly run past a family of Foxes with it. It'd raise suspicions."

"So?" I said. "What now?"

Wit pulled his tiny pink squirt gun from the side of his shorts. "Now get out there." He motioned to the front of the house. "Let's stick to our plan."

"*Your* plan," I corrected.

"*Our* plan," he said with a wink and then was gone.

I rolled my eyes and tried to pull off a casual walk outside. Michael and Sarah were in the hammock, talking with Aunt Christine about wedding details (and wisely sipping cocktails), Honey was adjusting the place settings on the long porch table, and luckily, it looked like my little cousins and Kate hadn't made much progress with the corn. They were sitting together on the porch's wide steps, which was the best Wit could hope for; they weren't under the cover of the roof.

But while I was gone, Peter had handed Nell back off to Kate. *Nope*, I thought, moving forward. *No babies allowed in the line of fire.*

"Oh, thank you, Meredith," Kate said when I swept Nell out of her arms. "We forgot her bottle, so Peter ran back to Lantern to grab it." She turned and smiled at Ethan and Hannah. "Now we can *really* get cracking on these. Watch me, Epstein-Foxes."

This side of the Big House faced the water, but I settled

in the grass with Nell in my lap and my back to the million-dollar view.

Because the *billion*-dollar view had begun. Pretending to watch my cousins learn to husk corn, I kept flicking my gaze up to the second floor, where Wit was now carefully maneuvering himself through the window and out onto the shingled rooftop. He stood there for a second, as if to take a deep breath, then dropped to his knees. When we made accidental eye contact, he blew me a kiss...and I swear I felt it hit my cheek, a light tickle followed by a rush of heat.

Shit, I thought, worrying someone would notice.

But it appeared everyone was oblivious, especially Wit's target. "No, wait a sec, Han," Kate was saying. "You gotta make sure you get all the silk." She took Hannah's piece of corn and demonstrated, tugging off the rest of the threadlike fibers. "Like this, see?"

Now Wit was doing a slow army crawl down the roof, pink squirt gun in hand. He'd move several inches, maybe a foot, then pause and listen to make sure all was still good. My heart was hammering when he stopped at the gutter line, lying on his stomach with Kate directly in his crosshairs. He was in position.

I felt giggles rising, but I forced myself to swallow them. No way could I ruin our plan. It was too freaking good.

But Kate didn't feel the first squirt, still absorbed in Ethan and Hannah husking the corn.

So Wit squirted her again.

This time, her hand went to the back of her neck. *She thinks she's imagining it*, I thought. Those tiny guns were as subtle as you could get with their water stream.

Wit obviously knew this, too, the side of his mouth quirking as he sprayed Kate a third time. He wasn't going to announce himself as her assassin; he wanted her to discover him.

Kate rubbed her neck again, looked up at the blue sky, and then over at me. "Is it my new-mom brain," she said, "or is there a sun shower happening? I feel this mist—"

Wit ambushed her. Squirt, squirt, squirt!

"Are you kidding me?" She sprang from the steps and turned to see him on the roof. "You've got to be kidding me!"

"What?" Peter came banging out of the house with Nell's bottle in hand. "What happened?"

"My stepbrother assassinated your wife," Michael said, now standing next to me in the grass. He smiled proudly, so not impartial. "That's what happened."

"No." Peter shook his head and looked up to see Wit spinning the water gun around on his index finger. So obnoxious, but I couldn't control the laughter that bubbled out of me. "No," Peter repeated as Wink, Honey, and everyone else came out to see what was happening. "No, he didn't, because 'outside' means at least ten feet away from a door." He gestured from the screen door to the steps. "There is no way that's ten feet."

Kate nodded. "Not a chance."

"I don't know." Aunt Julia eyed the distance. "It could be."

"Hmm, Jules might be right," Uncle Brad weighed in. "As much as I don't want to agree with her—"

Aunt Julia rolled her eyes. "Shut up, Brad."

"Hey, hey." My dad tried to mediate like the middle child he was.

Michael and Sarah exchanged a look while Peter and Kate kept insisting the steps were only seven or eight feet from the door. Nine, tops.

Still on the roof, Wit shifted into an intimidating crouch. "Okay," he said coolly, jutting out his chin a little. "Then let's get a measuring tape."

"Gladly!" Wink clapped his hands, beaming because of the disagreement. It was his favorite part of being an Assassin commissioner.

And thus, the investigation commenced.

"Kate, dear," Honey said once Wink disappeared inside, "please sit back down exactly where you were when Wit shot you..."

Kate sighed and took a seat on the porch's top step.

"That's not—" I started to say, but then Ethan chimed in from below.

"No, Kate." He shook his head. "You were sitting down here with me and Hannah, remember? Teaching us to husk corn?"

Yeah, I thought, watching Kate reluctantly move to the bottom step. *Take that.*

Wit was now whistling to himself, seemingly not concerned in the slightest. Part of me wondered if he'd snuck over here to measure out the distance earlier today.

Wink reemerged from the house. "Okay, here we are."

"How much?" I heard Uncle Brad mutter to my dad. "Ten flat?"

"Ten and a half," my dad muttered back.

"Twenty bucks?"

"Deal."

They fist-bumped.

Wink extended the tape measure from the house's threshold to the back of his granddaughter-in-law's neck. "Well?" Kate's voice was shrill.

"What's the verdict, Wink?" Peter asked.

I held my breath as my grandfather squinted to make out the measurement. "I think I need my glasses," he said after a second. "Honey, could you—"

Everyone groaned, knowing he was joking. Wink didn't wear glasses.

"Ten and a quarter," he announced. "Ten feet and a quarter!" The tape measure snapped shut. "It's a legitimate kill!"

"Boom!" Wit shouted from above and then proceeded to shimmy down one of the porch columns all the way to the ground. He went up to Kate and smiled at her. "Good to meet you, Kate. I'm Wit."

"I know," she said through clenched teeth, digging around in her pocket and producing her target slip. She handed it over with a grumble. "Best of luck."

"Thanks." Wit slipped the piece of paper into his own pocket, then saluted us. "I'll get out of your way now. Enjoy your dinner."

I caught Honey looking at Wink, and he replied with a nod. "Wait a moment, Wit," my grandmother said. "Why don't you stay? We have plenty of food, and as long you don't mind a tight fit at the table..."

"A tight fit meaning you'd be sitting on the stool," Sarah translated and gestured to the table. Since there were so many of us, it was a mishmash of outdoor furniture, kitchen chairs, a bench from the mudroom decoupaged with family photos, and at one corner of the table, a tall wooden stool. The infamously uncomfortable stool.

Claire had always volunteered to sit there.

"Oh," Wit said. "That's really nice of you." He ran a hand through his hair like he was worried about intruding. "But—"

Michael stepped in and shook his stepbrother's shoulders, then covered Wit's mouth with a hand. "He'd love to stay, Honey," he said. "Thank you for inviting him."

"Yes," Wit echoed after his stepbrother removed his hand. He elbowed Michael in the ribs. Both of them grinned. "Thank you for inviting me."

Sure enough, Wit got stuck with the stool. Wink and Honey settled at the head and foot of the table, while I took my usual seat: the antique Edgartown Yacht Club captain's chair from Wink's small study. It happened to be right next to Wit. Claire's stool stood taller than my chair, tall enough for Wit to eat with his knees if such a thing were possible. "I take it this is the seat of honor?" he said after he noticed me staring at him.

"Yeah," was all I said, my voice a whisper.

"Well, I'm very honored," he said back, whispering, too.

I forced a smile before picking at my salad; I'd never been a salad fan. Claire hadn't either. "Rabbit food," we used to call it and would always order soup over salad in restaurants.

Across the table, Sarah noticed me pushing around the lettuce, and even though she'd prepared the salad, she laughed. "Not inspiring enough for you, Mer?" she asked, every other conversation falling silent. My cousin's sparkling laugh was impossible to ignore. If she laughed, you wanted to know why.

"No, no," I said, shaking my head. "It's good...really, uh, fresh." I looked at Michael. "The cucumbers are a nice touch."

Sarah leaned forward to grin at me. "Liar." Then she straightened to address the entire table. "Claire did the funniest thing in New Orleans," she said, smile now bittersweet. "We took her to one of our favorite restaurants for dinner with a bunch of people, and she was so overwhelmed by the menu that she let someone order for her..."

I put down my fork, appetite gone. It's this place called Basin, my sister had said during our last text conversation. Sarah says it's in the Garden District, but afterward she and her friends are giving me the grand tour of the French Quarter! Bourbon Street! How jealous are you?

The French Quarter was the oldest neighborhood in New

Orleans, and Bourbon Street was famous for its nightlife. Jazz clubs, bright lights, and bars with crazy cocktails. Our cousin was helping Claire celebrate New Year's and her early acceptance to Tulane while I was stuck at home. Ridiculously jealous, I'd texted back. Why aren't I there?!

"Danielle had no clue about the salad thing," Sarah told us, now in full storytelling mode, "and of course Claire was too polite to tell her."

Most of the table laughed. "Our sweet Claire," Honey said as I stole a glance at my parents. They were listening with pleasant expressions, but I noticed my dad had put a hand on my mom's shoulder. She kissed his fingers.

Sarah kept speaking. "So after inhaling her appetizer, the crawdad mac 'n' cheese—*amazing*—the oyster Caesar salad arrives, and I swear she didn't take a *single* bite. She pretended. I forget who she was sitting next to..." She thought for a second, then shook her head. "But Michael and I watched her move her knife and fork around her plate, all the while keeping up a conversation with whomever. She was talking so much that they didn't notice she hadn't chewed or swallowed anything." She giggled. "When the server came and collected our plates, it really looked like she'd eaten most of it!"

Again, laughter circled the table. My heart was aching. *Do they not know?* I wondered as I felt Wit shift next to me, probably uncomfortable on the stool. *Are they pretending? Or do they truly not realize the timing?*

"Rabbit food," Sarah added, nudging my foot with hers

under the table. "That's what she told me right after we left. She said you two secretly call salad rabbit food."

"Well, it's not much of a secret anymore," I tried to joke, but it came off as cold and deadpan...because I knew what had happened next.

Everything turned to white noise as I remembered my phone buzzing at 3:00 a.m. that night eighteen months ago. Somehow, I'd answered without opening my eyes. "Hello?" I said groggily, only to hear Michael at the other end of the line.

"Meredith, Meredith," he said quickly. "Your parents. I've been calling your parents. Where are your parents?"

I yawned. "Knocked out asleep. We had a party, and my dad made his famous margaritas—"

Michael cut me off. "Please wake them up."

"What?"

"Wake them up!" His voice was frantic; he didn't sound like Sarah's composed fiancé at all. "Sarah," he said. "My Sarah, and Claire." He wavered like he was crying. "Claire..."

At the mention of my sister's name, I snapped to attention, throwing back my covers and racing down our dark hallway to my parents' room. "Mom!" I flicked on the lights. "Dad!"

My mom screamed after I handed her the phone, and even though I couldn't hear what Michael was saying, I *knew*.

Claire is dead, I thought, falling to my knees with tears already rushing down my face. *My sister is dead.*

It had been a drunk driving accident. One cocktail had

been enough for Claire during her Bourbon Street bar crawl, but apparently Sarah was three sheets to the wind, so she had handed my sister her keys. "You be my chauffeur!" Sarah had said. "I'll even sit in the back!"

Together, they'd made it back to my cousin's car, which was parallel parked right outside the French Quarter. Claire was a capable and careful driver, always double-checking everything before going anywhere, even if it was just pulling out of our driveway.

But that night, she didn't get the chance to adjust the mirrors and assess her surroundings. Claire had buckled her seat belt, turned to check that Sarah had buckled hers, and then had barely put the key into the ignition before a massive SUV came hurtling out of nowhere and smashed into them. The driver's BAC was three times the legal limit.

Sarah suffered several broken bones, a serious concussion, and was left with scars.

But my sister was killed instantly.

Instantly.

The next day, my parents were on the first flight to New Orleans, but I stayed home, absolutely petrified. Ben came over, and I hugged him and cried until Wink and Honey arrived. "Sweetie," my grandmother said, and while I expected her to say more, she didn't. She bit her lip and blinked back her own tears. Because really, what was there to say?

Claire was gone.

Now I felt my eyes stinging and Wit's hand on my back, a few fingertips subtly and smoothly brushing through my hair. He intuitively knew I needed steadying. I wanted to reach for some part of him, too, even if it was only his T-shirt hem. But before I could, I heard my name. "Meredith!"

Luli was climbing the porch steps and waving her phone. "Why haven't you been responding in the chat?"

"Because we don't allow phones at dinner," Wink answered for me. He motioned to the table, its centerpiece a tower of iPhones. "Family time."

"Oh, understood." Luli nodded, then refocused on me. "Your target—"

"Don't worry, Luli." It was Aunt Julia who spoke this time. "We all know who Meredith's target is." We made eye contact, a twinkle in hers. "No need for secrecy."

Luli's cheeks pinkened, realizing my aunt knew about our "shuffling the deck" strategy. "Anyway"—Luli cleared her throat—"apparently your target is in Edgartown, and Pravika thinks you can get them. Like, *tonight*."

"Wait, what?" I asked and looked at Wink before getting up from the table.

He nodded. Permission granted.

"Daniel Robinson is in Edgartown with his girlfriend," Luli repeated once we were alone in the kitchen. "Jake scooped their ice cream at Mad Martha's, and Pravika is predicting they'll visit her at Murdick's next."

"Okay," I said. "Let me think a second."

Daniel Robinson—this morning, Jake and I had joked that he was a John Doe, but after my dad had eliminated Pravika, she had appointed herself lead researcher for our alliance. I'd received a text earlier saying that Daniel was staying in Moor House, and an Instagram picture had also been included of him with Michael's younger sister, Nicole. Of course I already knew those details. Wit had also told me that Daniel was studying to be a marine biologist, so I was planning to off him by the Oyster Pond under the guise of showing him the horseshoe crabs. Understated but artful.

But now...I could get him *now?*

Claire would get him now.

"All right," I said to Luli. "Tell Eli to get the Jeep, and meet me outside the Annex."

Because Claire would also say this mission called for the Super Soaker.

I took a deep breath and returned to the porch after Luli confirmed the plan with Eli. "Can you guys save me some pie?" I asked. "I've gotta take care of business."

"Sure, sweetie," Honey said at the same time Uncle Brad and Dad went, "No promises!"

I rolled my eyes and turned to Wit, still on the stool. *Are you coming?* I almost said, but then I remembered that we weren't collaborating. Today had been a one-time thing. We weren't known accomplices.

"I'll save you a slice of strawberry rhubarb," he told me when I'd looked at him too long, and I grinned in response, knowing that meant *Good luck.*

"Meredith!" Eli shouted. "Everything all right?"

We were speeding down Paqua's driveway in Wink's battered old Jeep, the car we had all learned to drive when we were still years away from getting our actual licenses. It had no roof and no doors, so the wind raged all around us. I was doubled over in the front seat with my eyes squeezed shut, hugging the neon-colored Super Soaker to my chest. *Slow down*, I thought, stomach in knots. *Please slow down...*

"Faster, Eli!" I heard Luli call from the back seat. "Pravika's saying they walked into Murdick's!"

The Jeep didn't slow down until we rolled into Edgartown proper, with its white clapboard and cedar-shingled houses, the Old Whaling Church, the brick sidewalks, and the yacht club down by the water. Tonight, town was teeming with people wandering in and out of stores and licking ice cream cones. We could hear laughter from Alchemy Restaurant's balcony. I used to think of it as *our* balcony, since the Foxes always celebrated big birthdays there. The last one had been Claire's eighteenth. I'd made her wear this obnoxious light-up tiara. She was gorgeous.

"Okay, unbuckle," Luli said once Eli turned onto North Water and we passed Mad Martha's Ice Cream. Murdick's Fudge was two doors up the street. "Unbuckle your seat—"

"Oh my god!" Eli interrupted, head spinning over his shoulder. "There he is!"

"Who?!" Luli and I said. "Daniel?!"

"No, the man of my dreams!" He craned his neck further, and the Jeep suddenly swerved. My heart did, too. "He's back there, in the seersucker tie and blue blazer!"

"Eli, the road!" I punched his arm. "The road! Focus on *the road*!"

"Meredith!" Luli leaned forward and pointed to the Murdick's storefront, where Nicole Dupré and the afore-mentioned Daniel Robinson had pushed through the doors, hefty white fudge bag in hand (I admit my mouth watered as I wondered what flavors they'd chosen). The couple looked like they were going to continue up the sidewalk, but then, lucky for us, they decided to jaywalk to the jewelry store across the street.

The rest happened in about three seconds:

Eli slowed the car to a crawl.

I unbuckled my seat belt and, before thinking twice, shot up into a standing position.

"Hey!" Luli shouted as I situated my water gun over the Jeep's windshield. "Daniel!"

Daniel glanced over at us, at the Super Soaker now aimed straight at him. His eyes widened. "Run, Dan!" Nicole pretty much shoved him. "Run!"

But it was too late.

"Watch this, Claire," I whispered and pulled the trigger.

Somehow there was plenty of pie left by the time we made it back to the Farm. I'd insisted on driving home, so I pulled the Jeep straight up to the Big House, right in front of the porch. "How'd it go?" my mom asked while I looked for Wit. His stool was empty.

"Bloody brilliant," Luli said in her best British accent. "It was like something out of a James Bond movie."

We ended up reenacting the takedown for everyone, casting Sarah and Michael in the roles of Nicole and Daniel. "She won't stop texting me," Michael said afterward when checking his phone. He turned to Wink. "She's saying it's not a valid kill because it happened in town, not here."

Wink chuckled. It was his second decree of the day. "Remind her of the three rules, Michael." He served himself more peach pie. "One, game play is twenty-four hours a day." He plopped a scoop of vanilla ice cream on top. "Two, all eliminations must occur outdoors." He took a big forkful. "And three—"

"Nothing is to interfere with wedding events," Aunt Christine finished for him. She sipped her wine. "Meredith's takedown in no way conflicts with those parameters. There's technically nothing that restricts Assassin activity beyond Paqua property lines."

Honey patted my aunt's hand. "You're going to make a wonderful commissioner one day."

Aunt Christine smiled.

Michael bit his lip as he tapped a text back to his sister and let out a deep sigh when she responded. "She still doesn't think it's fair," he reported, "but Daniel says he'll drop his target off in the Annex's mailbox later tonight." He coughed. "Lots of angry emojis, too."

We laughed. "Everyone better watch out," Aunt Julia said. "Day one isn't even over and Mer has two kills under her belt. She's a threat."

"Wait, *two*?" Luli's eyebrows knitted together. "I thought Daniel was your first target? You didn't mention anyone else at tubing."

There was a beat of silence, my cheeks warming with shame. Why hadn't I told my friends? They were my alliance! "Well, um, I also eliminated Aunt Rachel," I said. "Early this morning."

"While I was meditating," Aunt Rachel added, definitely to defuse the tension. "I didn't even see her coming and asked her to keep it quiet for a while." She kissed Aunt Julia's cheek. "I didn't want to disappoint Julia so soon."

"Oh," Luli said. "So you weren't *really* on a run with Michael and Wit."

I shook my head.

"But speaking of Wit," Uncle Brad said, "he's another one to keep an eye on—he did double duty today, too." He gave us a look. "And that move earlier..."

"What move earlier?" Luli asked.

Kate, as the victim, took it upon herself to explain, and when we were walking home long past sunset, my dad brought it up again. "It was so *clever*," he said, "and the execution was excellent. I wonder if he's working with anyone..." He trailed off, and

I felt him give me some serious side-eye. "I mean, how did he know? How did he know that we were having dinner tonight?"

My mom laughed. "Tom, *everyone* knew we were having dinner tonight!"

"Okay," he conceded, "but what about everything else? How'd he know that Kate would be outside and that Uncle Richard's bedroom window was the perfect point of entry?" He sucked in a breath through his teeth as we reached the Annex. "Brad's right, the kid's dangerous."

"He doesn't like being called *kid*," I murmured.

"What was that, Mer?"

"Nothing," I said, then paused. My dad was holding open the screen door for me, but I didn't want to go inside yet. Especially when I thought about sleeping in the bunk room alone...

It was silent and suffocating.

"Meredith?"

I blinked. "I'm going to go out for a while," I said, even though it was nearly midnight. "To, you know, hang out."

My dad waved his hand across the horizon, his way of saying, *Do what you will!* I was eighteen; there weren't any Farm rules for me anymore.

"Have fun!" my mom said after I'd checked the mailbox for my new target. She probably thought I was going to the circle of tents to be with my friends. Eli's Nylon Condo Complex.

Which wasn't entirely off base. I *was* going to see a friend.

Just not one sleeping in a tent.

The Cabin was dark, the groomsmen definitely still partying in Oak Bluffs with the bridesmaids. Sarah and Michael had left the Big House to go meet up with them, but Wit...

I headed for the last room in the row, and once I saw light seeping through its blinds, I pulled open the door to see Wit in bed. He was under the covers reading what looked like a travel guide to New Zealand, but it fell from his hands when the door's hinges announced my arrival. "Jesus, lady!" he said. "Ever heard of knocking?"

"Apologies, my lord," I said, smiling. "But there is no *knocking* on Paqua Farm."

Then I did a goofy curtsy.

Wit laughed and beckoned me over to his bed. "This is the second time you've been in my chambers today," he commented when I joined him. He closed the New Zealand book and handed me the ice pack on his nightstand. "Come to tend to my wounds?"

"Yes, indeed." I humored him by pressing the pack against his bruise, snorting when he moaned melodramatically. "Remember," I told him, "your portrait is being painted come the end of this week!"

Wit smirked. "So what's up? More target talk? I saw the video of you nailing Daniel."

I raised an eyebrow. "There's a video?"

He nodded. "Your friend Pravika took it, I guess. It's all over Instagram."

"Hashtag HurrayShesADupré."

"Quite."

I smiled and shook my head at him.

@sowitty17.

"What's up?" he asked again.

The corners of my eyes prickled. "I want to tell you something," I said, my voice shaking some. "But you have to swear not to tell anyone."

Wit was quiet.

My heart hammered. "Okay?"

"Okay." He nodded and held out his pinkie. "I swear."

TUESDAY

EIGHT

I woke up to what sounded like someone breathing deeply and blushed when I realized it was Wit. I was in Wit's room, in Wit's bed, under his covers with him. *He's a mouth breather*, I thought, since his mouth was wide open, like he'd fallen asleep halfway through saying something. Which he probably had—we'd talked so late into the night.

And we weren't cuddling exactly, but my face grew warmer when I noticed that both of us had an arm flung out, unconsciously reaching for the other person. His was aimed for my waist while mine had gone for his chest. For a moment, I imagined what it would feel like to roll over and burrow into it, to feel his heartbeat.

The thought made my own heart catch, and then I felt a deep and longing tug.

"Time to leave," I whispered to myself and slipped out from under his quilt before even more carefully escaping through the door. Those ancient hinges...

They screeched, of course. Wit didn't wake up, but

Michael's head snapped up over by the firepit, where he was stretching for his morning workout. At first, he didn't say anything, just raising an eyebrow at my outfit—the same eyelet dress I'd worn to the Big House for dinner. Except now it was wrinkled, and it didn't help that my sandals dangled from my fingers by the straps. All signs pointed to a walk of shame.

"Nothing happened!" I blurted.

"I didn't say anything did," he replied.

"We fell asleep talking," I explained. "It was completely innocent."

Michael nodded, but he looked like he was holding back laughter. We eyed each other for a couple of seconds before he smirked and said, "Completely innocent, huh?"

I scowled and gave him the finger, which only made him smirk more. "Listen here, Michael Dupré," I started, but when a door down the porch squeaked open, I took off for the Annex without another word. The paranoia was sinking in now—who *was* my assassin? Not a single rumor had circulated. It could be anyone, hungover groomsmen included.

My parents were already awake, eating scrambled eggs and toast with Honey's homemade blackberry jam at the small table in the sitting room. "Good morning," they said to me, but they didn't ask where I'd spent the night, probably assuming I'd been with Luli and Pravika. It didn't look like they'd gotten much sleep. My dad had bags under his eyes.

"I'm going to the Camp," I said suddenly. "To meditate with Aunt Rachel."

That made my mom brighten. "Okay." She smiled. "Sounds good."

"Don't forget to take your gun," Dad said after I'd changed clothes. He sipped his coffee. "You never know who you're gonna run into."

Instead of parading across the wide field in clear view of the houses, I snuck through the woods and around the back of the Camp. There was hustle and bustle inside—I heard Aunt Julia say something to Ethan about too much whipped cream on his waffles—but like yesterday, Aunt Rachel was at peace by the flagpole. "Hello," she said once I sat down crisscross-applesauce next to her. "Ready for more?"

"Not today," I told her, shaking my head as a lump formed in my throat. Because Claire—this was just so Claire, and I didn't think I could truly focus yet. Memories flashed through my mind of my sister waking me up post–yoga class. She'd jump on my bed all sweaty and tickle me until I couldn't breathe. Now my heart ached to think of it. "But I'd like to sit for a while," I said quietly, "if that's okay."

Aunt Rachel leaned over and kissed the top of my head. "Of course it is, Mer," she whispered. "Of course it is."

Although maybe letting my aunt take me under her wing and teach me meditation techniques would've been better, because sitting silently with my eyes closed allowed me to drift back to last night, to Wit and what I'd admitted to him. "Sometimes I'm so mad at her," I'd said after our pinkie promise and after he'd switched off his bedside lamp. Somehow, the darkness made it easier to speak. "I don't hold grudges, but sometimes..."

I trailed off to let Wit ask who I was talking about, but he didn't.

He knew.

"It was the same night," I went on, my voice cracking a bit. "Why did she have to tell that story? About the salad and stuff? It was the same night, *that* night. Claire texted me *that day* saying they were going to the French Quarter after dinner." My eyes prickled, and a moment later, I felt a few of Wit's fingers gently twine with mine. Tears spilled over when I squeezed them.

"You don't blame her," he said—a question but not phrased as one.

"No, I don't," I said back, all choked up. "I really don't. She didn't do anything wrong. She didn't get Claire drunk, she didn't try to drive, it was a freak accident, but I'm still *angry*. Claire was only eighteen. Why did Sarah have to find her a fake ID and take her to Bourbon Street? Why couldn't they visit during the day like tourists?" My heart pounded. "I love Sarah, and I'm so happy she's okay, that she's marrying Michael, but...sometimes I'm a terrible person. I think that if she hadn't brought Claire there, she would still be here. She would be *here* right now. With me, with us. You would've met her." I wiped away more tears, my eyes already swollen. "I wish you could've met her."

Wit swallowed hard enough for me to hear. There was a long pause, and then he murmured, "You're *not* a terrible person. You're a *person*. Believe me, I understand how you feel. I've been there." He twined more of our fingers together. We were nearly holding hands. "I've been there..."

Now, after several minutes, I straightened my shoulders. "Actually, yes," I said to Aunt Rachel. "Please, teach me more."

—

"It's so easy," Pravika told Luli. "Go over and do it."

Luli sighed. "But that's the *thing*," she said. "It's *too* easy. I want my first kill to be front-page news." She looked at me. "Like Wit's rooftop assassination, or your 007 moment."

The three of us were floating in the Oyster Pond on the loud-and-proud rainbow unicorn tube. We'd stolen it from the Pond House's back deck after the bridesmaids had left for a bayside lunch at Atlantic with the groomsmen. Maid of honor Danielle had posted a video of Sarah and Michael together, feeding each other oysters. The caption read: 5 MORE DAYS! #HurrayShesADupré.

Wit and I still hadn't exchanged numbers, so I'd messaged @sowitty17 and advised him to order the lobster guacamole as an appetizer. It was served in a stone mortar with the best tortilla chips. That had been a few hours ago.

Now Luli, Pravika, and I were doing recon on Cousin Margaret, Luli's target. She was related to the Foxes, but you'd need a family tree to figure out how. All I knew for sure was that she was in her thirties, that she told the most hilarious stories after a few of my dad's margaritas, and that Pravika was right: it would be a piece of cake for Luli to oust her. Right now, she was sitting in a beach chair with her head in a romance novel, wearing a floppy hat and big round sunglasses.

"Look," I said after a few more minutes of watching Margaret flip from one page to the next. "Unfortunately, this move isn't going to be flashy." I shrugged, remembering the letdown of assassinating Aunt Rachel. It had been a stepping-stone, nothing more. "If you really want drama, maybe do a cartwheel or something."

"Yeah," Pravika agreed. "Do a cartwheel, then shoot her."

Luli bit her lip, then nodded. "Okay."

We paddled back to shore and quietly dispersed. Pravika went to devour a PB&J from our cooler as Luli returned to her towel to unearth her squirt gun. Then she hid it again by pulling her waist-length dark hair into a loose ponytail and tucking the gun into her colorful scrunchie.

Meanwhile, I grabbed a crabbing net and joined Ethan and Hannah in the Oyster Pond's shallows. They were scooping up crabs and depositing them in the "tanks" they'd dug in the sand. Each one had a tributary running into the pond so the water would be refreshed.

"No, Ethan!" Hannah shouted. "Don't make them fight!"

"Wait, fight?" I turned away from Luli, who was saying a casual hello to every cluster of people on beach chairs on the way to Margaret's lone one. "You're making them *fight*?"

"Yeah," Ethan said and gestured at one of the pools with his net. It contained only two male crabs, both big and blue. They appeared to be in a standoff. "This is the center ring." He poked one of them with his pole as if to say, *Make your move!*

"Okay, no." I shook my head. "There's no fighting allowed, Ethan—*ever.*" I netted one crab and moved him to the tank Hannah had finished digging. Because whether provoked or not, sometimes the male crabs went at it.

Ethan huffed, then waded back into the water. I refocused on Luli, only a yard or two away from her target now. If she had indeed cartwheeled, I'd missed it. Now she faced the ocean. "I think I'm going to take a dip!" I heard her say. "Wanna join, Margaret?"

Margaret didn't glance away from her book, instead holding up a hand. "I'm almost finished with the epilogue."

Luli tugged her scrunchie and dramatically shook out her hair—she caught her squirt gun before it fell to the sand and concealed it behind her back, pointer finger on the trigger. "Are you sure?" she asked. "Meredith says the water's amazing."

Come on, Luli! I thought. *I haven't been near the ocean today!*

Margaret's gaze shifted. "Did she?" she said lightly, raising her sunglasses to look at Luli. "Because I actually haven't seen Meredith go for a swim yet."

That made Luli panic. She scampered several steps forward, straightened her shoulders, and suddenly, she had her gun aimed at Margaret.

Who once again simply held up her hand. "Last page, Luli," she said. "Last page in the book."

Luli's gun began to shake. The beach was riveted, my dad and Uncle Brad leaning forward in their seats. *This is taking a while*, I thought. *Maybe Margaret's savoring the ending, but...*

And then it happened.

In the blink of an eye, Margaret sprang up from her chair, karate-chopped Luli's squirt gun from her hand, and took off down the beach. The breeze swept away her floppy hat, which twirled in the air before landing in the sand.

"Dammit!" Luli shouted, then grabbed her gun and raced after Margaret. Everyone else broke into laughter, even me. It turned out there had been room for some drama.

Ethan returned from the pond with a whopping three crabs in his net. He was pretty talented for a six-year-old. I watched him deposit them in the largest pool, one's claws tangled in the netting. Then he whispered something that sent chills up my spine. "What?" I asked. "Repeat that?"

"I heard my moms talking," he replied, kicking up wet sand. "About you—they know who has you."

My heart went still. "Who?" I tried not to waver, to keep my cool. "Who has me?"

Ethan shrugged. "Ask them."

Ask them?

No, I couldn't ask them. If my aunts hadn't already given me a heads-up, it meant they weren't on my side. I couldn't fully trust them.

"No, Ethan," I said, shaking my head. "I'm asking *you*."

He hesitated.

"Ethan..."

"Ian," he mumbled. "They said Ian has you."

I released a deep breath. Well, that explained it. Sarah's brother was Aunt Julia's godson. Of course her loyalty would lie with him.

You need to leave, Claire's voice inside my head advised. *He's here, remember? He skipped lunch at Atlantic to surf.*

Shit, I thought after spotting my cousin floating in the ocean with his surfboard. Claire was right; I had to go, because there was no way Ian's only motive for passing on oysters was to catch some waves. He would call it quits soon enough, and if I was tanning on my towel or busy building sandcastles...

I didn't make an announcement that I was heading home. I quickly and quietly packed up my tote bag, draped my towel around my neck, and slipped into my flip-flops.

Nevertheless, I heard Aunt Julia shout through Uncle Brad's beloved megaphone, "Bye, Meredith!"

My pulse pounded. Was Ian out of the water?

Don't turn around, Claire said as I fought the urge. *Don't turn around and make a run for it. It'll give everything away. They'll know that you know!*

So I raised a stiff arm in farewell.

But as soon as I'd disappeared from sight, I broke into a sprint.

My life depended on it.

Once I was safe in the Annex, I took a piping-hot outdoor shower—complete and utter bliss—and afterward threw on a tank top and my favorite faded pair of J.Crew shorts. I unplugged my phone from the sitting room outlet and flopped down on the couch to check any notifications, wondering if @sowitty17 had replied to my suggestion about the lobster guacamole. Had he ordered it?

But instead of an Instagram message notification, I had five missed texts.

All from Ben.

"What the fuck?" I said aloud, typing in my passcode to read them. "What the actual *fuck*?"

First: Hey, Mer.

Second: How's everything going?

Third: Seems like you're having a lot of fun.

"Yeah," I mumbled. "Because you're not here."

Fourth: You looked really pretty yesterday.

Aha! I thought, entire body simmering as I switched over to Instagram, to @meredithfox's profile. *And* there *we have it!*

Last night, I'd posted a picture from Wink and Honey's dinner. My mom had taken it after Luli, Eli, and I had returned from Edgartown. The three of us had our arms around each other with the pink-and-orange sunset in the background (*a pink-lemonade sunset*, Claire would've called it). I was smiling in the middle, my cheeks flushed from the rush of Assassin adrenaline and my hair blowing in the breeze. Cousins! I'd captioned the photo, completely forgetting about the wedding hashtag. It had gotten a ton of likes, but I'd turned off those notifications ages ago. Now, though, I couldn't help but notice the top comment: @benfletcher had left behind three fire emojis. I rolled my eyes. Ben had loved me, but I'd realized that it never went very deep for him. His compliments always revolved around my looks.

I reopened my texts to read Ben's final one: I think we need to talk.

"No, we certainly do not, Shithead," I muttered and debated whether or not to throw my phone across the room. But no, I settled for deleting Ben's texts. Then I swiped back to my Instagram profile and did a little identity changing.

I scrolled through my feed for a few minutes. Instagram stories of my former classmates picnicking on Clinton's town square, videos of my favorite bands performing on tour, photos of cute dogs, and funny memes. I double-tapped Timothée Chalamet's most recent post. He was on vacation in Italy.

Although the next picture caught my eye even more than Timothée...because it was of *me*. Not me now, but me from *years* ago. I was maybe ten, with my hair in braids and a napkin tucked into my shirt, and I instantly recognized the wicker chair I was sitting in. On my knees, I knew, since I'd been too tiny to reach the table.

And I'd *needed* to reach the table, to reach the giant stone bowl in front of me, filled with Atlantic's famous lobster guacamole. But rather than using my best manners and politely dipping a tortilla chip, I'd grabbed a gob of guac and smeared it across my face. Someone had dared me.

What?

I stopped gawking long enough to blink and see who was responsible for such blasphemy. Just delightful, @sowitty17 had written. Thank you, my lobster, for the recommendation! #HurrayShesADupré.

I immediately DMed him: WHERE DID YOU FIND THAT PICTURE?!?!

And then: You watch *Friends*?

Because "my lobster," Wit's term of endearment for the day, was not only a pun about his meal but also a direct reference to the old sitcom. Phoebe had a theory that when lobsters linked claws, it meant they'd fallen in love and would mate for life. "She's your lobster," she always said to Ross about Rachel. It was iconic.

Wit! Half of me wanted to kick him in the face again while the other half wanted to smile and laugh with him. But my only option right now was to check if he'd messaged back.

Not yet.

Where did he get that picture? I wondered again as I glanced around the sitting room at the photos covering the walls. The one of me wasn't here, but Fox family photos decorated *every* house on Paqua Farm. I smirked to myself. Every house, but Wit was only staying in *one*.

Several minutes later, I marched into the Cabin's empty main room with its mammoth stone fireplace, collection of cracked leather couches, and teeth-bearing tiger painting. I'd taken the back way through the woods in case Ian was lurking nearby. *Relax, relax,* I now told my pulse. *You're inside. You're safe.*

I surveyed the room, once, twice, three times before I noticed the series of framed photos displayed on the fireplace's mantel. Most of them had been taken two centuries ago, but there was a pop of color amid all the black and white.

Of course, it was me.

"Gotcha," I said and crossed the room to grab the frame as I felt my phone vibrate in my pocket. I dug it out to see a DM from @sowitty17.

Did you swipe right? it asked.

Swipe right? @claires_sister tapped back. Excuse me, but I don't recall us matching on Tinder.

You wouldn't, he said. I don't have Tinder.

Neither do I, I almost replied, but another message from Wit popped up:

I meant here, on the good old gram. Did you swipe right on my post?

Swipe right on his post? I frowned and tapped back to his throwback shot of me, only to realize that he'd uploaded multiple photos.

Two photos.

No way, I thought, thumb hovering over my screen. *There's no way he could have...*

But he had. When I swiped, I was treated to nineteen-year-old Wit Witry full-on imitating little Meredith Fox. Just like me, he had a blue napkin tucked into his shirt collar with a heavy mortar of guacamole on the table in front of him, and also like me, he'd taken a glob and smeared it across his smiling face.

My stomach swooped.

Wit must've messaged again after I'd liked the photo, but I was too busy to respond, risking another run-in with Ian to steal something from the Camp.

Hannah's red lobster stuffed animal.

She won't notice, I told myself as I raced back to the Cabin, to the last room in the row. *She has so many toys, she won't even notice!*

Wit hadn't made his bed, but I bypassed that to decorate his nightstand. I moved last night's ice pack in favor of arranging my picture frame just so and then placed the lobster on top of his New Zealand guidebook. *A trip with his mom?* I guessed. *Maybe to close out the summer?*

I noticed his unmade bed again before I left...and by that, I mean I stopped and borderline-creepily stared at it. His covers were kicked to the foot, some sand on his sheets, and you could still see where we'd slept. Our indentations in the mattress were a little too close to be fully platonic. I remembered this morning, waking up next to him and seeing our arms stretched toward each other.

Yes, I thought. *I want to smile and laugh with him...*

My heart flipped, realizing that wasn't *all* I wanted to do.

I also wanted to kiss him.

I wanted to kiss Wit.

NINE

I trekked over to the Nylon Condo Complex around 4:00 that afternoon. The village of tents was off one of the winding roads not too far from The Farm's only McMansion: Moor House. "I'm sure the Duprés are *thrilled*," someone joked when I'd stopped by yesterday. "Could our campground be any more of an eyesore?"

Which was kind of true—the twelve tents did obstruct Moor House's crystal-clear view of Job's Neck Pond. Now Eli and I were zipped up in his tent talking. Pravika and Jake had left for work, and I'd not seen hide nor hair of Luli since the beach. "Do you think she's still on the hunt?" I asked. "Maybe waiting out Margaret somewhere?"

"Mmm," Eli replied. "Could be." He looked up from the book he was half reading. "She might be hiding from her own assassin."

I groaned. Ian had also disappeared for the day, but that didn't make me feel any better—if anything, it put me more on edge. After leaving the lobster in Wit's room, I'd triple-checked that the coast was clear before sneaking back to the Annex.

"At least you know who has you now," Eli commented and then went back to reading. I glanced around to see a new pile of books near his sleeping bag.

"Eli..." I said slowly. "Where were you this morning?"

No response.

"You weren't at the bookstore, were you?"

Eli gripped his book tighter, almost white-knuckling it.

I laughed. "If he works at the yacht club, he's not going to be at the bookstore during the—"

"I went at lunchtime!" His voice jumped a few octaves. "Because you never know!"

"And?" I asked. "*Did* your sailing instructor make an appearance?"

Eli's shoulders slumped. "No." He shook his head. "But the guy working today was cute...black hair, tortoiseshell glasses, the bookish type." He paused. "Shy, though. He said hello but then went back to whatever he was reading behind the register."

"Doesn't sound like great customer service," I commented and thought of Claire. If she'd worked at Edgartown Books this summer, she would have made recommendations to anyone and everyone. Nobody would have left the store without a bag in hand. They would've loved her.

"I bet he gives the sailing instructor great customer service," Eli grumbled.

"Oh my god, Eli!" I tossed a book at him. "How do you even know they're gay?"

Eli made a face before changing the subject. "Are you going to the Varsity Room tonight?" he asked.

"Yeah," I said. "Provided Ian doesn't ambush me on the way there."

"Nah, he'll be too busy. He's the host now, remember? Since what's-her-face graduated?" He cocked his head at my confused expression, and then it dawned on him. "Ah, right," he said gently. "You weren't here last year."

"Nope." I shook my head and ignored the slight twist in my stomach before checking my phone to see that it was nearly 4:30.

Almost go-time.

"Good luck," Eli said when I unzipped the tent's flap. "Let me know how it turns out."

"I will," I said and did some of Aunt Rachel's deep-breathing exercises as I weaved through the tents toward Moor House. Because it was nerve-racking—the thought that I was both hunting and being *hunted*. My brain was telling me to abort this mission, to revert to my defensive stance and go hide somewhere. I mean, who knew? Ian could be carefully tailing me. It also didn't help that the piece of paper in my pocket read: OSCAR WITRY.

Last night, I'd been so anxious to tell Wit that I now had his dad, especially after what we'd talked about, but when I finally came clean, he'd laughed. "That's hilarious," he'd said. "Honestly, really funny." He yawned. "There's a prime time to get him, too, since he's in total vacation mode."

Thinking of Wit's laugh suddenly made me miss him. I hadn't seen him all day; after the most leisurely lunch ever, he'd messaged to say they were touring Chappaquiddick for the rest of the afternoon. The island was right off the coast of Edgartown, only five hundred feet across the channel. Of course a bridesmaid had posted a photo of everyone on what was affectionately called the Chappy Ferry. Wit wasn't looking at the camera, his sandy hair whipped up by the wind and his head turned to study whatever had caught his eye.

He's always on a swivel, I'd thought, remembering our bike ride to Morning Glory, how he'd observed everything. *He wants to appreciate it all.*

I liked that.

My stomach flip-flopped when I reached Moor House, the forest footpath I'd taken spitting me out into the side yard. "He'll be alone," Wit had told me. "Well, alone with a cigar and some bourbon. He likes sitting outside and taking in the day, enjoying the silence."

But right now, instead of silence, there were *voices*. My pulse pounded when I heard them in the backyard. *Bocce ball*, I suspected, and I pressed myself up against the house's white clapboard siding to regroup. If they were playing bocce ball, it meant there were at least four people out there. Three additional wedding guests to warn Wit's dad to run.

Close, but no cigar, I thought, deciding I would try again tomorrow.

Then I heard a woman laugh. "Oscar, what was *that*?"

Kasi Dupré said as I peeked around the corner of the house to watch the game play out. The bocce ball court was sixty feet long and twelve feet wide, covered with the same green crumbly clay as a tennis court. Michael's older sister stood at one end with their younger brother, Wit's dad and stepmom at the other. They both had tumblers of bourbon, and Oscar was indeed smoking a cigar.

He chuckled. "There's a learning curve to this, Kase."

"And we have all progressed," Michael's brother deadpanned as he rolled his heavy ball across the court, knocking one of Oscar's out of orbit. "Except you."

Oscar huffed in that way dads did.

"Ah, *cher bébé*," his wife said, kissing his cheek. "Don't you worry."

Out of nowhere, my face burst into fire, and I made sure my water gun was secure in the back of my shorts. I'd come to assassinate Oscar Witry, and that was exactly what I was going to do.

"I understand how you feel," Wit had said after I'd told him about my gnawing grudge against Sarah. "I've been there." He gave my fingers a squeeze. "I *love* the Duprés. Jeannie, Kasi, Michael, Nicole, and Lance—I love them, but it took a while." He paused. "My mom and dad split up when I was fourteen; we stayed in Vermont, and he moved to New Orleans. We kept in touch—or tried to at least—but we never talked about anything important." He sighed. "'How're things? How's school? Been skiing a lot?' Every call ended with, 'We should get you down here for a visit.'"

"When did that visit happen?" I asked after he went quiet.

Wit coughed. "Two years later," he said. "I always thought the 'we' meant him and me, but he wasn't talking about *us*. He was referring to himself and Jeannie." He started playing with my fingers. "Because when he finally bought me a plane ticket, it was for their *wedding*."

"No," I breathed. "You're kidding."

"I am not," he replied. "They began dating a few months after he moved there and never thought to mention it." He dropped his voice deep. "Welcome to New Orleans, son! Meet your soon-to-be stepmother!"

My heart sank. "Wit..."

"I was so upset," he whispered. "So angry that I thought about flying home right then and there."

"What happened?" I whispered back.

He shrugged. "They got married. They got married, and I suddenly had four siblings who made me feel like shit at first. Four siblings who made me feel forgotten, because watching my dad with them..." He trailed off. "It was obvious how much he loved them."

"You felt replaced," I said.

"Yes, I did, and I held that grudge for a long time—long after I fell in love with the Duprés myself." I could almost see him smiling in the darkness. "They're very easy to love."

"Yeah," I agreed, thinking of Michael. How effortlessly he'd fit into the Fox family from the moment Sarah had introduced him. "They are."

Then we were both silent for a long time, so long that I thought Wit had fallen asleep, but eventually I heard him say, "I picked Tulane for him. I know I said I chose it for the adventure, but it isn't one, and I *knew* it wouldn't be. Not with my dad living only fifteen minutes away." He let out a deep breath. "I picked Tulane because I thought it would get him to notice me."

"And has he?" I asked. "Noticed you?"

"Yes," Wit said. "He's noticed me, I've noticed him, we've noticed each other." He paused, then added in a softer voice, "And now I want an adventure."

I tried to pull off a casual walk across the yard to the bocce ball court, but inside, my heart raced. "Hi, Meredith!" Kasi called out. "Are you looking for Wit?"

"Um, yeah," I lied. "Do you know if he's back yet?"

Kasi shook her head. "Not yet. Nicole texted that they're thinking of grabbing dinner in one of the other towns. Chill-something?"

"Chilmark," I said. "Probably Chilmark Tavern."

"Are we missing out on much?" Jeannie asked, a pleasant smile on her face. She and Michael had the same brown eyes, eyes that put you at ease.

"Not really," I said. "The food's delicious, but the restaurant's *extremely* loud." I found myself returning her smile. "My sister used to say that listening to all those voices was the equivalent of banging your head against a wall."

There was a collective groan from the group. "Wit's going to be miserable," Oscar remarked. "He likes peace and quiet." He turned to exchange a look with his wife.

So I took the chance to grab my gun, and when he looked back at me, I raised it. "It's not personal, Mr. Witry," I said, "but it must be done."

Oscar nodded. His stepchildren shouted for him to make a run for the house, but Wit's dad closed his eyes and then faked a fall once I'd squirted him square in the chest. I stifled a snort; it reminded me of something his son would do.

"I haven't the faintest idea who this is," he said, handing over his target. "I asked Michael, but of course he's pretending to be impartial, and Sarah apologized profusely when I inquired."

I read the name and smirked.

"You know?"

"I do."

"Well, best of luck, Miss Meredith." Wit's dad offered his hand for a shake.

I took it. "Thank you, Mr. Witry."

⌇

My stomach rumbled as I walked down Moor House's crushed-seashell driveway, so instead of slowly making my way back to the Annex—hiding behind trees and glancing over my shoulder every five seconds—I decided to throw caution to the wind and race home. I figured if I was hungry, Ian was probably hungrier. Maybe he'd even driven to Chilmark to meet the rest of the wedding party for dinner.

I was jogging past the turnoff to Job's Neck Pond when I caught a voice that had me skidding to a stop. "No, it's absolute *bullshit*," a woman was saying, and I pivoted to see her pacing near an oak tree with AirPods in her ears, talking on the phone. "I'm sleeping on a couch in a house with her little cousins, who wake up so goddamn early."

This is too good to be true, I thought, making sure my gun was at the ready before I quite literally skipped over to Viv Malitz— one of Sarah's good friends but not good enough to be a brides- maid. "I keep saying that's not true," Sarah had told us. "But she's still so salty about it that I almost wish she weren't coming."

Now I was confident Viv was wishing the same thing. "I need to call you back," she said dully after I sprayed her. A merciful kill, a mere splash on the arm.

But she still shot me the dirtiest of looks.

"May I have your target?" I asked meekly.

"I was on the phone," she responded, gesturing to her AirPods.

"I know," I said. "But, um, the game's twenty-four hours a day." I avoided eye contact, afraid her icy stare would pierce me. "And you're, uh, outside, so..." I swallowed. "Your target, please?"

Viv stared at me, and her eyes did indeed cut like knives. "I don't have it."

"What?"

"I don't have it," she repeated. "It's in the Camp, probably covered in peanut butter, thanks to your cousins."

Ethan's allergic to peanuts, I almost said, but I didn't want to get off topic. I shifted from one foot to the other. "Can we meet later?" I asked. "Or maybe you can leave it in my mailbox? Or I'll pick it up from yours? It's important, to continue—"

"Oh my god!" she interrupted. "Yes, fine, whatever! Relax, I'll find it for you!"

Then she adjusted her AirPods and Face ID'd into her iPhone.

I took that as my dismissal.

"I need your help," she said as I walked away, back on her call with whomever. "I *need* you to get me off this island."

⌒

It turned out that instead of heading up-island to Chilmark, the wedding party came back to The Farm for dinner while my parents suggested we go to Coop de Ville. It was an open-air seafood shack in Oak Bluffs, famous for fried clams, steamers, and chicken wings. Instead of scattered tables, there were long narrow ones with benches and high-top stools, and the walls were decorated with international soccer flags and faded signs that said stuff like SCALLOPS TODAY! and CLAMBAKE TONIGHT!

Coop's had been one of Claire's favorites. My dad always had to twist her arm to get her to share her clams.

The three of us snagged stools overlooking the harbor, and after ordering our wings, my dad brought up Assassin. He'd eliminated a cousin and inherited yet another, while my mom admitted she was waiting for the right moment to pursue Nicole Dupré. "It's difficult with her being a bridesmaid," she said. "They're always on outings, and soon the wedding duties will ramp up."

Later, I had both my parents cackling as I told them about my visit to Moor House to take out Wit's dad. "He took it like a man," I said through a mouthful of spicy chicken. My lips were probably stained with hot sauce.

"Well, he's a very nice one," Mom commented before I could mention my encounter with Viv. "We spoke to him on the beach for a couple of hours yesterday." She sipped her water. "You can tell how much he adores his son."

At that, my leg began bouncing up and down. Wit, Wit, Wit—why hadn't I said goodbye this morning? I should've and *would've* if I'd known I wouldn't see him at all today.

No, wait, scratch that, I thought, leg bouncing faster. *I'll see him tonight.*

There's this thing later, I'd DMed him before leaving Eli's tent this afternoon. At the Varsity Room.

Thing? He'd written back. Does that translate to party?

Yes, I typed. It starts at 9.

No offense, he said, but I might pass. After spending all day with these people, I'm a little sick of them.

No, no, this is different, **I replied.** I promise.

A few minutes and then: Pinkie swear?

I smiled to myself. Pinkie swear.

"So what's that make, Mer?" my dad asked, pulling my attention back to dinner. "How many?"

"Four," I said without hesitation. "Four targets taken down."

Dad raised his beer. "I'll drink to that."

"Who's going to be number five?" my mom asked after we clinked glasses.

"I don't know," I told her, frowning a little. Would Viv drop her target in the mailbox? Or would I have to track her down for it? "I actually don't know."

The Varsity Room was right next to Paqua's tennis court, and while it was traditionally cedar-shingled on the outside, it wasn't like the rest of the houses. It wasn't even a house per se. Inside, it looked like an unfinished basement whose purpose was so unclear that the space was used for many purposes. There were only two rooms, the larger one filled with workout equipment, lumpy couches, an old TV that no longer worked, an even older stereo that somehow still did, and a perplexing wooden structure that my dad and Uncle Brad insisted was a bar—they'd built it themselves in high school. A bumper sticker–covered fridge now stood behind it to make things more obvious.

On the other side of the wall was a Ping-Pong table and a big blackboard to keep track during tournaments—Wink was our unrivaled champion. String lights covered the ceiling, and there was a pinball machine in the corner (Honey's forte).

In short, the Varsity Room was the perfect place for a party.

So when my family got back from Oak Bluffs, my parents wandered over to Lantern House to hang out with Uncle Brad and Aunt Christine while Luli, Pravika, and I took over the Annex to get ready.

"Eyeliner!" Luli shouted. "Tout suite!" She was still amped up from this morning; Margaret had indeed gotten away from her.

"Coming!" I called back, unplugging the blow-dryer and digging around in my makeup bag. Then I went into my parents' room; it had the best mirror in the little cottage.

Luli turned, and we made eye contact.

"What?" I asked, suddenly a little self-conscious.

"Nothing," she replied.

"People still dress up, right?" I asked. It had always been tradition for the girls to dress up and for the guys to wear... whatever. "Or has that changed?"

"No, it hasn't changed."

Then she casually asked if Wit was coming.

"Yeah, I invited him," I said.

Luli nodded. "Nice."

The back of my neck warmed. She didn't make it *sound*

nice; she made it sound like I'd done something wrong. "He's really cool," I said, trying to keep my voice light as I handed her the eyeliner. "Maybe tonight we can all—"

"Holy crap, Meredith!" Pravika walked into the room. She'd been painting her nails in the kitchen. "How *sexy* you look." She gestured to my dress, which admittedly was kind of sexy: a black halter with a back that dipped so low it was almost nonexistent. Sarah had sent it to me for my birthday in April. "You wearing it for anyone special?"

"Just myself," I replied, a white lie. "Sarah gave it to me."

To mesmerize someone, she'd written on the card.

This was my first time wearing it, and never had I been happier that Ben hadn't gotten a glimpse. I'd worn plenty of nice dresses with him, but never this one. Maybe I'd subconsciously known that he wasn't "someone."

My stomach twisted a little, remembering his text today: I think we need to talk.

Then it untwisted as I also remembered that I'd deleted the message.

Out of sight, out of mind.

As soon as Pravika and Luli were ready to leave, I pulled on my dad's hooded raincoat. It wasn't raining, but I didn't want Ian seeing me until I was safe from his crosshairs.

Although once we arrived at the Varsity Room, I realized there was no need for the disguise. Ian was too busy playing bouncer by the deck's steps, blocking some guests from passing through the sliding doors. "Seriously, Ian," Michael was saying,

Sarah at his side and most of their friends waiting eagerly behind them. "Let us in."

My assassin folded his arms across his chest. "Are you over the age of twenty-one, Michael?" he asked his almost brother-in-law. He jerked his chin at their group. "Aren't you *all* too old?"

Sarah groaned. "Ian!"

He whistled. "You know the rules, Sis!"

Pravika, Luli, and I laughed as we slipped past them and through the wide doorway. I'd told Wit this party was different, and I hadn't been lying. It *was* different, meant for The Farm's "younger set," as my grandparents called us.

But yes, there was some drinking. It was supposed to be a secret from our parents, but since most of the Paqua adults had once been Paqua teenagers, it was the worst-kept secret; I mean, Dad and Uncle Brad had built that so-called bar for a reason. "Wink stopped by," Eli and Jake said by way of a hello, handing each of us a White Claw seltzer. "Made the speech."

We nodded. My grandfather had strict rules, and he always showed up at Varsity Room parties to remind us of them. "If someone doesn't want to drink, do *not* make them drink," he'd say. "No hard liquor, only beer or that fizzy stuff. None of those stupid card games, please, and do *not* turn my Ping-Pong table into a beer pong table." He cleared his throat. "And finally, if *anyone* gets in a car—even if you're not driving—I will find the keys and throw them in the Oyster Pond myself!"

"Cold, Meredith?" Jake took a gulp of his beer.

I hadn't realized my body had started shaking...and not because I'd ditched the raincoat. "A little," I told him, blinking quickly and then popping the tab on my spiked seltzer. It was black cherry flavored, and I wouldn't take more than one sip.

"I put our names down for Ping-Pong," Jake told his sister as I surveyed the room. Music was pulsating through the medieval stereo, and some people were already dancing while Nicole Dupré and the terminated Daniel Robinson whispered to each other on one couch. Clusters of cousins chatted by the bar. It was crowded.

"Hell yeah," Luli said and motioned her seltzer toward the other room. A round of cheers erupted. "Let's go check out the competition."

She and Jake disappeared into the Ping-Pong arena, and a few minutes later, Eli pulled Pravika out onto the dance floor (really a hideous shag rug from the seventies). "Mer!" They waved for me to join them. "Come on!"

But suddenly the music and their voices turned to white noise, because a group of girls moved away from the bar to reveal a familiar figure standing by the far wall. Not awkwardly or anything—it looked like he was waiting for someone.

With a hammering heart, I made my way over to him.

TEN

Wit was leaning against the rustic wood wall but straightened up when he saw me. "Well, hello," he said. "You get through the door okay?"

Ian is my assassin, I'd messaged him earlier. I got Ethan to tattle.

Six-year-olds coming in clutch, he DMed back and then: We'll figure it out.

Not *you'll* figure it out, but *we'll* figure it out.

"Uh-huh." I nodded. "Ian's dealing with a situation back there." I motioned over my shoulder at the doors. Sarah and Michael hadn't given up yet, still arguing with my cousin.

Wit chuckled, and I couldn't help but stare at him. The guys really did wear anything to this party—Jake was still in his purple, ice cream–stained Mad Martha's shirt—but Wit had on slim jeans and a striped button-down. Dark green and white. It was unbuttoned with a gray T-shirt underneath, and the sleeves were rolled up to show his leather watchband. My pulse skipped like a stone across Paqua Pond.

"Hey, your bruise looks better," I commented; the blue was beginning to fade to green. "Aunt Christine will be pleased."

"That's because I iced it last night," he replied.

I raised an eyebrow. "*You* iced it?"

Wit winked, and I just about sprung at him. With the string lights shining above us, his blond hair gleamed, and so did his fantasy-novel turquoise eyes.

Then I caught him checking me out, too—my long loose hair and backless dress. I waited for him to tell me I looked pretty.

He didn't, and as strange as it sounds, that made me happy.

Instead, he said, "Are you sure those are the best shoes for tonight?"

"Oh," I said and glanced down at my wedges. If Ian decided to chase me home, I wouldn't stand a chance. "Well..."

Wit smiled and took a sip of what looked like red wine.

"Wait, wine?" I asked. "Where did you get *wine*?"

"Nowhere," he answered. "This isn't wine." He offered me his glass to taste. "It's cranberry juice. I found it in the fridge." He shrugged. "Beer isn't really my thing."

"Huh." All the guys I knew liked beer.

A beat of silence passed.

"Thank you for my gift, by the way," Wit said, all casual. "I'm gonna sleep with it every night."

I snorted with laughter, the sip of juice I'd taken almost coming out my nose. Hannah's lobster stuffed animal. "You are not."

He smiled wryly. "No, I'm not. I returned it while you were at dinner. You could genuinely *hear* the meltdown happening in the Camp."

"I bet," I said, thinking of Hannah's high-pitched sobs—I was silly to think she wouldn't notice the theft. Even with so many toys, the lobster was one of her favorites.

"How was the rest of your day?" Wit asked, leaning back against the wall. It put some distance between us, so I moved forward to close it and more. I kind of kicked his feet apart so that I could stand in between them. "My dad told me about the bocce scene," he said, clearing his throat. "He appreciated your manners."

"And I appreciated that he didn't run away," I replied before telling him about Viv. "I was jogging home, and suddenly, there she was on the phone, walking in circles under a tree..."

By the time I finished, one of Wit's hands was resting on my waist. His fingers were warm through the thin fabric, setting off that spiraling sensation. I vaguely heard Pravika call my name and say that Luli and Jake were up for Ping-Pong.

"We should go watch," Wit said, hand moving from my waist to my lower back. Both my heart and I leapt at the skin-to-skin contact. "Whoa, sorry." He paused, then said smugly, "Cold?"

"Yeah, freezing," I joked.

When we made it into the packed Ping-Pong room, we found ourselves in another corner. Luli and her brother were battling it out against Nicole and her boyfriend, with Eli as referee. I was watching but at the same time *not* watching. Wit's hand had left my back, and now our fingers were mingling. *Hold my hand*, I thought. *Hold my hand...*

"Do you want to go back?" I asked after the first half. My friends were ahead, and they had plenty of fans. "It's getting a little loud."

It wasn't that loud.

Wit nodded, and soon we were back where we'd begun. My seltzer was untouched, so I abandoned it—I was already giggly and smiley enough. Wit's lips were dark red from his drink, and they quirked at the corners when I reached out to trace them with a finger.

"You have very nice lips," I said.

Amused, he put down his glass to encircle me in his arms. "I do?"

"Yes," I nodded, then whispered, "I kind of want to kiss them."

"Kind of?" He laughed. "Only *kind of*?"

My breath caught. That was it. That was the cue.

But as I leaned in, Wit ducked out of the way. "Not here." He shook his head and glanced toward the door. "Follow me."

My heart fluttered, and I let him lead me and my giddiness to the sliders—where Ian promptly blocked our path, his water gun jammed in his pocket. "Hey, Mer," he said. "Leaving so soon?"

"No," I said, moving to hide behind Wit. "Not yet." I quickly bent down to unbuckle my wedges. Left foot, right foot. "Just a change of scenery." I stepped out of my shoes. "Wit and I are going to hang on the deck."

Ian followed us out there, of course; he hadn't been born yesterday. "Where's this going?" Wit whispered while I texted someone.

"Wait for it," I whispered back.

Five seconds later, Pravika burst through the door. "Ian!" she exclaimed. "Get in here! Sarah and Michael are trying to break in through the back door!"

"Okay, run," I said to Wit, tugging him down the deck steps while Ian stormed back inside to investigate. "Run!"

***

We burst into laughter after reaching the Cabin, both flopping down on Wit's bed. "Ian's gonna be out for blood," Wit said once we'd calmed down some. "Pravika's performance was Oscar-worthy."

I agreed, and then it went quiet. Both of us knew what was going to happen next, but some of the earlier magic had dissolved. The fairy lights, the quiet corner, the flirting fingers. Escaping Ian had shifted the mood.

My way of finding it again was to stand up, gesture to my dress, and ask, "Do you mind if I take this off?"

Wit's eyes widened, and he fumbled to stand, too. "Uh, sure," he said. "If that's what you want." He scratched the back of his neck. "There's no pressure..."

I laughed and shook my head. It was fun watching him sweat. "No, you idiot," I said. "Maybe in your dreams." I pointed to his dresser. "May I borrow a T-shirt?"

Wit nodded and moved to sift through his top drawer. He tossed me something blue.

"Turn around, please," I said.

He obliged.

Already wearing a pair of spandex shorts, I let my dress fall to the floor and quickly pulled on his shirt. "Okay," I said. "Ready."

Wit pivoted around, but again, it was like neither of us knew how to proceed. He was just standing there across the room.

I tiptoed forward.

Then stopped.

He caught my drift, taking a couple of steps himself.

I took a few more.

He took a few more.

My stomach was swoop, swoop, swooping when we met in the middle, especially when Wit half grinned and began gently tracing my face with his fingertips. My eyebrows, my eyelids, my nose, my cheekbones—he saved my lips for last. "I kind of want to kiss you, too," he murmured. "Would that be all right?"

"Yes," I murmured back. "Definitely all right, and preferably soon."

"Hey." He held up his hands. "I'm being chivalrous."

I sighed. "Preferably *now*, Wit."

"Okay, no need to beg—"

I didn't let him finish, instead scrambling into his arms and locking my legs around his waist so I could kiss him myself. He laughed, and I felt his lips smile against mine as I started running my hands through his thick hair. He tasted sweet, like the cranberry juice he'd been drinking earlier, and something burst beneath my skin, small spirals and then seismic waves rippling through my body. A groan escaped when we finally broke apart.

Wit smirked. "I'm going to take that as a compliment."

I blushed.

His smirk spread into a crooked grin.

I kissed it.

WEDNESDAY

ELEVEN

I woke up with a slight headache and heard something buzzing on the floor. It was pitch-black in Wit's room, but unlike yesterday morning, our flung-out arms had found each other—Wit's curved around my waist and mine holding on to his T-shirt. Both of us were fully dressed, having reluctantly fallen asleep after making out for not long enough. I smiled to myself.

The vibrating stopped, then began again. I carefully shimmied out of bed to find my phone near my discarded shoes and dress. *What the hell?* I wondered, yawning as I bent down to grab it. *It has to be past two in the morning...*

My legs almost gave out when I tapped the screen. While 2:00 a.m. had indeed come and gone, I saw that I had a few missed calls and one voicemail from Ben.

No, I thought, a chill creeping up my spin. *Why?*

Why couldn't those texts have been the end?

I wanted everything with him to *end.*

Don't listen to it, I told myself as I contemplated the voicemail. *Block him, and let that be it.*

But curiosity got the better of me. I glanced over at Wit, he and his hilarious mouth breathing still sound asleep. "Be right back," I whispered and then slowly slipped through his screen door. Thankfully, its hinges cooperated this time.

There were no stars in the sky. It was completely covered by clouds, and the wind whirled through the air. I stepped off the porch and strayed onto the front lawn, away from the house. My fingers shook as I typed in my phone's passcode, and my whole body started shaking when Ben's voicemail began to play.

"Hey, Mer," he said, his voice slow and slurred. I could almost see the drunken glaze that always washed over his face. "We're all at Finn's house." There was music and laughter in the background. Ben took a breath. "And I wanted to say I miss you, babe. I really do. Like, so much. That picture you posted the other night, you looked so pretty." Another deep breath. "I'm thinking maybe we were too hasty about things. Maybe we shouldn't have made that decision yet."

My cheeks flamed. *We?* I thought. *You broke up with me, Ben Fletcher. Don't you dare put this on me.*

"I would've come with you," he continued. "Babe, I really would've come to the wedding." He chuckled and repeated what he'd said the night he'd dumped me: "You're still my favorite girl to have on my arm."

You're still my favorite girl to have on my arm.

I used to love that line, but now I hated it. That was it. *This* was it, once and for all. I ended the message and hit redial, and when Ben answered, I said what I should've said last month. If only I'd had more strength. If only I'd realized that our relation-ship was imbalanced, the scale always tipping in Ben's favor.

If only I'd truly listened to Claire.

But now I made sure to speak loud and clear. "For the record, Shithead," I said, "I wouldn't have been on *your* arm." I swallowed and gripped my phone as tightly as possible. "You would've been on *mine*."

Then I hung up and blocked his number.

It felt like a chain had been unlocked from around my heart.

Daylight streamed through the windows the next time my eyes opened, and I was nestled into Wit's warm chest with a leg draped over his thigh. "Wake up," I whispered and kissed him. "Wake up, cutie."

Wit grunted something.

"What was that?" I asked.

"I said, hard no on *cutie*," he mumbled. "I'm not Ethan's age."

"But you're still cute," I said, stealing a kiss on the lips when his eyes fluttered open. "Incredibly cute."

He kissed me back, and I squealed when he trapped me in his arms and began tickling me. "How about handsome?" he asked, fingers somehow already knowing all my ticklish spots. "Can't I be handsome instead?"

I giggled. "You're that, too."

Because he was—even with the bedhead, wrinkled T-shirt, and blue-green bruise, he was so damn handsome.

Wit smirked and kept tickling me until I squealed again, which prompted a bang on the wall from next door. "Dammit, Wit!" Michael's best man shouted. "It's not even seven!" Pause. "But, like, good for you, man."

That only made Wit and me laugh. He rolled me onto my back and pulled the covers up over us to stifle it. "I should go," I said after a while, even though I loved the feeling of Wit's lanky body on top of mine and his soft lips on my neck. "I have to go."

"No, you don't," he replied. "Stay here with Handsome."

"Okay, I am *not* calling you 'Handsome,'" I told him. "It's so superficial—it says nothing about you." I thought of Claire and her penchant for personal, affectionate, inside-joke nicknames. She believed they made a relationship more intimate.

"I was only kidding," he said, propping himself up on an elbow. "That'd make me sound like such a douchebag." He gave me a long look. "But I must say, you are quite pretty."

My heart stopped.

Pretty.

Wit started drawing spirals on my skin. "I didn't get to tell you last night," he went on. "I mean, I was *nervous* to tell you last night, but yes, you are so—"

"Don't call me pretty," I interrupted, pulse spiking. "Please don't call me pretty or cute or…anything like that."

His eyebrows furrowed. "Why not?"

I shook my head. "I have to go. Aunt Rachel's probably waiting for me, to meditate."

"No way, Killer," Wit said. "You aren't going anywhere."

"Wit," I whined and tried to wiggle out from under him.

"Meredith." His voice was no-nonsense. "You're *actually* going to risk going over to the Camp?"

It took a second, but then it clicked.

"If your aunt Julia's really on Ian's side," he said, taking the words out of my mouth, "I bet you anything she's tipped him off and that he's in full stakeout mode."

I sighed. Wit was probably right, and it was disappointing, especially since I'd had a meditative breakthrough yesterday. With Aunt Rachel's help, I really had been able to zone out and relax. It had helped put me on track for the day. "Will you do some recon to make sure?" I asked him.

Wit pushed back the blankets. I shivered when he climbed out of bed, body heat no longer radiating onto me. He dug through his dresser for a sweatshirt, and before heading out the door, he turned and gave me a look. "Stay here."

I pulled his blankets back up like I planned on going back to sleep.

But because I also wanted to see him sweat like last night, I dramatically stripped off his T-shirt and tossed it at him. Now my bare shoulders were visible above the sheet.

Wit opened his mouth, then closed it.

"Recon," I reminded him, and his cheeks reddened. He

nodded slowly, then turned to leave for war. I blew him a kiss that he couldn't see.

The door groaned shut, and then I heard him say to himself, "Holy *fuck*."

I fell back against his pillows, covered my face with my hands, and laughed.

⁓

He was gone all of ten minutes, but I was up and back in my dress by the time he returned. "Wait, what?" he said, seeing me buckling my wedges. "I thought I told you not to leave."

"And I haven't," I said and did a twirl. "I'm right here."

Wit ran a hand through his hair.

I smirked. "Oh, come on. I was teasing."

"Yeah," he mumbled, "and it wasn't very considerate."

I went over and hugged him, both arms around his waist. "I'm sorry."

He responded by tiptoeing his fingers down my back.

"Wit!" I exclaimed, but my voice came out breathy.

"What?" he asked. "I was teasing."

"So not funny." I knocked my head into his chest a few times. He laughed and kissed my shoulder. We swayed for a minute, and then I asked the big question: "Was he there?"

"Yep," Wit said. "With his own yoga mat, too."

"Probably Aunt Julia's," I muttered.

"I figured."

I broke out of our hug. "Well, no meditation for me today."

Wit raised an eyebrow. "You were really going to meditate in that ensemble?"

I jokingly raised my fists, as if raring for a fight.

He smirked. "Where're you going now?"

"Home," I replied. "I should check in with my parents." I leaned in to kiss him, wanting to burst when he deepened it. "But meet me at the tractor barns," I added with a wink. "I'm taking you to breakfast."

"Breakfast with Wit?" my dad said once I was back at the Annex, changed and drinking a glass of water by the sink. He nodded. "That's a good move, Mer. Get him off The Farm, make him feel comfortable, get him to open up."

"Tom, something tells me this has nothing to do with Assassin," my mom said. "Absolutely *nothing*." She gave me a look, amused. "Is that where you've been the past couple of nights? The Cabin?"

I thought about lying. I had a strict curfew at home: midnight, and if plans changed and I wanted to stay over somewhere, I had to call them.

And, I mean, I wasn't always honest. A few times, I told my parents I was sleeping over at a friend's when in reality I was staying at Ben's house.

But now I didn't lie. My parents' rules were lax at Paqua, and they seemed happy this morning. "Yes," I said. "I've been hanging out with him. We just...fall asleep talking." I shrugged.

"Well, I'm not sure—" my dad started, but Mom put a hand on his arm. Her amused expression had turned into a smile.

"Have fun," she said, and I raced out the door with my backpack before they could ask any other questions.

⁓

Dock Street Coffee Shop was where all the locals had breakfast, but luckily Wit and I only had to wait a few minutes before snagging two seats in the narrow restaurant. With its iconic sign out front, Dock Street had an old-fashioned diner vibe with just the right amount of grunge factor. An eclectic mix of photos and drawings hung on the walls, and all the seating was red stools along one long counter. Directly behind it was the kitchen, with a colossal grill and red-and-white checkerboard curtains covering the lower cabinets. You could watch your breakfast being made.

Our stools were in the back, on the very end. We had a few minutes to flip through our menus before a guy came up to take our order. *Whoa*, I thought, since he was seriously built. An Adonis, but younger-looking than Michael. "All right, what can I get you guys?" he asked. Reddish-blondish hair peeked out from under a navy blue baseball hat. BULLDOGS, it said across the front. "Drinks to start?"

"Coffee," Wit and I both said.

"Cream? Sugar?" he asked, and after a beat of hesitation, "Maple syrup?"

I made a face. "Maple syrup?"

Our server scratched his ginger-colored stubble. "I don't know," he said. "My brother swears by it."

We played it safe by asking for milk and sugar. "Do you know who that is?" Wit asked once he walked away to get our coffees.

"Uh, no," I said. "Should I?"

Wit nudged my knee with his. "Do you follow college hockey?"

I shook my head, and he sighed. He clearly lived for college hockey.

But Ben had played basketball, so I'd followed basketball. For three years in a row, I had won our March Madness bracket. Villanova did not disappoint.

The hockey hotshot returned with a pair of mugs and a coffee decanter. "Now, food," he said once we were stirring in sugar with spoons. "What're we thinking?"

I ordered my usual, a stack of pancakes with home fries and bacon, but Wit couldn't decide between a sausage-egg-and-cheese and the Monte Cristo sandwich. He asked our server, with awe in his eyes, what he recommended.

"Well, both are epic," he replied. "But I'd get the Monte Cristo." He smiled, a dimple appearing in his cheek. "It's my girlfriend's favorite."

Wit nodded, and twenty minutes later, I watched him bite into his sandwich. Melted cheese oozed out and dripped down onto his plate. "Good?" I asked.

Mouth full, Wit shot me a look—an incredulous *Are you*

kidding me? look. "Good?" he said after swallowing. "*Good?*" He tilted his head back to shamelessly shout, "Where has this place been all my life?!"

"Not in Vermont!" a woman shouted back, and another added, "Or in the Big Easy!"

Their voices were familiar...*too* familiar. "Oh my god!" I grabbed Wit's arm when I noticed Honey and Sarah sitting several stools down the counter. They were both ignoring their menus in favor of spying on us. "Hide!"

"Where?" Wit asked as he waved at them. "Why?"

"Because they are the two biggest gossips on the island!" I told him.

Wit smirked, powdered sugar still on his lips. "But what," he said lightly, "could they possibly have to gossip about?"

"You and me," I whispered.

Wit widened his eyes. "Ah."

"It's not a joke. Sarah's going to go back to The Farm and tell Michael that—"

"—she saw us having breakfast," Wit said, putting his hand on my knee. "Which means Michael will keep grilling me about you." He cocked his head. "Apparently you've run into him while leaving my room these last couple of days?"

All I could do was blush.

Wit stole a strip of my bacon to munch. "Eat up," he said, pointing to my fluffy pancakes. "Another big Assassin day ahead."

"Shoot," I said.

"I've learned that's the point, yes."

"No." I shook my head and drizzled maple syrup over my pancakes. "Shoot as in, '*Shoot*, everyone will think we're accomplices.'"

"Why?" Wit asked. "Because we're breakfasting together?"

I gave him a look. *Well, yeah.*

He took a long, thoughtful sip of coffee before shrugging. "Okay, so let them." He spun my stool to face his, widening his legs so that they bracketed mine. Suddenly Sarah, Honey, and the café vanished; it was only us. "We don't need to publicly confirm or deny anything," he said. "But sure, let them think we're this Assassin power couple."

His words sent shivers through me. *Power couple.* I knew he meant it as nothing more than an expression, but still. "We do have a pact," I reminded him.

Wit chuckled and took another bite of his sandwich. "How was that only three days ago?"

"I have no idea." I smiled, and then I couldn't help myself—I leaned in and kissed him, kissed powdered sugar off his lips. "I like you," I whispered. "I really like you."

"I really like you, too," he said back, grinning. "I like you quite a lot."

﹋

After paying our bill, Wit asked if we could take a lap around Edgartown. "Sure, I'd love to," I said, but my eyebrows knitted together. "You were here all day yesterday, though."

"Yeah," he told me, "but I couldn't *explore*—I was shepherded from place to place." He put his hands on my shoulders and pushed me up the brick sidewalk. "Nope, straight ahead, Witty," he imitated Michael. "We have reservations!"

I giggled and shook him off so I could take his hand. "I'll give you the grand tour, then," I said. "We'll go anywhere and everywhere." I paused to feel the sun shine down on us. "But I insist that we start at a certain someone's favorite spot."

The bookstore. Whenever Claire and I had biked into town, we'd locked our bikes at the nearby rack and gone to Edgartown Books first. It was a beautiful white house with black shutters and a green-and-white awning shading its peaceful porch. Right now, two little girls sat on the porch chairs with their grandparents, reading the books they'd bought. I watched them for a moment, grateful when Wit squeezed my hand.

We walked inside to hear a bell chime above us and see the staircase leading up to the second floor. Books of all different colors were painted on each step's riser, along with a genre written in delicate script. *Yes*, I thought. *Yes, here we are.*

My sister's wonderland.

"This way," I said and led Wit through the archway on the right. "Claire called this the parlor."

Because back when this was a family home, the main room probably *was* the parlor. The big windows made the space light and airy, the walls a creamy yellow and lined with maple bookcases. MARTHA'S VINEYARD, the plaque above one read—the local interest section. Wit, like the explorer he was, let go of my hand and made a beeline over there. Meanwhile, I just basked in the warm glow.

Until I heard someone speaking at the register by the bookstore's big front window. Not a customer but the bookseller on duty. He had a book flipped open in one hand and held his phone to his ear with the other. "No, I can't eat another lobster roll," he said in a low voice. "How about you get sandwiches from Skinny's and meet me here? We'll find a spot outside?"

Holy crap, I thought when I noticed the tortoiseshell glasses and flop of black hair. "The bookish type," Eli had said.

This guy was a dead ringer and pretty dang cute.

"Turkey with pepper jack on sourdough, please," he said. "Lettuce, tomato, onion." A pause. "Oh yeah, and honey mustard." He rolled his eyes. "Uh-huh, you know me better than I know myself." He smiled. "I love you, too."

Okay, okay, I thought as Wit mentioned he was moving to the travel section. *So he's in a relationship...*

After the bookseller hung up and stuffed his phone in his pocket, I wandered toward the travel shelves to find Wit with a Martha's Vineyard history book under his arm, now perusing something Australia-related. "I'm heading upstairs to look at the young adult stuff," I told him, ruffling his hair.

He nodded, then pointed to his cheek without taking his eyes off the page.

I gave it a good old grandmotherly pat.

"I wanted a kiss," he said once we met back up at the register. The shy bookseller quietly scanned our stuff, putting a turquoise Edgartown Books bookmark in each one before slipping them into our bag.

"Hmm, did you?" I said dryly. "I didn't catch that."

But then I pointed to my own cheek.

Wit lightly flicked it.

"Ouch!" I exclaimed.

"Fifty-three eighty-eight," the bookseller said, and I caught him glancing at his watch. Wishing for lunchtime with his love. It'd be tough to break the news to Eli later; thank goodness he was partial to the sailing instructor. Again I thought about Claire and how she would've amazed customers here with her endless energy and passion for books.

You could do that, too, Mer, she said, a whisper in my mind. *I'm not the only one with that energy and passion...*

"Where to next?" Wit asked once the bell dinged us outside. He swung our bag back and forth. "What's the next stop on Claire Fox's tour?"

Claire Fox's tour.

I immediately brightened. "The Candy Bazaar," I said, our hands finding each other again. "Down by the yacht club docks."

Wit nodded. It seemed a little stilted, but he nodded all the same. "Lead on," he said.

"Okay." I stretched and kissed his cheek. "Follow me."

TWELVE

Wit convinced me to let him drive the Jeep home, and he faithfully followed the speed limit...until we hit The Farm road. Then he pressed down on the clutch to shift into a higher gear before letting out an excited whoop. I laughed at first, but the faster we flew, the harder my heart hammered. "Can you slow down?" I asked. "Wit..."

He couldn't hear me, and thick clouds of dust kicked up in our wake. I clenched my teeth, worried Wink's old car might topple. It had happened before, back when my dad and Uncle Brad were in college. They'd been messing around in one of the fields and accidentally rolled it. No one had been hurt, but still, the car had ended up on its side. My grandfather had been livid.

And Claire—I mostly was thinking about Claire and how fast that SUV had been going when it smashed into Sarah's car. Even though the lane was barely wide enough, Paqua's driveway was technically a two-way street. What would happen if we had to swerve around another car?

"Wit," I tried again, and this time, I put my hand on his knee and squeezed it. "Wit!"

Something flashed in his eyes when he turned and saw the terror on my face, and before I could count to ten, he'd eased on the brakes, pulled onto the side of the road, and put the Jeep in park. "Shit, shit, shit," I heard him mutter as he hopped out of the car and came around to my side to pop open my door. "I'm sorry." He looked up at me, high off the ground in the passenger seat. "I'm an asshole. I'm sorry."

Don't cry, I told myself. *Don't cry.*

But it had taken him less than ten seconds. It had taken him *less than ten seconds* to connect the dots, while Ben had *never* connected them. "No, I'm sorry," I managed to say. "I just..." I glanced away, unable to look at him. "I like to be in control. Ever since..." A tear escaped, and my cheeks burned. "I feel like I need to be in control."

Wit gestured to the driver's side. "Absolutely," he said. "Please, take over."

"No," I told him. "You wanted to drive." I took a deep breath and settled back into my seat. "I have to get over this."

Because I did—I couldn't continue living in fear whenever I wasn't the one behind the wheel. I needed to trust other drivers again.

"It doesn't have to be today, though," Wit said. "It's okay."

I kept my seat belt buckled.

He nodded, then walked back around the front of the Jeep and climbed up into the driver's seat. He turned over the ignition, put the car in first gear, then pulled onto the road after Aunt Christine's Range Rover drove by us.

The speedometer's needle didn't go above twenty-five the rest of the way back, and we parked the Jeep outside the tractor barn. Wit walked me back to the Annex, his arm curved around my waist and carrying my Edgartown treasure trove (books, candy, and a new Black Dog T-shirt) like a gentleman. "Anything?" he asked as I checked the mailbox for my new target. When Viv had come up empty-handed last night, I'd texted Commissioner Wink. What a load of horseshit, he'd replied. If you don't have it by tomorrow, let me know, and I'll take care of it.

"Nothing," I said with a sigh. "Nada."

"Seriously? That's ridiculous."

"What's ridiculous?" someone asked, and we turned to see Luli rounding the cottage.

Wit gave the top of my head a sweet kiss. "See you soon," he whispered before saying Michael needed him for something.

I thought he was a little afraid of Luli, so I giggled once she and I were alone...but my friend didn't laugh with me. Instead, she watched Wit retreat to the Cabin. "Bye-bye," she said, her voice almost wistful. "Bye-bye, Benny Boy."

My stomach stirred. Again, Luli was bringing up Ben. Why? I picked up my shopping bags and shot her a look. "Could you call him by his actual name, please?" I asked.

Luli laughed. "Meredith, what happened to 'I'm here to celebrate Sarah and Michael and spend time with my friends and family'?"

"Nothing," I told her. "That's exactly what I'm doing." I nudged open the Annex's door, and Luli followed me inside. My parents were gone, probably at the beach. It was *h-o-t* hot today, at least ninety.

"Yes," Luli said, "but how about your no hookups thing? You told us—"

"Relax," I cut in, feeling this needling on my neck. "Wit isn't a hookup."

Luli raised her eyebrow. "Isn't he? You guys were the talk of The Farm this morning. Everyone saw you leave the Varsity Room together."

I fumbled for a good response, because I wasn't sure what Wit and I were yet.

Then I remembered what my dad had said earlier when I mentioned Wit and I were going to Dock Street. *That's a good move, Mer. Get him off The Farm, make him feel comfortable, get him to open up.*

"Relax," I said again. "Yeah, we're having some fun, but I'm also pumping him for information." I straightened my shoulders. "Assassin information, to help our alliance."

It felt so wrong to say, but when Luli's lips curled into a scheming smile, I knew it was the *right* thing to say. At least for now. "Ooh, that's so evil. Getting personal with the enemy. I love it." She flopped onto the sitting room's couch. "Speaking of which, I need your help this afternoon. Obviously, I still have Margaret, but I'm thinking I can get her—"

"I'm sorry," I said, stomach twisting. "Wit and I have plans later...so, um, can Pravika or Jake sub in for me?"

"They're both at work," Luli said flatly.

"Eli?" I suggested.

"Sure, I guess so," she said after a beat and then, "Do you know Wit's target?"

"That's my goal for today," I lied.

She smirked. "Good."

I winced.

"Text us when you find out?"

"Yes." I nodded quickly, trying to muster up enthusiasm. "Of course."

Instead of joining everyone on the main stretch of beach, Wit and I headed for Paqua Pond. "You'll like it," I said when he met me back at the Annex. "Hardly anyone goes there. Claire and I call it Secret Beach."

"Sounds awesome," he said and slung my canvas tote over his shoulder. It was packed with all the beach essentials: towels, sunscreen, books, ice-cold waters, sandwiches, and other snacks. Wit winked. "You had me at *secret*."

We walked across the fields but veered onto the wooded pathway in the opposite direction from the ocean and the Oyster Pond. Both of us had our water guns, just in case. I listened as Wit relayed the new intel he'd collected from the other groomsmen. "The bridesmaids are dropping like flies," he said. "Uncle Brad bombarded their breakfast and took out Danielle."

"Ouch, really?" I said. Birds were chirping, and sweat was already dripping down my back. "The maid of honor?"

"Uh-huh. She tried to argue that it was an official wedding event, since they were all there, but Wink rejected that in about three seconds."

I laughed.

"Ian is still in, so we gotta watch out for him, and I think you should text Sarah to get that nightmare's number."

"Calm down," I said and pretend-punched him in the arm. It was slick with sweat, too. "Viv isn't a nightmare. She's just—"

"—the worst," Wit finished. "Sarah and Michael have dragged me to dinner with her before in New Orleans. Trust me, she's the worst." He shook his head. "Of course she hasn't delivered her target."

"Mmm," I mumbled, not exactly eager to reach out to Sarah. "Wink said he would take care of it."

Wit nodded, then slipped into silence with a pensive expression on his face. "Who do you think has me?" he asked, sounding unnerved. "I'm starting to freak out a little."

"I don't know," I answered. "My dad is picking off cousins, my mom has Nicole, Jake's new target is a groomsman, Uncle Brad now has whoever Danielle had, and Luli..." I bit my lip. "Your name hasn't come up at all."

"Sorry about Luli, by the way," Wit said. "I totally abandoned you back there." He chuckled. "Part of me suspected *she* had me, and the other part is scared of her."

"She does not have you," I assured him.

Although I'm supposed to tell her who you *have...*

Wit and I had agreed to neither confirm nor deny any alleged Assassin allegiance, but where did that promise to Luli fall? I already knew who Wit's next mark was, so I technically could've told her right then and there. Ugh. I wasn't actually going to break Wit's confidence, was I?

Either way, I couldn't tell him.

"Hey, this is a cool tree," he said, snapping me out of my thoughts. He'd stopped in front of a tree with thick branches and outlandish vines twisted around its trunk. My heart flipped. Dad had taken Claire and me on so many walks when we were little and always pointed out the "jungle tree."

"Watch this!" I broke into a grin and sprinted past Wit to scramble up the tree in record time. Using one branch as a balance beam, I pushed through a patch of leaves to see him staring up at me. "What?" I asked.

He smiled. "Nothing."

I laughed. "I love climbing trees."

"Yes," he said, the corners of his mouth curling. "Just like you love climbing *me*."

My breath caught.

Just like you love climbing me.

"You're wicked," I said.

"And you go wild for it," he said back as I jumped to the ground.

⌁

Secret Beach was beautifully deserted. Paqua Pond shimmered in the sunlight, with its wooden float just waiting for Wit and me to wade into the water and swim out to it. "We need to let the sunscreen soak in first, though," he said and sighed when I gave him a look. "Listen, I can't get burned." He pointed to his bruise. "Michael told me that Aunt Christine is still debating cutting me from the wedding photos. If I'm both maimed *and* fried, I'd say the odds won't be in my favor."

I grumbled. "Fine."

So we spread out our beach towels, ate our roast beef sandwiches, and read our books for a while. I'd bought the final installment in Claire's favorite fantasy series, but I kept peeking at Wit, shirtless and all stretched out with his New Zealand and Australia books.

"Okay," I said eventually, "when do you leave?"

He glanced over at me. "Oh, Michael told you?"

I shook my head. "No, but you're obsessed—I mean, you got *another* one today." I laughed. "When do you go Down Under?"

"The end of the summer."

"And when do you return?"

Wit hesitated, slowly closing his book. "Next May."

"Wait," I said, sitting up on my towel. "What?"

Wit sat up, too. "My adventure," he said. "Remember? The one I want to go on?"

I nodded silently.

"Well, this is it," he explained, holding up his guidebook. "I'm taking a year off school and going to New Zealand. My parents and I agreed that it's the best thing for me right now." He paused. "Because Tulane..." He shrugged. "I don't know... maybe I'll go back there, maybe I'll transfer. I need to think."

Again, I just nodded.

Wit looked at me. "Meredith?"

"A whole year?" I blurted.

"No, not a *whole* year," he said. "Just late August to late May. A school year."

For some reason, my head was spinning. Perhaps it was the extreme heat. "What are you going to do there?" I asked.

"Everything," he answered. "Travel, of course, but first I'm going to work as a tour guide at a national park. One of Michael's friends did that in college and helped me set it up. I'm going to Australia, too." He smiled. "It might sound ridiculous, but I want to work on a farm for a bit. It's on my bucket list." His lips quirked. "Don't laugh."

I didn't laugh. Because it was hitting me now, *really* hitting me. "Wit isn't a hookup," I'd told Luli, but yes, that was *exactly* what he was—exactly what we were to each other. After Sarah and Michael said "I do" on Saturday and drove off into the sunset, Wit and I would go our separate ways, him halfway around the world and me to Hamilton. Suddenly, I felt like I was treading in unfamiliar waters, and I didn't like it. Ben and I had dated for *four years*—I had no true understanding of or experience with casually hooking up.

"Hey," Wit said now. "Sunscreen be damned. Let's take a dunk."

"Yes, finally." I jumped up from my sweat-soaked towel, sighing contentedly when the cool water hit my skin. Wit immediately submerged himself in the shallows and did a goofy handstand before taking off for the pond's float. I flipped onto my back and did my best backstroke to follow him.

He pulled himself up onto the float first, and once on the edge, he stretched out a hand to help me before we swiftly fell back against the worn wood planks and kissed. The float was warm from the sun, but I shivered a little. Wit's slick skin felt so *good* against mine. His fingertips danced up along my waist as I tangled my hands in his wet hair, and our kisses sent slow spirals through me before I had to break away for air. "Holy fuck," I breathed.

"Payback for this morning," he said.

I laughed when he fiddled with my bikini strings. "You are so *not* subtle."

He shrugged. "Only if you're comfortable."

"Yes, of course." I ran my hands over his shoulders, down his wiry arms. Because yes, with him, I was comfortable, and if we only had a few more days together, I did want this. "Just not here," I said and kissed his collarbone. We might've been the only ones at Secret Beach, but it wasn't like we were *really* in private. "Later?"

"Mmm, yeah," Wit murmured. "Later. Right, all right." He sounded like he wasn't thinking straight. "Good, all good."

And then he just stiffly rolled off the float, flopping into the pond. A type of cold shower, I supposed. It was hilarious.

"You are wicked," he said when he broke the surface.

"And you go wild for it," I said back, moving to dangle my legs off the float.

Wit splashed water at me.

I kicked water at him.

How did we only have four days left?

THIRTEEN

Later that afternoon, my mom decided to march me straight into enemy territory. Wit and I had stayed at Secret Beach for another hour or so before wrapping ourselves in towels and packing up our things to make some Assassin progress. Well, Wit could make progress—I remained in limbo, the Annex's mailbox *still* empty. *What the hell, Viv?* I thought.

But even so, I led Wit to the storage shed and offered him Claire's huge high-pressure multi-nozzle jetpack gun. I'd stick with the simple Super Soaker. This one would weigh me down if I ever tried strapping it on my back. It was *that* elaborate. "Word has already spread that you're dangerous," I told Wit. "Take it and flaunt it."

"Are you sure?" he asked, admiring the water gun almost reverently.

I nodded. Claire would want him to use it.

Wit kissed me—*really* kissed me. I ran a slow hand through his hair and smiled when I felt goose bumps grow on the nape of his neck. "We should go," he whispered afterward. "I need"—he paused—"some time."

I raised an eyebrow. "Some time?"

He nodded, cheeks coloring a little. "To collect myself."

I smirked. "Collect yourself?"

"Yeah, collect myself," Wit smirked back, his hand going to the back of my head to smoosh my face into his chest. I could feel his heartbeat. "You know, refocus myself." He cleared his throat. "For Assassin."

"Sure," I said, biting back a smile. "You do that."

Although a wave of jealousy washed over me then. Because not only was I on the sidelines, but Wit and I had also reviewed our pact on our walk back from the beach: we wouldn't help each other execute eliminations.

So I ended up in the Annex, where my mom promptly handed me a grocery list. "Julia and Rachel are going to the store," she said. "I need you to go with them to pick up a few things."

I froze. *Aunt Julia and Aunt Rachel.*

No.

No!

They were helping *Ian*, not me. Going anywhere with them could be a trap.

"Um, why can't you go?" I asked.

"Because I think I finally found my chance to take out Nicole," she replied and gestured to the door. "I said you'd meet them at the Camp."

"Mom," I whined.

She sighed. "Meredith."

I grabbed my bike and took the longest route possible to the Camp, riding deep into the woods and racing along trails I wasn't sure Ian even knew existed. By the time I made it to my aunts' house, they already had Ethan and Hannah strapped into the minivan. I literally hit my brakes and dove into the car.

"Meredith!" the kids cheered.

"Hi," I said cautiously and checked the trunk as I buckled myself into the way back. Was being in a car the same thing as being inside a house? A safe zone?

I needed to text Wink and Honey.

Thankfully, the trunk was empty.

"All right," Aunt Julia said from the driver's seat. Aunt Rachel and her swollen stomach barely fit into shotgun.

"Will this kid just get here already?" she mumbled.

Aunt Julia laughed, and then we were off. My insides swirled all three miles down the driveway, terrified that Ian would be waiting for us at the Stop & Shop. "Are you okay, Mer?" Aunt Julia asked when she turned onto West Tisbury Road.

"Yeah," I heard myself say. "Fine."

I was so paranoid that I had to suppress a screech when my phone vibrated on my lap, but I exhaled when I saw that @sowitty17 had messaged me. It kept slipping my mind to ask for his actual number.

Who, he'd written, is Anne O'Brien?

What? I thought. *He's already killed the Dupré cousin?*

Margaret's mom, I replied, wondering if Luli had eliminated my distant relation yet. How'd you get Michael's cousin?

I'll tell you when I have my arms around you, he said.

My breath caught. He was so casual, so easy with his affection. There was no stupid winky face emoji or a hundred obnoxious hearts following his words—he wasn't teasing or even flirting. He was just being open and genuine.

Open and genuine were part of Wit's brand.

Any advice? he asked when I didn't respond. Oh, wise one?

Try the tennis court, @claires_sister told him. She and Honey play most afternoons.

Once I sent that, everyone in the car groaned—we'd arrived at the Stop & Shop. Or, as the Foxes called it, the "Stop & Plop."

"Plop" insinuating that you weren't moving anytime in the near future.

"Ugh," Aunt Rachel said as Aunt Julia weaved the car through the supermarket's packed parking lot. There were no empty spots to be seen. "Does being eight months pregnant count as a handicap?"

"Right there, Mommy!" Hannah shouted once we'd circled the lot a few times. "Someone's leaving!"

"Good eye, Han!" I stretched forward to high-five her.

"Okay, kids," Aunt Julia said once we'd parked and were crossing the lot. "You know the rules..."

"Hang on to the cart," Ethan and Hannah recited.

Or else you'll be swept into the stampede, I silently added, because the crowd of cars was just a warning for what awaited us inside: pure chaos. Now there was no time for me to be paranoid about Ian—I had to focus on navigating the store without getting trampled.

"We'll meet back at the van?" Aunt Rachel asked me.

I nodded. It went without saying that with different shopping agendas, we would be separated. The grocery store was buzzing like a beehive. Music was probably playing over the speakers, but you couldn't hear it. People were *everywhere*, some straight off the beach. One guy was shirtless, only wearing board shorts and an obnoxious bucket hat.

Here we go. I took a deep breath and inserted myself into the rush hour. The store was a gridlock today, only one shopping cart able to move at a time. The first item on my mom's list was toilet paper.

So naturally, I worked my way toward aisle four, the breakfast food aisle. That was other major problem with the Stop & Plop: *nothing* was where it was supposed to be. I would push my cart past the Cheerios, Reese's Puffs, and Golden Grahams only to find the Charmin next to the granola bars. The shampoo and conditioner were with the salad dressing, the coffee in the produce section among the fruits and vegetables.

Wit buzzed in again after I'd secured the TP (and a box of Nature Valley bars). In the middle of another traffic jam, I unlocked my phone to see: Eli's brother drives the tractor in the afternoons? Where?

Wait a second, I typed back. What happened to Auntie Anne?

Almost immediately: You said to go to the tennis courts, so I did.

I sighed. Wit was having a blast out there, and here I was, literally stuck. *Maybe I should ransack the Camp for Viv's target? Take matters into my own hands?*

"Hey, miss!" someone behind me shouted. "You going to move or what?"

I looked up to see that I was blocking a whole line of shoppers. "Yes!" I squeaked. "Sorry!"

Forty-five minutes later, while I waited at the deli counter for turkey, ham, and cheese and listened to the lovable Ukrainian workers argue with one another in their thick accents, Wit DMed me again. I'm sitting in a chair outside the Pond House's front door, it said, waiting for Sarah's brides-maid Haley. She has a haircut in an hour.

I snorted. So Eli's bro is no more?

Terminated, he confirmed. Shortly followed by Michael's favorite uncle.

WTF?

Claire's monster of a gun, he replied. It's been a game changer.

I snickered. You know the Pond House has more than one door.

Don't worry, I've rigged the others, Wit wrote. Chairs under each knob.

I poked another hole in his plan by typing, She could climb out a window. The Pond House was a ranch house; you could easily escape through a window.

Okay, he said, I mean this in the nicest way possible, I really do, but I've been dragged to dinner with Haley...and she's not going to think of climbing through a window. Her brand is not your brand!

My deli number was called. "Seven-one-seven!!"

I'm touched, I quickly sent back, smiling at my screen. Have fun waiting her out.

———

After two and a half hours—yes, *two and a half*—Aunt Julia slowed the minivan to a stop in front of the Annex. My mom greeted us, looking totally stone-faced. "Did you get the Funfetti frosting?" she asked as we unloaded my bags.

"Yes, ma'am," I said, even though it hadn't been on the shopping list. It didn't need to be; my dad was so obsessed with Pillsbury's vanilla-and-sprinkles frosting that it went without saying—if you went to the supermarket, you bought it. "What's wrong with Dad?" I asked, since he broke out the frosting whenever he was stressed or upset.

"Just come inside," Mom answered. "You'll see."

Plastic bags in hand, I found my dad collapsed on the couch with a spoon. And a defeated look on his face...

Assassinated, I realized. *He's been assassinated.*

"Who was it?" I ventured carefully once he was a spoonful or six into the frosting. My mom sat next to him, rubbing his back.

"Who was it?" He gave me a look. "Who *was* it?"

My shoulders sagged. *Damn.*

Dad sprang up from the love seat. "He is on a different playing field *entirely*," he said. "Brad called it." He shook his head. "He has ten kills, Meredith—*eight* of which happened while you were gone."

"Jesus," I breathed. The last I'd heard from Wit was right after he'd eliminated Haley the bridesmaid. His plan had worked, and next on his list had been Aunt Christine's sister.

"He's wearing a bandanna, too," Dad added. "To mask his face."

I quickly messaged Wit. A bandanna?

"And somehow he talked Wink into borrowing the binoculars."

But of course, **Wit responded.** A little anonymity never hurts.

"Did you give him Claire's gun, Mer?" Mom asked.

"Oh." I felt myself flush as I tucked away my phone. "Um, yes, I did." I looked at my dad. "Sorry."

He scowled while Mom laughed. "I'm sure she's happy it's getting some good use."

I couldn't help but grin. "That's what I thought, too."

But eight eliminations, Wit? Really?

Perhaps a bit obnox—

Someone knocked on the kitchen door. My ears perked up, knowing right away it wasn't a Fox. They knew the long-standing no-knocking rule. "It's open!" Dad called through a mouthful of frosting. "Always open!"

The door squeaked, but Wit had barely crossed the sitting room's threshold before Dad flipped out. "But not to you," he said and pointed outside. "Absolutely not."

My mom moved to escort Wit through the screen door. "Too soon," I heard her whisper. "It's a little too soon, Wit." She turned and nodded for me to follow him.

We met under the trees. "Aunt Christine is going to *murder* you," I told him. "Literally, she's going to assassinate you herself."

Because while Wit's red bandanna now hung around his neck, the top half of his face was not only freckled but also deeply sunburned. It was, to say the least, an interesting combination with his murky bruise.

I *tsk-tsk*ed him. "Looks like someone didn't reapply their sunscreen."

"It slipped my mind," Wit said as I traced the bridge of his nose. "I was busy."

"Yeah, being a *serial* killer."

"Well, isn't that the goal of the game?"

"My dad is pissed at you."

"So it seems." Wit scrubbed a hand through his hair. "Will he, um, *stay* pissed at me?"

I hesitated a moment to build the suspense, then shook my head. "He'll be fine once he finishes his frosting."

Wit exhaled. "Phew." He slid his arms around me, and I smiled.

"Now you have to tell me," I said. "You have to tell me about each takedown. You said you would when you, and I quote, 'had me in your arms again.'"

He blushed—through his bruise, through his sunburn. He *blushed*. "How about dinner?" he murmured. "How about I tell you over dinner tonight?"

"Dinner?" I slung my arms around his neck. "Like a date?"

"Yeah, dinner." Wit nodded. "Like a dinner."

My fluttering heart wavered.

So *not* a date.

Although it sure *felt* like one later when Wit opened the Raptor's driver's-side door for me. He smelled like his orange shampoo, freshly showered and wearing chinos with a light-weight blue button-down. It kind of billowed in the breeze.

"Where're we going?" I asked once he was buckled up next to me.

"I don't know," he replied. "How about anywhere you want?"

I chose Home Port in Menemsha, one of the Vineyard's smaller fishing towns. The restaurant was famous for its lobster, and since I hadn't been invited to Atlantic the other day, I was seriously craving some. Wit and I hadn't made a reservation, so we strolled along the docks while waiting for a table. "Claire and I loved to race down these," I told him. "She would always win, but I was close one time and probably would've won if I hadn't tripped and skinned my knee."

Wit took my hand.

In response, I tugged it away and sprinted ahead of him. Luckily, I wasn't wearing my wedges tonight, just a pair of gladiator sandals.

But Wit caught up in no time. We ran toward the end of dock, and the race ended in a tie. Our reward was a text from the Home Port's hostess, saying our table was ready.

She seated us by the windows, the natural-wood interior and usual blue water glasses a warm welcome back. There were four chairs at our table, and Wit pulled out the one next to mine. "What?" I said. "Don't sit there."

"Why not?" he asked.

"Because you should sit across from me," I said. "So I can see your face."

"Meredith, my face is a *wreck*."

I giggled. It was, but it also wasn't.

"Besides," Wit said, sitting down next to me, "if I sit here, I can do this..." He put his arm around my shoulder. "Or this..." He brushed his fingers through my hair. "Or even *this*..." His hand went to my knee. "But, I mean, if you aren't—"

"Nope," I cut him off, tangling our fingers together under the table. "You've made some valid points."

We both ordered the lobster clambake: freshly boiled lobster with steamers, corn on the cob, and baby potatoes. Then Wit told me about today's eliminations, including hiding under Moor House's grill cover to overtake someone on a bike. The back of his neck was *also* sunburned from his stakeout at the Pond House, and he'd stalked my dad like a wolf in the woods.

"Did you get him from a tree or something?" I asked.

"Uh, not exactly." He scratched his neck. "I actually"—he lowered his voice—"got him coming out of the outhouse..."

"No!" I let my forehead drop onto his shoulder, overcome with laughter. "You didn't!"

Wit laughed, too, shoulders bobbing up and down. "Sorry, but I did."

Our dinner came a few minutes later. Two big steaming plates of deliciousness. "I've been waiting two summers for this," I said when we cracked open our lobster shells. "Oh my god." I moaned with pleasure.

"Oh, wow," Wit said. "Should I give you a minute?" He pretended to push back his chair. "You and your *lobster*?"

"Haha, so clever." I rolled my eyes, but my heart was hopping. While Wit dunked his first bite in melted butter, I unlocked my phone and asked a passing busboy to take our picture.

"Okay," the kid said when he had the camera positioned. "Smile."

And I did smile—a smile so filled with happiness, happiness I hadn't been sure I'd ever be able to feel again. But then out of the corner of my eye, I spotted butter dripping down

Wit's jawline, and I was overcome with the *need* to lean over and lick it off. The busboy would take a burst of photos, after all. It wasn't like we would post this one.

"Oh, hell yeah we will," Wit said after we'd scrolled through all the pictures. We'd agreed to post one on Instagram. "It's this or nothing."

"But I'm licking your face," I said, pointing to the screen. "I'm *licking* your face."

He smirked. "And what a beautiful face it is."

I snorted.

"Come on," he said. "Post it. It's us."

It's us.

What did he mean by that? Were we really an "us" if we weren't meant to last past this week? I looked at the photo again—Wit's hair roguishly mussed and those turquoise eyes electric but also alarmed. Alarmed because I had one hand on his chest and the other on the back of his neck to pull him close so I could lick up the melted butter. You could literally see tongue.

And a happy smile.

"Okay, fine," I said, excitement shooting through my veins. "Let's do it." I tapped my screen a few times, having offered to do the honors. My first upload as @claires_sister. "What should the caption be?" I asked as Wit leaned over to see the screen. He rested his chin in the crook of my neck, and I ran a hand blindly through his hair. *Hopefully we aren't ruining too many dinners*, I thought, knowing people must be judging our PDA. I'd felt some stares.

"No caption," Wit answered.

"So just the hashtag?" I said. "Hurray She's a Dupré?"

He sighed.

"Sarah and Michael," I reminded him. "It's for Sarah and Michael."

"Wrong," Wit said. "This is for *us*."

Then he stole my phone, thumbs flying over the touch-screen. I nervously watched him scan whatever he'd written before he tapped to post the picture. He smiled crookedly and handed back the iPhone.

"Feast your eyes," he said.

"Must I?"

He dug his chin into my shoulder. "Look at it!"

So I did. Underneath our ridiculous photo, there was an even goofier hashtag: #HitchMeToWitry.

My jaw dropped.

He laughed.

"Again," I said slowly, since I could hardly speak, my heart was fluttering so fast. "Aunt Christine is going to hunt you *down*."

"I know," Wit said. "But I'm a Witry, not a Dupré." He nudged me. "And we're partners in crime."

"Which I thought we previously agreed to neither confirm nor deny," I said but then grinned before kissing him on the cheek. "You just totally—"

"Hey, lovers!" someone shouted from somewhere in the restaurant. "This is a family setting! If you wanna get it on, get out!"

Wit kissed me goodnight outside the Annex. It was late. By the time we'd gotten back from dinner, my dad had indeed finished his Funfetti frosting and forgotten his bad blood with Wit, so we'd spent the last couple of hours hanging out with my parents. I'd noticed that Wit was calm around them in a way that Ben had never been, from the way he relaxed in his armchair to the way he got really animated when he spoke. I don't know—with Ben it had always felt like talking to my parents was all politeness and pleasantry, while with Wit, we were a family having fun together. At one point, he and my dad even recounted the whole outhouse scene. My mom laughed so hard she cried, and I smiled so hard from seeing her laugh so much. It felt good; it felt almost like old times. Not quite, of course.

But close.

"I'll see you later," I said, giving him one more hug. We melted together, both of us sweaty. Usually the Vineyard's temperature dipped at night, but the air was still as balmy as it had been this afternoon.

"Later?" Wit hugged me back. "Or tomorrow?"

It was a good question. I'd spent almost every night this week in his room, whether by accident or on purpose. I glanced back at the cottage. "Tomorrow," I said, since it would be very on purpose if I walked away with him now. My parents knew we were no longer just friends—instead of sitting in my own chair, I'd perched on the arm of Wit's so

I was only a reach away from ruffling his hair or putting my hand on his shoulder and shaking it.

"You really like him, don't you?" my mom had asked when we'd gone into the kitchen for ice cream, and when I didn't answer, she added, "I saw the Instagram post."

"Yes," I admitted, nodding. "I do."

The look that flashed across her face was almost sad—sad that I would have to say goodbye to him at the end of the week. "It's going to be difficult," she said quietly.

"I know," I whispered, and that was it. We scooped Moose Tracks ice cream into four bowls and brought them back into the sitting room.

"I'll see you later," I told Wit, and after watching him disappear into the night, I walked to the mailbox. Chances were Viv had still not delivered; I was going to text Wink again in the morning, but what was the harm in checking?

Third time's the charm, I hoped, and I was *stunned* when I turned on my iPhone flashlight and pulled open the rickety door to find a message—my new target slip with a purple Post-it Note on top. It read: *You got your dear old granddaddy involved? Grow up.*

"Fuck you," I muttered before shining my light onto my target slip.

And at first, I was confused.

But I already... I thought. *I already killed...*

Then it dawned on me, and the shock set in; my face felt like it had been slapped. I read the paper again and again—there had to be some mistake. It *had* to be a mistake, because the name...

The name.

His name.

⁓

I stared at the ceiling from the top bunk, sweating in my T-shirt. The Annex had no AC, so my window was open, and I had two fans blasting. *Tell me what to do*, I said to Claire. *Tell me what to do.*

She was everywhere tonight. I swear I could hear her shifting on the mattress below.

But when she didn't answer, I sighed, sat up, and after pulling my sweaty hair into a topknot, found myself sneaking barefoot out of my house and over to the Cabin. It was supposed to rain tomorrow, but the sky was enchanted with stars.

It sounded like Wit also had a fan whirring when I arrived at his room. No lamplight seeped through his blinds, so I suspected he was asleep. *Do I go in?* I wondered before I heard a sleepy, "I knew you'd come."

That was all I needed to slide through his door. In the starlight that shone through the screen, I saw the fan on his dresser and Wit in bed, shirtless under only the sheet. The blankets had been kicked to the floor. Too hot.

I didn't join him just yet. "How did you know?"

"Because when we said goodbye, at first you told me you'd

see me *tomorrow*." He yawned and propped himself up on an elbow. "But then the next time you said it, it was *later*."

"Oh, I didn't notice," I lied.

He didn't believe me. "Whatever helps you sleep at night."

My eyes welled up.

A beat passed.

"C'mere," Wit said.

I blinked away my tears and crossed the floor to climb in with him...only to feel cold spots on the mattress. "Ice packs?" I guessed.

"Yep." He rolled me into his arms. "Everyone's eager to give them to me, so..."

A giggle slipped out, and I reached to touch his bruise. Wit let out an overdramatic yelp and jokingly jolted us both. More giggles escaped.

The best man banged on the wall.

"Sweet dreams, Gavin!" Wit called back, then whispered in my ear, "He's upset because Danielle has 'suspended' things with him."

"What?" I whispered back. "Why?"

"Dunno, but I'm sure they'll be back together by the rehearsal dinner." He tugged on my T-shirt. "Do you want a fresh one? This is soaked."

"No, that's all right," I said and sat up to strip off my sweaty shirt before nestling back into him. Even with the ice packs, his body was a thousand degrees, but I wanted his sticky skin against mine. It made me feel safe.

"Well, I suppose you did say 'later' to this, too," Wit said lightly, the scene at Secret Beach coming to mind: him asking to take off my bikini top, me saying yes but not until we were in private. Now Wit sketched something on my back before kissing my shoulder—it sent tingles all the way down to my toes. They even curled.

Soon I was on top of him, my hands running through his damp hair and his thumbs pressed into my hip bones. Spirals swirled under my skin.

"I didn't mean to sound presumptuous earlier," Wit murmured, breath warm between us. "I'm happy you came over." He kissed along my neck. "I really wanted you to come over."

For a second, I thought of what I'd found in my mailbox but quickly shook it away. "You *did* sound presumptuous," I said, then admitted, "I really wanted to come over, too."

Because god, I had—I'd wanted to come over. I'd needed to come over. It had only been a few days, but somehow, some way...

Even if this truly was just temporary, it felt like much more. Something special, something singular, something I'd been waiting for for a very long time.

So when Wit asked if I wanted to, I said yes without any hesitation. "Wow, quite enthusiastic," he commented, voice magnificently melodious. It had this lilt to it that just made you *melt*.

"Do you have something?" I asked.

"Yeah, yeah," he said and then slid us over to the edge of

the bed so he could reach underneath. "The best man, uh, gave us 'welcome packs' when we got here on Sunday."

"How thoughtful of him," I deadpanned as he rummaged around in the dark.

He sighed. "If it helps, I wasn't remotely expecting to use it."

I laughed, and once Wit found what he was looking for, he used one hand to tickle me so that I had to suppress a squeal. My heart was soaring.

"Are you sure this is okay?" he asked a minute later. "Really okay?"

Not with anyone else, I thought. *If Wit were anyone else...*

"Yes, it's okay," I murmured. "Like, way beyond okay."

Wit laughed, and then we tangled our bodies together.

~

"What's wrong?" he whispered a while later, both of us drifting in and out of sleep.

A lump formed in my throat. "How do you know something's wrong?"

He shrugged, shoulders curved around me. "Just do."

"I came here to be with you," I told him. "But also because I can't sleep there. I can't sleep in that room without her."

Wit was quiet.

"I still miss her so much," I told him. "And that room...it brings everything back. Like Sarah's story. I can't stop thinking about it and how I didn't even *talk* to Claire that day. We texted, but just about her plans—the restaurant, the French Quarter." Tears started to spill. "I didn't get to tell her I loved her, and she didn't get to tell me. We called each other every night and said it before hanging up."

I love you, Claire.

I love you, Mer.

Again, Wit was silent, but the type of silent that felt like he wanted to say something. "She did love you," he said eventually, sounding a little sorrowful himself. "She loved you very much."

I nodded and continued to cry. He hugged me to his chest and didn't let go even when I'd stopped crying. "Sleep," he murmured. "Go to sleep, Killer."

THURSDAY

FOURTEEN

Wit and I woke up early to go hiking but not early enough to avoid Michael stretching pre-workout. "Good morning," was all he said as I bowed my head, Wit's hands on my shoulders.

"Um, yeah, good morning," I stammered back.

"Are you embarrassed to be seen with me?" Wit whispered.

I smiled and shook him off. "More like *mortified*."

We stopped by the Annex so I could change into hiking clothes, fill up a water bottle, and grab the Raptor's keys. My parents were asleep, their bedroom door shut, but Loki was wide awake and bouncing around the cottage. The Jack Russell could barely contain himself when I clipped his leash onto his collar, knowing it was time for a walk.

The Menemsha Hills Reservation Trail was up-island in Chilmark, and Wit was almost as excited as Loki by the time I parked the truck. "It's one big loop," I told him and glanced up at the overcast sky. Hopefully, we'd beat the forecasted downpour. "Claire knew it better than me." I paused. "I'm not the best with directions."

"Well, lucky for us, I am," Wit said, pulling a map out of the nearby hutch. He unfolded it, scanned it for a few seconds. "Onward?"

I nodded. The cool thing about this trail was that it was woodsy but then out of nowhere, you'd pop out of the trees and have your breath taken away by the view. My favorite part overlooked the ocean with its wide-open beaches and rolling cliffs.

"I love this," Wit said once we got into a groove, our sneakers covered in the dusty sand we were kicking up. "This is exactly the type of thing I want to do in New Zealand."

New Zealand—I wished the thought didn't make my stomach turn so much.

"Tell me about when you were younger," I randomly said.

Wit raised an eyebrow. "When I was younger?"

"Yeah, like when you were in high school."

"So barely two years ago?"

I was thankful Loki jerked me ahead so Wit didn't see me blush.

"There's not much to tell," Wit said. "I lived in Vermont with my mom, I went to school—I didn't love it, but I didn't hate it—and I skied as much as possible on the weekends in the winter."

"What about your friends?" I asked. "Did they ski, too? Or snowboard?"

Wit hesitated for a moment. "To be honest," he said, "I only have a couple of good friends—Kevin and Caleb and I have known each other since kindergarten. But I'm always cool doing my own thing, too. There were people I hung out with from time to time and studied with, but not a huge group of friends." He shrugged and chuckled to avoid any awkwardness. "I guess that's why Michael and Sarah take me out with them in New Orleans. Since it's kind of the same way at Tulane. I'm not great at making friends."

"And I'm not great at keeping them," I found myself saying, reining Loki in—he'd caught a whiff of something and was trying to crawl under the path's split-rail fence.

"What do you mean?" Wit asked. "I bet you have plenty of friends. You're incredible."

My heart twisted. "I did have friends," I told him. "But somewhere along the way..." I trailed off and cleared my throat. "Somewhere along the way, I stopped paying attention to them. Everything became about Ben...especially after Claire died. I was so sad and checked out that I clung to the person closest to me and didn't let go. I shut out everyone else and didn't ever open the door again. Because Ben loved protecting me. He loved that I *needed* him, until he decided that he didn't need *me* anymore."

"Ben?" Wit asked. "What happened to Shithead?"

We reached another overlook and sat down on its bench, built from three slabs of stone. I quickly told Wit about Ben's drunken 2:00 a.m. voicemail and what I'd said when I'd called him back. "So he's just Ben again," I finished. "But in the sense that I don't care—he's beneath my consideration. I blocked his number."

Wit leaned over and kissed the top of my head, leaving an arm slung over my shoulder. It was freckled from the sun. "Good for you, Killer."

I shut my eyes. *Killer.* There it was—not one of our

ever-changing terms of endearment but my special, sweet, inside-joke nickname.

Now, did I have one for Wit?

That was more complicated.

Are we meant to last more than a week? I wondered, wishing I could ask Claire to consult her astrology charts and tarot cards.

"What about you?" I asked. "Have you ever had a girlfriend?"

"Yeah," he answered. "For a little while in high school."

I elbowed him.

He laughed. "What?"

"More details, please."

"Why?"

"Because it's important. Girls care about this stuff."

Wit sighed. "Her name was Brianna. We were in the same math class and agreed to go to junior prom together. It escalated from there."

"When did you break up?"

"Winter senior year, because apparently I didn't give her enough attention."

"That doesn't sound like you," I said.

His lips quirked. "What do you mean?"

I swallowed. "Oh, just that..."

You are affectionate without even thinking about it.

You let me talk for hours, and you listen for hours.

You make me feel absolutely golden.

But I couldn't say any of that, so I kissed him. "What about Tulane?" I asked afterward. "Any love interests there?"

"Really? *Love interests?*"

I gave him a look.

He shrugged. "Some girls, yes...but they weren't real relationships or anything. We would hang out a couple of times, and then..."

"Hook up," I finished for him. "You hooked up, and that was it."

Wit ran a hand through his hair, face flushed. "Meredith, why are we talking about this?"

Because, I thought. *Because I want to know if things...if things were different...*

"I don't know," I said quickly. "Sorry, I'm being stupid." I leaned forward to grab my water bottle from my backpack's side pocket. "Loki!" I coaxed him over, then squirted a stream into his mouth. He gulped and gulped.

"Neat trick," Wit commented.

"Claire taught him," I said.

He nodded thoughtfully. "Seems like something she'd do."

I laughed. "You sound like you knew her."

"Well," he said, shifting on the bench, "actually..."

"I talk about her a lot," I said. "I know." I gestured around us. "Every piece of this island is *her* to me, so I can't help it. She would've liked you."

Wit gave me a gentle smile. "Sarah said that, too," he said. "She thought we would be really good friends." He paused, not exactly looking at me, gazing at the horizon instead. His fingers were folded on his lap. "Meredith, I think I need to clear something up—"

The sudden crack of thunder drowned out whatever he was going to say.

"Crap!" I said and shot up off the bench. Finding the car and driving home in the rain was daunting. "Let's make a run for it!"

But I didn't know which path to take. Multiple trails led to our overlook.

Wit's hand found mine. "Don't worry," he said. "I know the way."

~

Our clothes were drenched by the time we reached the Raptor, and I gladly tossed Wit the keys when he offered to drive. I swung myself up into shotgun, a soaking-wet Loki settling on my lap. It was too bad I didn't have a beach towel to wrap him in, because his first inclination was to shake himself dry. *Perfect*, I thought, now also covered mud. *Just perfect.*

Wit didn't laugh; instead, he resumed our conversation from earlier. "I'm sorry for being weird about the girls," he said, coughing. "It's not something I'm proud of, and Michael's already chewed me out a bunch of times."

"You tell Michael about that stuff?" I asked.

"Yes."

I nodded but didn't say anything, remembering how Claire constantly told me I deserved more than Ben, that someone better for me was out there. "I don't know when it's gonna happen," she'd said once, after I came home from a fight with him. She and I were curled up together in her bed—her the big spoon, me the little. "But someday, somewhere..."

And then she'd murmured something in my ear.

It had stopped my sobbing for a second and made me smile.

"You're prettier than all of them anyway," Wit added as he turned the Raptor's windshield wipers up to full speed. "By far."

I squeezed Loki to my chest. "Don't say that."

"But it's true." He took a hand off the wheel so he could lick his thumb, then reached over and wiped some mud from my cheek.

My chest tightened. "I don't care if it's true," I said. "Please don't call me pretty."

Why not? I expected him to ask, but he didn't. Instead, Wit flipped the blinker before pulling the truck over to the side of the road. He threw on the hazard lights, then turned to me. And I could see it in his eyes, in their gold rings, that he remembered yesterday morning, us fooling around together. *Don't call me pretty*, I'd been quick to say, and then I'd managed to leave his room without an explanation.

"Okay," Wit said slowly, both hands still on the steering wheel but not breaking eye contact. My pulse raced. "What's the deal? Tell me, please."

I waited a heartbeat...then two...then three.

Wit's hands dropped from the wheel.

"Everyone says I'm pretty," I murmured.

"Well, they're right," Wit replied. "You are undeniably—"

"*Ben* called me pretty," I cut in. "Ben called me babe, Ben called me cute, Ben called me *pretty*." My eyes prickled. "He almost never acknowledged that I had something more to offer than my looks." I blinked away tears. "And I can't hear it anymore. I can't handle it." I paused. "Especially from you."

Wit was silent.

"I don't want to be 'pretty' to you," I tried again. "It means nothing. It's sanitized and superficial." I reached for one of his hands and squeezed it tight. "You pay me the most wonderful compliments. You say such interesting things no one has ever said before, like how affectionate I am, and smart and clever... and I can't even tell you how good that makes me feel." I kissed his fingers, which were warm despite the downpour. "Hearing *those* things make me so happy." I started kissing his palm, along his love line.

"Okay," Wit said after a minute. "I won't say you're pretty." He sighed. "But am I still allowed to think it? Because if not"—his eyes flicked up and down my body, all wet and splattered with mud—"that'd be a huge ask."

"A huge ask?"

"An *impossible* ask."

I laughed. "Even when I look like this?"

"Uh-huh," he said, leaning over to mess up my hair. "Even when you look like this."

Michael texted me just as we pulled onto The Farm road. I don't know where you two rogues are, it said, but everyone's invited to Moor House for board games and gumbo.

Wit groaned when I read the message aloud. "What?" I asked. "Do you have something against gumbo?"

"Not at all," he said. "Jeannie's gumbo is the *best* gumbo in New Orleans." He paused. "It's just, you know, with everyone in one house...like the whole Varsity Room situation?"

I nodded, catching his drift. "A massacre."

Because while Wit and I had fled early, so many people had been unable to escape elimination when the Varsity Room's party officially ended. According to Pravika, at least ten players were assassinated.

"We'll have to be creative, then," I told Wit. "Climb through some windows or something."

Hopefully Ian wouldn't consider that possibility, and if Jeannie's gumbo was as delicious as Wit claimed, then I'd happily wait out my cousin all afternoon.

"By the way," Wit said, "did you ever text Sarah about getting in touch with Viv? For your target?"

My heart scrambled up into my throat. "Oh." I could barely speak. "I...um, don't need to anymore." I bit my lip. "Viv... delivered it right after you left last night."

"Wait, she *did*?" Wit swerved a little but righted the Raptor quickly. His hand went to my knee, but for once, I didn't want it there. "Why didn't you tell me in my room?"

"Because I was too busy seducing you," I joked. "With my sweat-soaked T-shirt and such."

"Ah, yes..." Wit said but trailed off as if also thinking about me sobbing in my sleep—crying over Claire. "I'm an idiot."

"But a handsome one," I said.

"Handsome?" He gave me an incredulous look. "You can call me *handsome*, but I can't call you—"

"You *like* being called handsome," I said. "Yesterday morning, you pouted like a little boy when I said I *wouldn't* call you handsome."

Wit straightened up in his seat.

I tried to turn the subject back to him. "I'm guessing you're going to try to get your target today, right?"

"*Try?*"

I rolled my eyes. "Asshole."

"But a *handsome* asshole, right?"

"Yes, although handsome assholes do not compare to handsome idiots."

Wit laughed and nodded. "Yeah, yeah," he said. "I'm going to give it my best shot."

"Cool," I said, then went silent, wishing this ride could be over. I knew who Wit's next target was, and while it would probably be an easy execution, the repercussions would be difficult.

For me, not him.

"Speaking of," I found myself saying, "I think I'm going to take a step back."

He raised an eyebrow. "A step back?"

"Uh-huh." I nodded. "With Ian on the prowl, I'm going to play more defensively for a while. He's getting under my skin, and I want to be on my guard."

"But you *are* on your guard," Wit said. "You even know Ian's your assassin." He sighed. "I don't know who mine is, and that's *really* freaking me out, but I'm not letting it stop me."

"Wit," I said, his name now difficult to say. "You have *so many* people freaked out that I think even *your* assassin is freaked out. You can afford to be a bandanna-wearing bandit." I took a breath, rehearsing what I needed to say next. "Besides, there's an advantage to me switching to defense."

His voice was deadpan. "Enlighten me."

"Well, while I avoid Ian, my target will be doing most of the work."

"Most of the work?"

"Yeah," I told him. "Sure, they'll be out there having fun, but the more people they take out, the fewer people I'll have to deal with when the time comes."

Wit kept his eyes on the road, but I could almost hear the gears going in his head and see the scenarios he was envisioning.

Please, I thought, stomach stirring. *Please believe me. Get on board. This is how it needs to be...*

"Who is it?" he asked.

Blood pumped through my ears.

"Who's your next mark?"

I hugged Loki so hard he let out a bark.

"Fuck," Wit murmured. "It's me, isn't it?"

"No!" I said quickly, watching him run a hand through his hair. "No, oh my god, Wit"—I forced a laugh—"it's *not* you. Don't be ridiculous. Of course it's not you!"

His jaw tightened. "Then why did I have to ask twice?"

Words—I needed words, and *fast*. "Because even though it's not you," I answered, "it's still someone I'm close with." I mentally ran through the names of who was left, soon landing on one. "Someone I'm aligned with." I took a deep breath and hoped this wouldn't come back to bite me. "Luli—I have Luli."

He gave me a look. "Luli?"

I nodded. "Luli."

"Not me?"

"Not you."

Silence.

"That sounds like solid logic, then," Wit eventually said. "Focus on outwitting Ian, and let Luli have her fun."

"Yes." I looped my pinkie around his and locked them together. "That's exactly what I'm going to do."

FIFTEEN

Most people drove over to Moor House, but Wit and I grabbed an umbrella, and I led him down the forest footpath I'd taken to assassinate his father. We were both armed with our guns—Wit so he could carry out his latest plan and me to keep up appearances. No one could know about my newest strategy. *Because it is a strategy*, I kept telling myself. *Without an assassin on his tail, Wit can eliminate as many players as he wants, narrow down the pool of players.*

Then, eventually, I could kill him.

Not now, but eventually.

He was nervous, though—more nervous than I'd ever seen him, more nervous than *me*. Fidgeting and swiveling his head every few seconds. "Hey, relax," I told him. "Basically no one knows about this trail."

"Basically?"

"Claire," I said. "And the dogs, probably—but other than that, only Claire."

A single nod.

My stomach knotted. *Maybe I should tell him*, I thought. *Maybe I should tell him it's me, and then we can make some kind of deal. An addendum to our pact, some kind of deal where we work together so it's the two of us in the final showdown.*

But it was too late. He had asked me directly if he was my next target, and I'd directly said no. I couldn't take that lie back.

"It's going to be fine, Wit," I said, swallowing hard. His name sounded not quite right coming out of my mouth. "You are cool, calm, collected, and *clever*. Don't let the paranoia get to you. Do *not* let it get to you. All right?"

"All right," he said and let out a long breath. His face was scorched with sunburn, but somehow it still looked as pale as the gray rainy day.

"We're going to go in there," I said in my best *Rally the troops!* voice, "and do what needs to be done. I'm going to avoid Ian like the best of them, and your target won't even know what hit him."

"Games and gumbo, too," Wit added. "Don't forget."

"Right." I smiled. "So let's not keep everyone waiting."

"We can for one more sec," he said and hooked an arm around my waist before leaning in to kiss me. It was a light flutter of a kiss, but suddenly I wanted more, climbing up his strong, wiry frame until he held me and I had my arms around his neck. Now we were truly, deeply *kissing*. I had no idea where the umbrella had gone; neither of us was holding it anymore.

I kissed him one last time, and then Wit set me down and

we continued down the pathway, both dripping by the time it spit us out in Moor House's side yard. There were several people around the corner with their water guns, staking out the front lawn for new arrivals. Uncle Brad and Nicole Dupré were among them. I didn't see Ian.

"Okay, this leads to the downstairs bathroom," I told Wit as I pushed up one of the first-floor windows. "Ready?"

He nodded and gave me a boost inside, then hoisted himself up after me. There were several toothbrushes on the side of the sink and towels hanging on the back of the closed door—Wit and I used them to dry off a little. We stowed our water guns in the shower, the chevron-patterned curtain making a snaking noise when I pulled it shut.

A hundred voices swirled once we slipped into the hallway, whose walls were whipped-butter yellow and decorated not only with Fox family photographs but also beautiful watercolor landscapes. "No way," Wit whispered, seeing the initials BGF in the corner of one painting. "Uncle *Brad* did these?"

I nodded. "He has many talents."

And so did Jeannie Dupré, the smell of gumbo embracing us once we made it into the kitchen. Right away, I detected onions, peppers, and sausage. Pots and pans covered the stove, and my mom had thrown herself into helping, chopping up vegetables on the counter. I smiled—she loved to cook, but we had ordered a lot of takeout after Claire died. Now, though, it was like she'd gotten her groove back. I remembered almost falling to the floor several months ago when I'd come home from Ben's house to find her in the kitchen making my favorite fried chicken for dinner.

Wit noticed me watching her. "That's called the trinity," he said. "Onions, bell peppers, and celery—the essentials."

"Oh, Wit!" His stepmother spotted us. "Thank goodness! I already have a few pots ready, but more people are coming, so I've just sent Michael and Oscar out to make more groceries..."

"Buy groceries," he translated for me.

"Will you and Miss Meredith smother those once Liz is finished prepping them?"

"Miss Meredith?" I gave Wit an amused half smile as my mom confirmed the trinity was ready to go.

Wit rubbed the back of his neck. "Yeah," he said. "It's what my dad and Jeannie call you." He held up his hands like he was in trouble. "Not my idea."

I fully smiled and shook my head, remembering Oscar Witry telling *Miss Meredith* good luck after I'd assassinated him. "What does 'smother' mean?"

"It means we're gonna cook this stuff in more onions." He accepted the cutting board from my mom. "On high heat, for a *long* time."

Sarah was already at the stove, stirring a beige-colored substance in a saucepan. "Jeannie!" she called when the beige began rapidly turning brown. "The roux! It's—"

"—ruined," Wit said, then cocked his head. "Not for the first time, I'm guessing?"

She huffed. "It's only flour and oil," she said, pushing her glasses up her nose. "You think it'd be so simple." A groan. "This is my third try."

After Wit and I did some successful smothering, we served ourselves gumbo from a ready and waiting pot and searched for games to play. We'd decided on our walk here that we wouldn't play the same one. *Distance*, we'd agreed. Wit wanted to pull off a move today, and it was best if I wasn't anywhere near him if and when it happened.

While he wandered off to play Scrabble with Wink, Honey, and a few Duprés, I found Pravika, Eli, Jake, and Luli setting up Monopoly on the screened-in porch. As banker, Eli was counting out the money while Luli organized the property deeds.

Luli, I thought. *Good.*

I needed to talk to her—*really* talk to her. Yes, I'd apologized on Monday for ignoring her texts and stuff, but after hiking with Wit this morning and telling him about my friend troubles, I felt like she deserved something deeper. An explanation, to make sure the door between us could be fully reopened and stay open for a long time. I remembered when she, Claire, and I were little girls—the way we raced around The Farm together with our never-ending giggles. One of my favorite memories was the night we'd pranked Jake and Eli, drawing all over their faces with lipstick while they slept. I felt a twinge now at the thought of forever losing that closeness. I'd lost Claire; I couldn't lose anyone else.

"Hey, Mer," Pravika said now. "Thimble, boot, or top hat?"

"Thimble, please," I replied and took the empty chair next to Jake.

"Your taste buds aren't even ready," he warned as I raised a spoonful of gumbo to my mouth and blew on it. "Not. Even. Ready."

"Oh, wow." I actually moaned after my first bite, sweet and spicy all at once. The onions, peppers, celery, sausage, shrimp—a burst of fire in my mouth. Somehow I could *taste* the passion that had gone into cooking it. "This is…"

"Luli's had three bowls," Eli said, and I noticed all of theirs were empty. I scooped up more from mine. Perhaps I would have three bowls myself.

From my other side, Luli playfully scowled. "Can we start now?"

"I have to talk to you later," I whispered as Eli started dealing the money. "After the game?"

Her eyes sparked, probably thinking I meant Assassin—that I had some counterintelligence to share. Pinpricks needled the back of my neck. "Okay," she whispered back. "Can't wait."

Unfortunately, Monopoly was way less exciting than the gumbo. It played out as it usually did between the five of us: Jake quietly bought up all the cheap properties and built hotels, Luli landed on free parking a hundred times, and I found myself in jail over and over, all while Eli and Pravika kept proposing ridiculous property trades. Eventually, we abandoned the game altogether. "What do you guys think?" Eli asked. "Should I go to the yacht club and just introduce myself?"

"Not today," Luli said and gestured outside to the current break in the rain. "I'd bet all my Monopoly money that sailing was canceled."

Eli rolled his eyes. He'd been bummed about my Edgartown Books recon, the bookseller making lunch date plans. "There's always your sailing instructor," I had said to cheer him up. "You called him the man of your dreams, remember?"

"Yes," he'd responded. "Because he is..."

"Do it," I said now. "So we can finally find out this guy's name."

"Yeah, and who knows?" Pravika said. "Maybe it'll be love at first sight and he'll come to the wedding—"

I shot her a look. *Abort, Pravika. Abort.*

"Hey," Luli said, back from the bathroom. "Where'd Jake go?"

"Mer's place," Eli replied, gazing wistfully through the screen at Job's Neck Pond in the distance, which was of course distastefully obscured by the Nylon Condo Complex. Hopefully everyone's stuff wasn't ruined from the rain. "To get the old chessboard."

None of us were very good chess players, but we had decided to give it yet another chance. I knew I should've gone to the Annex to get the board myself, but Jake had jumped up and volunteered first.

And...

"He's been gone a pretty long time, hasn't he?" Luli commented. I suspected Wit's water gun was no longer in the shower. It wasn't a coincidence that he'd joined the Scrabble game, which was being played in the living room...the room *everyone* passed through when entering and exiting the house.

Eli shrugged. "Maybe he needed to stop and take a dump."

Luli and Pravika groaned. "Eli..."

"What?" He patted his stomach. "This gumbo's strong stuff—"

Shouts from the other room cut him off:

"Oh my god!"

"Look outside!"

"He's out of his mind!"

Our foursome flung ourselves from our chairs and hurried into the living room, where family members and wedding guests were pressed up against the windows. "Meredith!" My dad waved me over, and I squeezed in to see the driveway, where all the cars were parked. Wit was among them, popped up through the Raptor's sunroof. He had Claire's monster gun strapped to his back, but right now, he was in the middle of launching a rainbow of water balloons at his target.

"Did you give him the truck keys?" I asked my dad.

"I might've left them in the wheel well," he said lightly. "Did you buy him the balloons?"

"Touché," I muttered, because @sowitty17 had requested them when I'd gone to the store yesterday afternoon...and now he was pelting poor Jake with water balloon after water balloon.

I tried not to smile, but it was perfect, right down to the sunroof—an homage to how we'd first met. Plenty of people were laughing, but they had no idea that the takedown was an inside joke, something secret and special between Wit and me. I liked it that way, liked that certain things were only for us.

The group had a field day when Jake, dripping wet with bits of colorful rubber clinging to his clothes, came inside once he'd relinquished his target to Wit. "Towel, please?" he said. "Can somebody grab me a towel?"

"Coming right up!" I said, since it was the least I could do.

Then I felt Luli's hand on my arm. "I'll help you," she said in a pleasant voice, but the expression on her face was pure *fury*. Dark narrowed eyes, scrunched nose, pursed lips—even a vein bulging in her neck. I knew she would be angry, but *this* angry? She pointed above us to the second floor. "The fluffiest ones are up there."

"Cool." I tried to smile. Earlier, I'd wanted to talk to her, but not like this. Not when it looked like she wanted to actually avenge her brother's death. "Let's go."

Her face did not soften. "Yes, let's."

My lungs expanded, but they did not contract when I followed her upstairs.

SIXTEEN

I thought the best course of action was to apologize first, no matter how hard it might be. "Listen, Luli," I said when she shut the bathroom door behind us, "I've been doing a lot of thinking lately—"

"Oh, you have, have you?" she interrupted. "Let me guess." Her hands went to her hips. "You've been *thinking* about yourself and *only* yourself."

My eyebrows knitted together. "Um, excuse me?"

Luli rolled her eyes. "Don't play dumb, Meredith. You and your traitorous ways just got my brother eliminated!"

"No," I said. "That's not true, so not true. Jake volunteered to get the chessboard. I didn't do anything."

"Yeah, but you knew. You *knew* Wit had him, and you didn't tell us." She laughed dully. "Some alliance, huh? I can't believe I fell for that BS about you only flirting with him to get information. You probably switched sides the second you slipped on that little black dress."

The back of my neck blazed. *Actually, Wit and I were* always *on the same side*, I thought about saying. *We made a pact Sunday night to be open with each other.*

Not that I was exactly being open with him right now.

"I have not switched sides," I tried again. "I'm still loyal..."

Luli shook her head and pulled her phone from her pocket. I gritted my teeth, already knowing what she was going to show me. "Hitch me to Witry?" she said when the Home Port Instagram post loaded. "That pretty much says it all, no?"

I didn't answer, instead just looking at the photo—how the two of us sat on the same side of the table, with me grinning and licking butter off Wit's beautifully wrecked face.

"And it's not just about Assassin, Meredith," Luli said. "It's so much more than that." She paused. "It's always about you. Always about what Meredith wants, always about what Meredith needs, always about Meredith and her guy!"

Meredith and her guy.

Her *guy.*

Suddenly, I realized why Luli kept bringing up Ben this week, why she'd called Wit by his name. She wasn't teasing me about getting dumped before the wedding. She thought Ben and Wit were one and the same.

"Luli," I said carefully. "It's not like that."

"Yes, it is!" she fired back. "Ben might've broken up with you, Meredith, but you broke up with us long before that." She turned away. "Your friends never left you. *You* left *us.*"

I nodded, unable to deny it. I'd told Wit the same thing— that after Claire died, I'd taken Ben's hand and pushed my friends away. The only friend I wanted by my side was my sister, and she was gone.

But I couldn't find those words for Luli. I felt myself shutting down, quivering and anxious about being trapped in this small space with her.

"And now you're doing the same thing with Wit," Luli said, like I knew she would. "Ben says goodbye, and along comes Wit. You've known him what, five minutes? And you're already all in with him."

"I am *not* all in with him," I said, hoping my voice didn't falter as I grabbed a towel for Jake and moved toward the door. "We're just hanging out for the week."

Luli was silent for a moment, then used the last weapon in her arsenal. "He's going to break it, you know," she said. "He's going to break your heart." She took her brother's towel from my arms and brushed past me into the hallway. "Don't count on me when you need help picking up the pieces."

After shivering and staring at myself in the bathroom mirror, I took Moor House's hidden staircase up to the third floor—the attic reading room. *Don't cry*, I thought, curling into a ball on the upholstered window seat. *You don't need to cry.*

But I sobbed, covering my face with my hands before caving and using one of Honey's handmade quilts as an oversized tissue. The clouds outside had almost fully cleared by the time the door creaked open. "Mer?" someone said. "Are you in here?"

Sarah stepped into the room with a small blue box in hand. Her eyes widened when she spotted me huddled up alone. "Yes," I said weakly as she set the box down on a bookshelf. "Hi."

A blink later, she had wrapped me in her arms. I buried my blotchy face in her pink-and-orange Lilly dress and breathed in her Sarah scent. The usual vanilla, but infused with spice from the gumbo. Somehow it worked. "Everyone is frantic," she said when I finally looked at her. "There have been a *ton* of attacks—Ian crawled out the dog door—and no one's seen you for ages, so Wit..." She tilted her head and half smiled. "Wit is worried. He's paranoid that Ian cornered you somewhere."

More tears escaped. "I *was* cornered somewhere," I warbled, and then it all rushed out: Luli accusing me of treason toward our alliance, dropping my friends for Ben, and Wit—well, I started and stopped there. Honestly, I wasn't sure I wanted to talk about him with her, didn't want to know her thoughts on what he'd do to my heart.

Did he have it? Because the more time we spent together, the more it felt like he did. I wasn't in love with him, but I knew I was falling. His voice, his laugh, his jokes, how natural things were between us right from the start. I thought about his tender hand on my knee, sleeping with his arms around me, his lips on mine, and the words he'd whispered that had made me feel like I could do anything and everything.

Yes, we'd only known each other a few days, but I was

sliding down one of Aquinnah's age-old cliffs and gaining speed by the second. Luli had no idea how much of a chord she'd struck with her last blow. Although Wit's mind was a mystery. *Were we on the same wavelength? If I said I wanted to stay together after this week, would he agree?*

My head was against Sarah's shoulder when I finished speaking, and she held my hand with both of hers. I waited for her to say something, but it was several long seconds before she did. "I'm sorry," she eventually said. "I'm sorry for being so distant this week."

Distant? I thought. *More like I've been avoiding you.*

"Oh my god, stop," I said. "You've been busy with wedding stuff!"

"That doesn't matter," she replied. "You're my cousin, and I know how much you've been struggling. I should've been there for you. I should *be* there for you."

This time, it was me who was quiet, debating whether or not to ask her something that would go right to her gut. "Then why," I whispered, "did you tell the salad story? Why did you tell that story about Claire not eating her rabbit food in New Orleans?" My voice was thick, something coating my throat. "It was the same night, Sarah. *That* night." I looked at her, unable to avoid staring at her long scar. "Why would you do that?"

My cousin glanced away. "I didn't mean to," she told me. "At least not at first. You avoiding your salad just made me think of her and how funny it was, and suddenly I was halfway through telling the story and knew I couldn't stop—knew that if I did, everyone would make the connection." She squeezed my hand. "I hoped you hadn't."

"Of course I did." My heart hammered. "She's my sister, my best friend." I paused. "We texted *every day*. I woke up that morning knowing that you'd be having breakfast at the Ruby Slipper and were going to visit the bayou afterward."

Sarah burst into tears. "I'm sorry," she said. "Meredith, I'm so sorry. For telling that story like it was a harmless joke...and for taking her out that night in the first place. I never should've done it. She was only eighteen, but I forgot—she always acted so much older." She shook her head. "When I woke up in the hospital and Michael told me..."

I hugged her, any and every little grudge suddenly gone. Because my parents and I weren't the only ones who were still recovering from losing Claire. Sarah had lost her cousin—her *favorite* cousin. "You didn't know," I whispered. "How were you supposed to know what would happen? It was a freak accident."

"I know," she whispered back. "I know, and I remind myself every day—especially here, especially now." She took a deep breath, then rose from the window seat and crossed the cozy library back to the bookshelf. I watched her pick up the blue box. "The next day," she said after rejoining me, "we were supposed to go to brunch, just the two of us, and I was going to give her this before asking her to be a bridesmaid."

My pulse slowed.

"You know how much I love you, Meredith," Sarah said,

as if reading my mind. "I love you to pieces, but Claire was my mini-me."

"I know," I said, because I did. Sarah and I were close, but she and Claire had something special. While Claire was my older sister, everyone considered Sarah *Claire's* older sister. Their bond had been knit tighter than a winter scarf. I'd been jealous when I was younger, but later I loved watching them be their perfectly quirky selves together. They were beautiful, singing silly made-up songs and dancing barefoot around the campfire.

Sarah smiled faintly. "This belongs to you now," she said, handing me the blue box. "I want you to have it."

My heart twisted as I lifted the lid to see a delicate gold necklace inside, its pendant engraved with what I suspected were latitude and longitude coordinates. "Paqua," I murmured. "The Farm, right?"

Sarah nodded. "All the others are silver," she said, taking the necklace and fastening it around my neck. "But Claire's favorite color was gold—"

"Just like my hair," I finished for her. It wasn't an *exact* match, but Claire would always tug on my braids and say, "Your hair, Mer! Forever my favorite color!"

"Yes." Sarah's smile widened. "Just like your hair." She folded me into another warm hug and whispered that she loved me.

"I love you, too, Sarah," I said, eyes watery. "I'm sorry for everything."

She kissed my cheek. "Should we head back downstairs?"

Yes, I thought, but then pulled Honey's quilt up again and lay down. "Can we actually stay here a while longer?" I asked. "Just a little?"

"Sure, why not?" Sarah got under the blanket with me, and we spooned like Claire and I used to do—me the little one, her the big. She held me tight. "Let them search far and wide for us."

Wit was fading fast, but I kept nudging him awake. "Don't fall asleep," I said as his eyes fluttered open, then fell closed again. "They'll be here soon."

He yawned. "You've been saying that for the last two hours."

"Only because you've been *asking* for the last two hours." I hit him with one of the Annex's throw pillows. Tonight, we'd stayed in to eat dinner and watch a movie with my parents. They'd wandered over to Lantern House for a nightcap while Wit and I were waiting for Sarah and Michael. "Come," she'd said after our attic nap. "Michael and I want to do something alone before all the fanfare starts tomorrow."

Tomorrow's fanfare included the big reception tent going up on the Big House's sprawling front lawn (Aunt Christine was already fretting over whether or not the ground would still be saturated from today's rain) and then the afternoon ceremony rehearsal at St. Andrew's Church before the rehearsal dinner in Chilmark.

"Are you sure?" I asked. "If you guys want to be alone..."

Sarah shook her head. "Alone as in 'not with our entourage.'"

I laughed, and as promised, she and her fiancé arrived at the stroke of midnight. Michael beeped the Jeep's horn, and it was like Wit had been faking exhaustion—he leapt up from the love seat, threw me over his shoulder, and walked us out the door. It was chilly, the storm breaking yesterday's extreme heat. All four of us were wearing sweatshirts.

Once we were cruising down The Farm road, Wit asked where we were going. Don't tell him, I'd texted Sarah earlier. It should be a surprise!

Because I wanted to see the childlike wonder on Wit's face.

Now, by way of a response, Michael said, "You think the line will be long?"

"What a silly question," Sarah said from shotgun. "It turned out to be a nice night, so..."

"We probably should've brought chairs," I joked.

Wit groaned. "Seriously?!"

"Seriously," the three of us replied, and then it was only Assassin talk once we passed the Paqua obelisk and turned in the direction of Oak Bluffs. My mom had been taken down by a bridesmaid when leaving Moor House, Nicole Dupré basically tackled Luli and Jake's father, and Uncle Brad had profusely thanked Jeannie for gumbo leftovers before assassinating her in the driveway. No one had any updates on Ian; all we knew was that he'd fled Moor House through the dog door.

So he knows, I determined. *He knows his assassin.*

I needed to find out who it was, too. In the event that Ian was taken out before I was, I needed to know who would be gunning for me next.

"And here we are!" Sarah said, snapping me out of strategizing. She turned around in her seat. "Welcome, Wit, to Back Door Donuts!"

We passed under a streetlamp at the most perfect moment—I caught Wit's eyes widen in the glow. "Donuts," he said, and I swear I heard his stomach rumble with excitement.

"Yeah," I told him, grinning. "Donuts."

Then I pointed to what was normally a nondescript parking lot behind several stores, but tonight, it was filled with people—the winding line leading up to the local bakery's propped-open purple back door. Hence, Back Door Donuts. It was how everyone on the island satisfied their late-night sweet tooth. The first summer Claire had her driver's license, we came multiple times a week. The honey-dipped and coconut cream donuts were our favorites.

"You guys get out here," Michael said after circling town a few times, looking for a good parking spot. There were none in sight, since Oak Bluffs was where everyone and their mother ended the night. The restaurants, bars, and streets were swarming with people. "I'll find you."

Sarah leaned over the gearshift to quickly kiss him. "Good luck."

We hopped out of the Jeep, and Wit took my hand as Sarah led the way up the street, down some brick steps, and across the massive parking lot, stopping at the end of an incredibly long line. I squeezed Wit's fingers. "Now we wait."

He was bouncing up and down like a little kid, and when Michael joined us twenty minutes later, he nodded at his stepbrother. "Everything okay, Witty? You need to use the bathroom or something?"

Sarah and I giggled. "Where's the car?" she asked. "Far?"

Michael rubbed his jaw. "Let's just say we'll be walking off some calories."

My cousin smiled and rolled her eyes, then burrowed into his side. Michael slipped an arm around her and kissed her forehead. They began murmuring about this and that, off in their own loved-up world. "What if I trip walking down the aisle?" I heard her ask him, to which he answered, "Then I'll trip walking back up it."

The couple in front of them turned around. "I didn't mean to overhear," the woman said, "but are you two getting married?"

"Yes!" Sarah answered. "The day after tomorrow!"

Wit leaned closer to me. "And...*bam*!" he whispered at the same time Sarah flung out her left hand to show off her engagement ring, a halo of small stones surrounding a pear-shaped diamond big enough that I'd asked my dad how much Michael made working for the Saints.

The answer? A lot more than I'd thought.

We slowly but steadily moved up in line, Sarah and Michael now chatting away with their new friends, who had gotten engaged last month. Sarah sounded like Aunt Christine, all too happy to impart some wedding planning wisdom. Like mother, like daughter, even in the smallest of ways.

I shut my eyes and settled back into Wit, standing beside me like a human shield. The wind had picked up, but he gave off heat like a fire. His arms held me to his chest while his chin rested on the top of my head. I could feel his heartbeat against my back. "You're so warm," I murmured.

"And you're a liar," someone said, and my pulse surged before I realized it was *not* Wit who had responded. It was whoever stood behind us.

Relax, I told myself. *He doesn't know. He doesn't know you lied about Assassin, about having him as your target. He doesn't know, he won't know, he'll never know...*

But wait, was that true?

"No, it's not," came the voice again. "You are *such* a liar."

Yes, I am, I thought, shifting from one foot to the other and admitting to myself that Wit *would* find out sooner or later. Whether it was because Ian eliminated me tomorrow or because the two of us made it to Saturday's final showdown, Wit would learn that I'd lied to him. That I'd broken our pact and straight-up lied to his face.

My stomach knotted, but I exchanged a funny look with Wit. We were close enough to read the menu now, and the two boys behind us were bantering about the origins of the Charlie donut. It was so hilariously absurd that soon Wit's body was shaking against mine with silent laughter. "Are these guys for real?" he whispered.

"Apparently," I whispered back, then glanced over my shoulder to see a grinning boy with bright blue eyes and red-gold hair.

"Did you want to weigh in?" he asked as I noticed Edgartown Yacht Club's insignia embroidered on his windbreaker. "Tell my boyfriend who *really* invented the Charlie?"

He was holding hands with none other than the cute bookseller.

"Nope, I'm good," I said, also thinking, *Poor Eli.*

"Hey, Hitch Me to Witry!" Sarah called, and I spun to see her and Michael at a register. It was our turn to order. "Get over here!"

⁓

Donuts. We ordered so many donuts. Boston cream, honey-dipped, coconut cream, maple bacon, apple fritters—we ordered them all. They were so light and fluffy, the sugary sweetness bursting before melting in your mouth, but I might as well have been chewing and swallowing cardboard.

And not very much of it.

"Are you sure you don't want a fritter, Mer?" Michael asked on our walk back to the car. "There are a couple left."

"No, thank you," I said, holding tight to Wit's hand. A few minutes ago, he'd polished off his third jelly donut and offered to let me lick the rest from his fingers. Sarah and Michael cracked up when I accepted.

Now I didn't want to let go of those fingers. I *couldn't* let go of those fingers. Our time together was unraveling like a ribbon. *The day after tomorrow*, I kept thinking. *The day after tomorrow.*

I only had these fingers, this hand, this arm, this body, this *person* until the day after tomorrow. It wasn't enough. It wasn't even *close* to enough, and my heart was fluttering so fast it felt like it was going to fly out of my chest.

And I knew why.

FRIDAY

SEVENTEEN

"Hey, there you are," Aunt Rachel said when I unrolled my purple yoga mat and sat down next to her. "I've missed you the last couple of days."

"Yeah, well," I said, "somebody tipped me off that Ian's been keeping you company."

Wit had thought I was taking too big a risk by coming over to the Camp this morning, but I'd covered his mouth midprotest and told him I needed to do this. I needed to calm and center myself...and if that wasn't possible, I needed to *think*.

"You assumed we sided with him, didn't you?" Aunt Rachel asked. "Pledged our allegiance?"

I gave her a look. "Aunt Julia announced over a megaphone that I was leaving the beach!"

"Oh, Julia." My aunt laughed. "I probably shouldn't say this, but it was all part of her master plan—" She dropped off, took my hand, and pressed it to her belly. "The baby..."

"He's kicking," I breathed, feeling the little punting. "Like a baby bronco."

She groaned. "I'm so done with being pregnant."

"What were you going to say?" I asked a minute later. "Before? About Aunt Julia's master plan?"

Aunt Rachel smiled. "Ian's been assassinated," she told me. "*Julia* assassinated him last night. We invited him over to bake cookies with the kids, and when he left, she followed him back to the Cabin."

I gasped. "But he's her godson!"

"I know." She nodded. "That's why she didn't pursue him earlier. She said it was 'mutually beneficial' to leave him in the game—the more people he picked off, the closer she was to the showdown." She sighed. "But he wasn't making any progress."

So Aunt Julia and I think alike, I thought. *The same strategy, except one of us pulled the trigger, and the other...*

I needed to do it.

I needed to be like Aunt Julia.

I *needed* to kill Wit.

The thought made my stomach squirm.

"Although here's the twist," Aunt Rachel continued. "Ian never had you, Mer."

My eyes widened. "What?"

"It was a ruse so you'd focus on him and feel secure with everyone else."

A classic Claire Fox stratagem, I realized. Spreading false information around The Farm—after watching her win so many times, my cousin had caught on and learned something. Perhaps my alliance had failed this year, but Ian had played well.

"I don't know who he's working with," Aunt Rachel said before I could ask. "I just know the name on Julia's new slip isn't yours."

I released a deep breath.

"And on that note..." She smiled. "Shall we begin?"

"Yes." I smiled back. "We shall."

But when we closed our eyes, Luli came to mind. *You've been thinking about yourself and only yourself.*

I mean, she wasn't wrong there. Now that Wit and I were spending so much time together, our pact *had* become stronger than my alliance with my friends. It was an alliance in itself. I hadn't meant for it to happen, but it had. It was hard for it not to when we fell asleep together every night.

I couldn't find that vital balance between friends and boyfriend. Ben had been all I needed after Claire's death. I didn't need to go shopping or get coffee or just hang out with my friends. I should've, but I didn't. School, bagel shop job, and Ben—that was all I could handle. When Claire had died, fun died with her. It was like I was walking through a thick fog and needed to cling to someone so I didn't get lost.

Wit was different, though, right? I wasn't clinging to him; it was more like we were tangled together, an invisible string connecting us. He was my friend, my partner in crime, the person who made me laugh so hard before lulling me to sleep with his heartbeat and adorable mouth breathing.

I'm going to try, I wanted to tell Luli. *I've made so many mistakes, but I'm going to try my best to do better. We've been friends forever—I want to* stay *friends forever.*

By the time Aunt Rachel and I wrapped up our session, I'd decided that I would talk with Luli. Her hurtful comments still stung, but I regretted not saying more, not trying harder.

"Where're you headed next?" Aunt Rachel asked as we rolled up our mats, and I said I was going on a hike.

Because the Nylon Condo Complex was exactly that.

<hr>

After leaving the Camp, I set off across the lawn, only to encounter Michael walking down the Pond House's road wearing last night's clothes: the same black sweatshirt with the Saints' gold fleur-de-lis logo, the same jeans. I sped up, quick and quiet steps, and soon was at his side. "Good morning," I said casually and laughed when he flinched with surprise. "You get some good sleep?"

"Yes, as a matter of a fact," he said, fully owning his walk of shame. "I did finally." He yawned, then smiled to himself. "I never sleep well when we're apart."

A lump formed in my throat.

"Speaking of," Michael said, "where's Witty?"

"As far as I know," I told him, "he's still in bed."

"Great." He clapped his hands together. "I'm in the mood for a run."

All was silent at the Nylon Condo Complex when I arrived. It was early enough that most people were still sleeping, but some had probably gotten up and dragged themselves over to Moor

House for breakfast with the Dupré clan. That kitchen could hold an army, and Jeannie was more than capable of feeding one. "Yeah, the woman can *cook*," Eli had said after I'd raved about the gumbo. "You should try her spin on eggs Benedict."

I'll go over for breakfast, I decided before circling the tents until I found the magenta one, the tent Luli was sharing with Pravika and her sister. They were both early risers, but not Luli. Her longest sleep was sixteen hours straight.

Heart racing, I attempted to knock on the nylon. Of course we'd grown up not needing to knock on the house doors, but this was a tent, and I felt like I had to now. "Hello?" I said when my knuckles just slid down the thin fabric. "Luli?"

There was no response at first, but soon someone unzipped the tent's front flap. Luli's dark bedhead looked like a nest around her face. "Meredith," she said, voice a grumble. "Hi."

We stared at each other for a few seconds, and then I blinked and pretended my pulse wasn't pounding so hard. "Can we talk?" I asked. "I have something to tell you."

Luli grandly gestured inside. "Welcome."

Her tent was much messier than Eli and Jake's. I glanced around to see an air mattress, sleeping bag, and pillow arranged in each person's corner, but there were also exploding duffel bags and backpacks. Various clothes and shoes and towels were strewn across the floor, and sand had inevitably been tracked in from the beach. I suddenly felt guilty for not offering up Claire's bunk in the Annex—and, since I technically hadn't slept there, mine as well.

"Not exactly Moor House," Luli commented. "Or *any* house."

"But it's fun, right?" I said tentatively. "You're having fun?"

"Yes," she said. "The Nylon Condo Complex has seen plenty of fun."

I nodded back, and again, things went silent between us.

Luli broke it this time. "So you said you had something to tell me." She crossed her arms over her oversize T-shirt. "What is it?"

"Oh," I said, inviting myself to sit down. Luli stayed standing. "It's about Assassin. I have some news for you."

"From Wit?"

"No." I shook my head. "Aunt Rachel."

Luli arched an eyebrow.

I took that as my cue, telling her all about Aunt Julia and what had gone down between her and Ian last night. Her original strategy, the cookies, the delayed elimination—

"But how does this involve me?" Luli asked before I could finish. "Ian was *your* assassin, so now Aunt Julia has you. I have no part in this."

"Well, that's the thing," I said. "It was all a cover-up. Ian took Claire's false intel tactic to the next level, actually *acting* like he had me. Showing up at Aunt Rachel's morning meditations, tracking me in the Varsity Room." I shook my head. "It was a farce. Someone in his secret alliance has me, not him—and not Aunt Julia."

Luli sighed. "How do you know for sure?"

"Because I have this," I said, pulling up a photo on my phone: a laminated piece of paper with Luli's name on it. She stiffened. "It's Aunt Julia's," I continued. "Aunt Rachel snuck into their bedroom while she was still sleeping and brought it out to show me."

Don't spread this around, my aunt had said. *Use it wisely.*

I'd say I was using it as wisely as I knew how.

Luli stared at the photo, rubbed her eyes, then stared at it again. I kept quiet. "Thank you," she eventually whispered. "For the heads-up."

"You're welcome," I said and added, "I've always got your back."

Luli's face twisted into something I couldn't read, but I took my chance anyway—I apologized. I apologized for the last eighteen months. "You were the best," I told her, "reaching out so often, but I just couldn't respond most of the time." My eyes welled up. "I tried to, but I physically couldn't do it. My fingers would shake, my throat would thicken, or I would literally start crying." Tears trickled down my face now, too. "Being in my house was a constant reminder that she was gone. I mean, for a while, I tried to convince myself that she was just away at college, but I felt like talking about it with you would make things worse. Each text, each FaceTime, each Snapchat was another reminder that she's gone." I shook my head. "I'm sorry. I should've handled it differently. You didn't deserve to be ignored."

"No, I didn't," Luli said numbly and turned away from me.

"All I wanted was to be there for you, to be a good friend—a good cousin."

"You *are* a good cousin," I said. "You are so special."

Luli considered, her back still facing me. "Could you please leave, Meredith?" she asked after a few frantic heartbeats. "I need some space."

"Oh...okay, sure." I scrambled up from the ground and wiped away my tears, even though I felt another rush coming. "I'll see you later?"

By way of an answer, Luli nodded.

The wedding reception's white tent looked like a billowing cloud in the beyond-blue sky, and as I got closer to the Big House, I noticed Aunt Christine supervising the tent's construction while Honey also hovered on the lawn. But instead of eagle-eyeing the crew, she was offering the builders glasses of her homemade iced tea and chocolate chip cookies.

The Big House is truly perfect, I thought. *Truly perfect for a wedding.*

Apparently, there had been some back-and-forth about where on The Farm the reception should be held, but in the end, Wink and Honey's home trumped all. "It has the best view," Sarah had said. "The ocean, the ponds, the stars—you can see everything, and I want that night to be everything."

Wink was relaxing on the front porch, reading a book.

"Morning, Mer," he said as I collapsed on the hammock. "Any updates?"

I closed my eyes. "Yeah," I said, "I'm in a food coma from breakfast at Moor House. Jeannie made me her eggs Benedict. You know she adds fried green tomatoes and grilled red tomatoes?" I sighed. "It's delicious."

"Mmm, yes," my grandfather agreed. "When Honey and I went to visit Sarah and Michael this winter, she and Oscar invited us over for brunch. Tomatoes are a very Creole fruit, you know."

"She mentioned that," I said, then swallowed hard. I'd texted Pravika that I was coming for breakfast, so she, Eli, and Jake had saved me a seat at the long kitchen table, but their faces when they saw me...

I knew that they knew about Luli's and my fight. She must've told them yesterday. "She didn't mean any of it," Pravika said once I sat down and picked up my utensils. "Not a word."

"Did she tell you that?" I asked.

"No," Pravika said, "but—"

Eli cut her off. "Meredith, I wouldn't say she didn't *mean* it."

I waited for him to say more.

He didn't, so Jake sighed and stepped in. "You ghosting her really bummed her out, Mer. I mean, it really bummed all of us out"—he glanced around the table, and the others nodded—"but her the most. She's always thought of you and Claire as sisters...so after Claire..." He paused. "She wanted to be there for you, but she also needed you to be there for *her*."

I winced. He was right, and I was an idiot. I'd never thought of it that way before, that Luli wanted to be both comforting and comforted.

"Give her time to process," Eli said after I told them about my apology. He put an arm around me. "She's upset. It'll take her some time to calm down, but it'll happen." He gave me a look. "Okay?"

I bit my lip. "Okay."

It was silent for a minute, and then Pravika spoke up. "New topic?" she suggested. "Fun topic?"

"Like what?" I asked.

"Isn't it obvious?" she said, giggling. "Your hot-and-heavy wedding hookup?"

Now, in the Big House's hammock, my heart sank. "Well, do you think you're going to be able to do it?" Wink said.

I blinked. "Huh?"

My grandfather closed his book. "Do you think you're going to be able to do it?" he asked again.

All I could do was gape at him. *He knew?*

Wink nodded. "You started out so strong, Mer...Rachel and her meditation, Daniel in Edgartown—and from the Jeep, no less!—Oscar during bocce, and Sarah's *odious* friend Vivian." He leaned forward in his Adirondack chair. "But I've been watching you. You've been carrying around your Super Soaker"—he pointed his book at the water gun, propped up against a porch column—"for two days now yet have *nothing* to show for it." He leaned back in his chair. "So tell me, does he know?"

I sighed. "He guessed."

Wink whistled. "His nickname is apt."

"But I lied," I admitted, covering my face with my hands. "I *lied* to him and said I had Luli instead."

"Ah."

"I should've told him the truth," I said anxiously. "I should've been honest, and we could've made some sort of deal."

"But you didn't," my grandfather said, "and you're worried that if you come clean now, he'll feel betrayed."

I nodded.

Tell me what to do, I thought. *Please.*

"Hmm," was all Wink said before opening his book again. He wasn't going to tell me anything. And why would he? Yes, he was my grandfather, but he was also the Assassin commissioner! He couldn't advise or show any favoritism.

I stood up to leave.

His voice stopped me. "Keep in mind, Meredith," he said, "that only one person can win."

❧

Even though the wedding ceremony rehearsal was this afternoon, Wit had been more than game when I told him about driving out to Beach Road and jumping off the Jaws Bridge. It was the borderline between Edgartown and Oak Bluffs, but the landmark's true claim to fame was its appearance in the movie

Jaws, which had been filmed on the Vineyard in the 1970s. "You have to do it," I'd said. "It's pretty much a rite of passage for tourists."

The bridge sat twelve or fifteen feet above the water, and there were signs that read KEEP OFF BRIDGE RAIL! and NO JUMPING OR DIVING FROM BRIDGE! but everyone ignored those. Claire and I first made the great jump when we were thirteen and twelve. We jumped holding hands, and six launches later, we were doing swan dives and flips (with a few belly flops mixed in).

"Oh, I'm so down," Wit said once I'd explained the tradition, nodding quickly. "*So* down."

We agreed to meet at the Annex, so after slipping into a swimsuit, I sat down on the front steps to wait. All set, I DMed @sowitty17.

And then I just scrolled through Instagram, eventually finding myself on Sarah's account. Her latest post was from Back Door Donuts, a video I'd filmed of her double-fisting Boston cream donuts. "Watch it, cuz," I heard myself say. "You might not fit in your dress."

"Oh, I'll fit," she said through a big bite. "I might not be able to *breathe*, but I'll fit!"

#HurrayShesADupré.

Sarah doesn't have many videos, I realized, so I continued to scroll past pictures of her brunching with friends, on the sidelines of a Saints' game, at a Mardi Gras celebration, and posing with the Dupré family during her engagement party. Sarah had her hand on Michael's chest, her gigantic ring glittering in the light. Her smile was a mile wide.

But eventually, there one was—another video, buried deep among the photos. My heart stopped, immediately recognizing the person in the thumbnail. At first glance, it could've been Sarah, with the cascading auburn hair and glasses...but the off-the-shoulder blouse she wore?

It was mine. Claire had asked if she could borrow it when packing for her trip.

That was my sister, right there.

Don't watch it, I thought. *Don't even think about—*

I tapped the video. It didn't have a caption, but the location tag was Basin Seafood and Spirits Restaurant. My face prickled.

Claire's last night.

When I tapped the video to turn on the sound, Sarah was speaking. It was difficult to hear in the humming restaurant, but I did my best. "Watch her," she said. "Watch what's happening over there." She zoomed in on Claire and her salad, which she was enthusiastically rearranging with her knife and fork. "She hasn't taken a single bite."

"And I don't think he's noticed," Michael chimed in. "Do you?"

Sarah giggled. "I think he has," she said, tilting up to Claire's face. She literally could not keep her mouth shut; it was moving as fast as her utensils. "I think he's being sweet, polite—oh, look! His eyes just dropped down to her plate. He's on to her."

My spine straightened, because I suddenly had a feeling I knew who they were talking about...and when Sarah moved her camera again, there he was next to my sister.

Wit.

"Hey!" he shouted from across the table. "Are you filming us?"

He looked the same but different. His sandy hair was a bit shorter, and of course his face was unblemished. No bruise, no sunburn.

"I don't remember signing a waiver," he said. "Do you, Claire?"

My sister laughed, and just like that, my fingers began trembling, my phone shaking. I hadn't listened to Claire's laugh in over a year. Her gorgeous, dazzling laugh. The world felt so quiet without it.

I let my phone drop lifelessly to the grass, but I snatched it right back up once I heard Wit's voice in real life. "I'm ready!" he called out, walking toward me in striped trunks with a towel thrown over his shoulder. "Are *you* ready?"

He grinned and tried to kiss me after I rose from the deck's steps, but I twisted away from him. I held up my phone and managed to choke out, "What the hell is this?"

Wit's eyebrows furrowed. "Uh, your phone?"

"Oh." I realized I'd locked it, the screen now dark. "Hang on." I quickly entered my passcode and queued up the video, sound and all. "What," I repeated, "is this?"

I watched his face fall as the video played, my eyes pooling at Claire's laughter. "Listen," he murmured, "I can explain—"

"You knew Claire?" I interrupted, my voice shrill. "You *knew* my sister?"

A beat of hesitation, and then a nod.

Needles pricked the back of my neck. "I can't believe you didn't tell me," I said. "I can't believe..." I trailed off, unsure how to continue. My vision blurred with oncoming tears.

"Please let me explain," Wit said, putting a light hand on my arm. I shook it off and brushed past him into the open field. Part of me wanted him to tell me everything, but the rest didn't want to hear a word. "Meredith!" Wit caught up to me, matched his pace to mine. "I tried to tell you," he said. "I've been trying to tell you."

"When?" I snapped.

"Yesterday," he replied. "While we were hiking. You said it was like I knew her?"

I stopped walking. We were in the tall grass, both looking out at the dunes. *You sound like you knew her*, I'd said after Wit had complimented Loki's water bottle drinking abilities, but I hadn't thought much of it, chalking it up to me talking about Claire so much. But then, yes, something had shifted, and he'd looked away from me. *Meredith*, I vaguely remembered him saying, *I think I need to clear something up...*

Then thunder had cracked.

"Well you should've tried *harder*," I told him now, not caring how loud my voice sounded. "You should've told me on the way home, or before gumbo, or later that day!"

Wit scrubbed a hand through his hair. "I thought you

knew," he said softly. "You cut me off so abruptly, saying we had to run back to the car."

"No, the *thunder* cut you off," I countered, heart hammering. "We *did* have to run back!"

"Meredith, it was *one* rumble. I thought you knew what I was about to say and didn't want to hear it." He swallowed. "I wanted to respect that."

There was a weird crunching noise in the tall grass behind us, but I was too frustrated to look. It was probably Loki or Clarabelle or one of the other dogs.

I clenched my teeth. "So is that also why you didn't say anything on Monday?" I asked as another clue came to mind from Wink and Honey's dinner, where Sarah had told the story about the salad. She'd said she'd forgotten who Claire was sitting with at Basin—maybe that was true, maybe it wasn't, I didn't really care—and Wit had kept shifting on Claire's stool. "When we were talking about her?"

Wit was quiet. Again, I heard that crunching noise, but all I could focus on was waiting for him to speak. "You were shivering," he murmured. "It was warm out, but you were shivering." My arms were crossed over my chest, but a few of his fingers began brushing through my hair, subtly and smoothly, like they had that night. I resisted the urge to close my eyes and let myself cry. "I never would've done that to you."

"But you still kept it a secret," I said. "You kept it a secret for *way* too long. I mean, were you *ever* going to tell me?" I stepped away from him. "I gave you every opportunity—talking about her, telling all those stories." I shook my head. "Maybe if—"

I couldn't finish the sentence, because a surge of something hit me square in the back.

Well, not a surge of *something*.

A surge of *water*.

Wait, what? I thought as Wit and I turned to see Uncle Brad grinning like the most cunning of foxes. It took a second for things to sink in, but once they did...

I was speechless.

You've been assassinated, I told myself. *You've blown it.*

My stomach dropped. I was supposed to do this for Claire. I was supposed to *win* for her.

"Cough it up," Uncle Brad said, gesturing toward my shorts pocket with his water gun. "Tight schedule today, with the ceremony rehearsal and dinner and all."

"Yeah." My throat was dry. "Okay." I slid my hand into my pocket for my Assassin slip, but slowly, so I could throw a quick look Wit's way. "Run," I muttered to him.

Uncle Brad still had his gun raised, and my anger at Wit aside, I did not want my uncle knocking off two targets within a mere minute of each other.

Wit narrowed his eyes. "What?"

"Any day now, Mer..."

"Run," I mumbled again.

"No," Wit said as I tugged my target slip from my pocket. I held it facedown, name pressed against my chest. "We aren't finished talking. Just hand it over"—he motioned to Uncle Brad—"so we can work this out. I'm not leaving."

Body angled away from Uncle Brad, I flipped the paper over so Wit could see his name on it. His turquoise eyes widened while the rest of his face went slack. "Stephen," I said firmly. "Run."

EIGHTEEN

After Wit narrowly escaped elimination and I relinquished my target to Uncle Brad, I went to Secret Beach to sulk, but I wasn't quite sure what I was sulking *about*. Was it Assassin? Apparently, my name had been passed around a lot this week. Ian's mysterious ally was my first killer, but Uncle Brad had inherited me from Jeannie Dupré. "She hesitated before giving me your name," he said. "Even though you shot her husband, she hesitated big-time."

Now I swam out to Paqua Pond's float and flipped onto my back to stew in the sun. No one would be looking for me right now—I didn't have any plans until tonight's rehearsal dinner. *I'm so sorry, Claire,* I thought when the sun disappeared behind some clouds. *I'm so sorry I couldn't do you proud. I threw it all away for some guy.*

Why was I like this? Luli had been spot-on; I *had* gone from being with Ben to being all in with Wit. So committed that instead of effortlessly eliminating him from Assassin, I'd decided to delay and delay—I'd decided to *protect* him. I'd put myself second again. My eyes welled up, tears soon slipping down my face.

I started thinking about Sarah's Instagram video—Claire and Wit talking together, laughing together—and the fact that he didn't tell me about it. *Hey, I met your sister.* I honestly couldn't say how I would've reacted, but the point was that he'd never said anything.

Claire had said something, though. I'd realized it on my walk out here, when I'd opened our old text conversation that I couldn't bring myself to delete. The last message she'd ever sent me was: I have unbelievable news! The fates have finally aligned!

I hadn't responded right away, since our family was hosting a New Year's party. Ben and I had played games with everyone for a while, then there was dinner and dessert, and after that, we'd snuck away for some alone time. I hadn't checked my phone until a couple of hours later, once we'd settled down to watch Ryan Seacrest host *Dick Clark's New Year's Rockin' Eve.* My stomach had swooped at that text. *Unbelievable news!*

Have you met a boy? I'd written back, because after reading about endless love interests in her books, Claire more than deserved to have one of her own.

The message had been marked delivered, but by then, it was late enough in the evening that she'd been busy on Bourbon Street and hadn't had a chance to respond.

Of course, it turned out she *never* had a chance to respond. I'd wondered about that message for so long once she was gone. *The fates have finally aligned.*

What had she meant by that? I asked myself time and time again, but mostly I didn't give two flying fucks about the fates, instead just wishing she'd texted I love you, Mer before safely going to bed that night.

Finally I had my answer.

Yes, Claire *had* met a boy in New Orleans.

Just not one for herself.

"Stephen," she'd decided back when we were still young enough to match our outfits and joke about who I would marry someday. "His name will be Stephen!"

Now I felt as faint as I had when I'd first seen his name on my Assassin slip. *Stephen...*

I must've fallen asleep, because I lurched awake when a slick hand tugged my ankle. My eyes snapped open to see Wit treading water with his elbows resting on the float. "You're burnt to a crisp," he said. "Sunscreen slip your mind?"

I winced as I tried to sit up, my arms and legs scorched red. How long had I been out? The sun was no longer behind the clouds; in fact, it had moved across the sky.

"There's aloe," Wit told me. His voice sounded strangely formal. "I have that big bottle on my dresser, remember?"

"Your middle name is Oscar," I replied, a sudden epiphany. "Isn't it?"

He nodded.

@sowitty17, I thought. Not obnoxious, but admittedly *witty*. It had been there the entire time: SOW.

Stephen Oscar Witry.

"I like that," I said, dipping a few toes in the water. The cool rush was such a relief—even my feet were burnt. I took a deep breath. "Look, about earlier..."

"Yeah, about earlier," he said. "Why did you do that?"

The slight sharpness in his voice made my stomach twist. I was going to bring up Claire, but he was clearly talking about something else.

Assassin.

"I believed you, Meredith," Wit said. "When you said you didn't have me, I *believed* you. I even guessed the truth, and still." He splashed the water. "You lied to me."

"I'm sorry," I said. "Wit, I'm so sorry. I wanted to tell you, I really did, but..."

"But what?" he asked. "You thought everything would end if I found out?"

I swallowed.

He shook his head. "We could've worked out a plan— created some sort of arrangement to get us both further along, to get us to the finals together."

"That's what I've been doing, though," I said, because mistake or not, it was the truth, and I was going to defend myself. "It's exactly what I've been doing. I've never once approached you with a gun. I wanted you to take down as many people as possible so that it *was* us in the end."

"Yeah, but you went about it the wrong way," he said. "You broke our pact. We *agreed* to tell the other if one of our names came up." He shrugged. "And you didn't."

My voice had never been smaller; if I were Loki, my tail would've been curled between my legs. "Wit..."

He sighed. "I've gotta go. We're leaving for the rehearsal soon."

"When will you be back?" I asked.

"We won't," he replied. "We're going straight from there to dinner." He paused. "I'll bring our script."

"Okay, thanks," I said, thinking of the folded sheet of paper tucked in his New Zealand guidebook. "And, um..." I bit my lip. "Can we talk more later?"

Because I felt like nothing between us had been solved; our situation and communication had only become more complicated. He'd lied to me. I'd lied to him. For once, we weren't on the same page.

"Sure." Wit nodded. "I know I owe you a better...a much better..." He trailed off, took a deep breath, then looked me in the eye. "Yeah, we'll talk later."

Then he pushed away from the float and swam back to shore.

Sarah and Michael's rehearsal dinner was up-island in Chilmark, amid its bucolic hills at the Beach Plum Inn. Formal gardens and private cottages dotted the property's seven acres, but the rehearsal dinner was at the main house, where my cousin had taken her fiancé the first time he'd visited the Vineyard. They wanted to recreate that first island date and keep everything as simple as possible—long oak farmhouse tables on the back brick terrace with linen table runners and vases of Morning Glory's wildflowers. Unlike tomorrow's reception, there was no assigned seating. "This is beautiful," my mom said as we climbed the terrace steps. "Absolutely beautiful."

"Not as beautiful as you, Liz," my dad said before kissing her. It warmed my heart. Sarah and Michael weren't the only ones who were perfect for each other.

Ironically, the bride and groom and their entourage were among the last to arrive. "There was an incident at the church," Aunt Christine said, her high heels clicking loudly. "I *told* everyone wedding events were off-limits!"

"Mom, relax." Sarah smiled. She looked stunning in a white cocktail dress with gold wedges. "Nice shoes, Mer," she said to me and winked, since I wore the same pair. My dress was a light coral color, its off-the-shoulder sleeves fluttering in the breeze.

Said "incident" had been Nicole Dupré trying to assassinate one of the groomsmen at the ceremony rehearsal. "But it wasn't *during* it," she protested. "We'd all left the church and were getting into the cars."

Wink had yet to make an official ruling, but once cocktails had been mixed, Aunt Christine announced that if she saw any water guns tonight, there would be *serious* consequences.

My dad snorted into his drink and clapped Uncle Brad on the shoulder. "Excuse me while I run to the restroom," my uncle said, handing off his martini to his wife. "I'll only be a moment."

We all laughed, watching him speed inside. "The father of the bride, ladies and gentlemen," Aunt Christine deadpanned and took a long sip of Uncle Brad's drink. She affectionately rolled her eyes. "Also known as my husband."

I found Wit with his fellow groomsmen. "Wait, what?" I said when he turned to me. "Where's the..." I gestured to his face, which was completely bruise-less. Still sunburned but missing its swamp-green splotch.

"Oh, it's there all right," Wit said. "Just hidden under about fifty pounds of makeup." He rubbed some of it off for me to see. "Your aunt summoned me to the Pond House, where the bridesmaids used a mixture of foundation and concealer and whatever 'contouring' is to make sure I look wholesome for the pictures." He shrugged. "Not too bad, I guess."

"Not too bad at all," I said, kind of stunned. I'd only ever known Wit with his giant bruise. Now he looked more like the boy in Sarah's Instagram video. It was a little eerie.

God, was he handsome.

"Where're you sitting?" I asked.

With you, I hoped he'd say. We said we'd talk, we needed to talk, and I wanted us to talk.

"With my family," he said, his voice sounding so reserved again, like we barely knew each other. My stomach sank. "How about you?"

"I'm not sure yet." I matched his formal tone. "I should probably figure that out." I turned away, but Wit's warm fingers alighted on my elbow before I could take a step.

"It's right here," he told me when I glanced back at him, patting his suit jacket's breast pocket. "I didn't forget."

"I didn't think you would," I said.

He cocked his head. "We'll meet up?"

I nodded. "We'll meet up."

***

"No, that's impossible, Eli," Jake said. "It cannot be done."

"Yes, it can," Eli countered, shaking his head. "I've already been in *ten*."

"Ten what?" Aunt Julia asked, sitting back down with Aunt Rachel. The main course was on its way, but Aunt Rachel wasn't feeling well, so they'd gone on a walk in the gardens. It didn't look like it had helped much. Aunt Rachel's face was still scrunched with discomfort.

Is the baby bronco-kicking her again? I wondered. *Or is it more than that?*

"Ten photobombs," Pravika told them. "Eli has made it his mission to photobomb every wedding picture."

"Not *every* one," Luli said. "There's no way Aunt Christine will let him past all the red tape she'll put up tomorrow for the wedding party photos."

I laughed. "They've been tasteful photobombs, though," I added. "He doesn't do bunny ears or anything; he just politely poses with the group."

"Right," Eli said as our food was served: a New

Orleans–inspired dish. Jeannie had worked with the Beach
Plum's chef on a custom menu. "The idea isn't to *disrupt* the
photos but to make the guests ask themselves 'Who the fuck is
that?' when the album goes online."

More laughter, but I saw Aunt Rachel push away her dinner
and rub her forehead. Aunt Julia's spine straightened. "Rach—"

A rapid chime sounded, and like the flick of a light switch,
all conversation halted. I spun in my seat to see Jeannie Dupré
holding a champagne glass and microphone. Michael leaned
over and whispered in Oscar Witry's ear, and they exchanged a
thoughtful look before Oscar rose from his chair to stand beside
Michael's mother. "Hello, everyone!" she said. "I'm Jeannie,
the proudest mother of any groom that has ever existed!" She
smiled at her son. "And I want to thank y'all for being here
tonight. It's such a special occasion, and it's been made even
more meaningful by having each of you with us to celebrate…"

"Rachel," Aunt Julia murmured. "Are you all right?"

Aunt Rachel's hands were fully pressed against her face.
"No." She shook her head. "Contractions." She let out a low
moan. "I think my water's going to break."

My friends were wrapped up in Jeannie's toast, but Aunt
Julia and I made eye contact. "My parents," she said to me.
"Tell Wink and Honey."

I nodded and slipped out of my seat, quickly walking to
my grandparents' table. "What's up, sweetie?" Honey turned
when I put a hand on her shoulder. Wink turned, too. "You're
interrupting Jeannie's—"

I told them about Aunt Rachel.

They leapt into action. Honey immediately went to my aunts—Aunt Julia, Jake, and Eli were lifting Aunt Rachel from her chair—while Wink found Sarah and took her hands in his to explain. *I'm sorry*, he mouthed before kissing her forehead.

He was supposed to give a toast tonight.

Some people had picked up on the sense of urgency, but there was no shortage of applause when Jeannie raised a glass to the bride and groom. Jake and Eli returned to our table several minutes later. "On their way," they confirmed. "In the car, on their way to the hospital."

We all exhaled in relief, and Luli released my hand. I hadn't realized she'd been holding it. Maybe it was an old ingrained habit, or maybe we were getting back on track as friends.

I chose to believe the latter.

Dinner continued, and so did the speeches. Uncle Brad set up a whole slideshow of photos of Sarah, from the day she was born to her first day of school to her engagement party to the other day on the beach. Michael's favorite uncle talked about what an upstanding man he was but also that he needed to be a little more reliable when it came to securing free Saints tickets.

Wit signaled to me from across the terrace while we waited for dessert, raising his arm and waving. I gestured that he should join me at my table, and soon he was at my side, heat radiating off his body and onto mine. It reminded me of the lazy morning we'd spent in his bed composing the toast, our handwriting all mashed up—Wit's all-capital scribble and my loopy letters.

"Yes, we've got it," I remembered saying, leaning back against Wit's pillows as he lay in my arms with a pen raised. "I love that." I pointed to a few lines he'd written.

"Is it any good?" He had turned to give me a look. "I'm not the best poet."

"Yes, you are," I'd said, kissing him. "You just don't know it."

Neither Sarah nor Michael knew about our speech; we'd agreed it should be a surprise. Wit unfolded the paper, and I smiled at all the little memories on it. Between the two of us, we'd heard so many stories about their lives before they met and after they got together. "That's why he chewed me out about the Tulane girls," Wit admitted after cluing me in about Michael's wild fraternity days. "He was like that, too, until Sarah."

I'd been shocked. "But she always says it was love at first sight!"

Wit nodded. "Oh, he says that, too, but he adds that love at first sight doesn't mean she didn't need to whip him into shape."

"Do you want to do the honors?" I asked now, offering him my water glass. We had the microphone, too. "Or should I?"

"You," he said. "My fingers are shaking."

I took his hand to check—they really were trembling. "Public speaking makes you nervous?"

He didn't answer.

My heart knotted, and before I could stop myself, I kissed him. Just a light kiss on his lips—lips I had kissed so many times this week, lips I adored, lips I knew I needed to *stop* adoring.

"Pretend it's just us," I murmured. "Pretend it's just you and me, goofing off in the Cabin, like when we practiced. Okay?"

Wit closed his eyes. "Okay."

I waited to see their gold rings again before tapping my glass. Heads turned toward us, Sarah and Michael looking especially amused. "Hello, Sarah and Michael shippers," I said confidently, mic in hand. "I'm Meredith, Sarah's cousin, and this is"—I paused, about to say *Stephen*, but quickly recovered— "Wit, Michael's stepbrother."

"And while the competition's been pretty stiff tonight," Wit chimed in, "Meredith and I would like to try giving a toast. Does that sound good?"

Our audience applauded.

"Wonderful!" I nudged Wit's shoulder with mine. "Wit and I both happen to be aspiring poets, so, Sarah and Michael, we've written one for you!"

Wit held up our script for everyone to see, his fingers no longer shaking. I dramatically cleared my throat and spoke through my smile:

Sweet Sarah and Michael,
let's go down memory lane,
I guess to the beginning,
all the way back to Tulane

What was it about Michael,
instantly your number one pick?

His love for beef jerky,
or the infamous kick?

Laughter, whoops, and whistles filled the air. Michael hid his face in his hands as his groomsmen teased him, and even Sarah smirked. "The infamous kick" referred to a party at Sigma Chi where Michael had been so trashed that he accidentally punted a football through one of his fraternity house's windows. He'd straight-up shattered the glass.

Once things settled down, I handed the mic to Wit. He glanced at me and grinned his crooked grin before beginning his part:

What was it about Sarah
that brought you to your knees?
Her Sailor Moon costume
or need for late-night grilled cheese?

So many stories you've shared,
and now we've made it to this day
when we'll watch Michael cry as
he sees Sarah holding that bouquet.

There were more loud howls from the wedding party's table and an *aww* from everyone else. My heart skipped, and I leaned in close so Wit and I could perform the final stanzas together. His hand went to my lower back, mine to his wrist, and our breath mingled as we read:

The two of you will be forever—
of this there is no doubt.
Through honesty and humor,
you know each other inside out.

So now we'd like to raise a glass
with everyone sitting here:
Sarah and Michael, we love you dearly
and offer you this cheer!

NINETEEN

Michael's groomsmen hosted a rehearsal dinner after-party at the Cabin with a bonfire, s'mores, music, and plenty of beer and cigars, although I only stayed for a half hour or so. Long enough to watch Jake and Luli win a few rounds of cornhole but not long enough to get caught up in a conversation with Wit. I'd wanted to talk to him so badly at the Beach Plum, and now I just *didn't*. Because what did it matter? Everything was ending.

I slipped away to the Camp to help my mom "babysit" Hannah and Ethan. They were both asleep in their bunk room, the actual babysitter having put them to bed hours ago. Tomorrow, they would wake up to find out their baby brother had arrived.

My mom was sitting on the couch with me sprawled across her like a sad little girl. I still wore my coral dress, but my hair had come out of its updo, now loose and wavy—she was running her fingers through it. "What's wrong, Mer?" she asked when I sighed. "Why aren't you having fun with your friends and Wit?"

"Because things with Wit are shit," I mumbled.

Neither of us laughed at the rhyme.

"I told you it would be difficult," she said after a minute. "Saying goodbye to him."

I nodded, remembering the other night at the Annex— admitting how much I liked Wit and that troubled look she gave me. "But it's not just that," I murmured and rolled over so I was faceup on her lap. Our eyes found each other. "He met Claire," I said. "When she visited Sarah and Michael in New Orleans. He *met* her, and he never told me." My voice was thick. "He says he tried to a few times, but I interrupted him once, so he thought I knew but didn't want to talk about it. Mom, he kept the whole thing a secret. He lied."

"How did you find out?" my mom asked softly. "If he didn't tell you?"

"An old video on Sarah's Instagram," I said. "It was from that night at Basin. Claire was sitting across the table from Sarah, and guess who was sitting next to her?" A lump formed in my throat.

She pulled me closer and gently wiped away my tears when they inevitably fell. "Yes, he should've told you," she said. "Especially after how much time you've spent together, how close you've become." She kissed my forehead. "I don't believe he lied, Mer, but yes, he also wasn't truthful. If he tried telling you but didn't, I think he was"—she paused—"reading the tea leaves."

Reading the tea leaves.

Anyone else would say "reading the room," but *reading the tea leaves*—that was my sister. That was Claire.

My eyes spilled over again. "I just miss her so much," I said. "I miss her so much, Mom."

"Oh, Meredith, I miss her, too—we all do. My heart aches every day." She touched her hand to my cheek. "But being here this week, it's ached a little less. As impossible as it might sound, I feel her presence. I feel her all around us."

I thought about Claire's voice in my head this week, the hugs she gave me through the sunshine. "She's everywhere," I agreed, although that didn't stop my sobs. It might've worsened them, dredging up my Assassin elimination and its aftermath. "I'm so upset with Wit," I cried. "And he's upset with me, too."

My mom didn't say anything, waiting for me to explain.

"We made a deal right before Assassin started," I said. "Not an alliance but a pact to feed each other information and tip the other person off if our names came up." I swallowed hard. "I ended up inheriting him as a target, but I didn't say anything. I didn't *do* anything. I never went after him; I had this whole plan to get us to the end together." I paused. "But when he found out today, he was pissed—*really* pissed."

Again, my mom didn't comment.

"Which is stupid, right?" I asked, but my voice was weak. "Assassin is all about secrets and deception. You lie to survive. I mean, I lied to Luli and my *actual* alliance. I'm not proud of it, but I did." I rubbed my forehead. "Wit...he plays like Claire. He should understand."

"Yes, he should understand," my mom said. "It's only a game, and there should be no hard feelings when it ends." She tucked a lock of my hair behind my ear. "But in this case, I don't think Wit could help it. His emotions got the better of him."

My breath caught. "What?"

She gave me a bittersweet smile. "Mer, your pact started out as strategy, but now I think it means more than either of you expected it to. You both know that."

This time, it was me who didn't say anything. My heart was hammering.

"I'm very grateful to him," she added. "He's brought you back to us. The Farm and him. You've been in this sleepy haze this last year and a half—I know we all have—and I don't think I've seen you so awake and alive since that awful day. When the two of you are together..." She shook her head. "I think you should talk to him. If you part on poor terms, you'll regret it."

I burrowed into her side. "I can't talk to him."

"Why not?"

"Because—" I started, but I was cut off by my mom's phone buzzing on the coffee table.

Tom, the screen said.

She answered the call and looked at me after they hung up a couple of minutes later. "Oliver Isaac Epstein-Fox," she announced with a smile. "Eight pounds, five ounces."

I was just settling in for the night on the Annex's love seat when I heard the porch steps creaking outside. Not my parents, I knew. Aunt Julia was staying at the hospital, so they were going to sleep at the Camp with Ethan and Hannah.

"Hello?" I said.

"Hey," someone said back.

I pushed away my quilt and took several steps over to the door. Wit stood outside. "Where have you been?" he asked. "I must've taken a hundred laps around the Cabin."

"I wasn't there," I said. "Well, I was for a little while, but then I went to babysit Ethan and Hannah with my mom."

"Oh, gotcha."

"What are you doing here?" I asked.

Wit raised his hand and rested it against the door's screen. I instinctively did the same, our palms pressed together. "Because we never did it," he told me.

My eyebrows knitted together. "Never did what?"

"The dare," he said. "The driveway dare."

The driveway dare.

"You dared me on Monday, at Morning Glory. We agreed to do it sometime this week." He shrugged. "But tomorrow is the big day, so..."

I dropped my hand. *Tomorrow is the big day.* He'd hit the nail on the head and on the heart—that was why I couldn't do this. Crossed wires aside, our time together was rapidly dwindling, and I needed to be okay with that. I didn't care if we still had the wedding tomorrow—I needed to put space between us *now*. "Sorry," I told him, faking a yawn, "but I'm about to go to bed."

Silence.

"Please," Wit murmured. "Please, let's walk." He paused. "Let's walk and talk."

I laughed. Hollowly, but I laughed. "Okay," I said, thinking of what my mom had said about Wit—how I would have no closure if I didn't talk to him. "Let's walk." I lifted my hand and matched my palm to his for another moment. "And talk."

But for the first ten minutes of the walk, the only sound was our feet scuffing against the sandy dirt road and nighttime critters skittering away from our footsteps. We kept an easy pace, walking side by side without holding hands. If the backs of our fingers brushed, it was an accident. Neither of us spoke.

Until out of nowhere, Wit did. "I'm sorry," he said. "I'm sorry for not telling you about Claire. You were right. I had so many chances, but I was worried about overstepping and making you sad, and then as more time went by, I convinced myself that you probably figured I'd met her with Sarah and Michael."

I sighed. "I was really shaken when I saw that video, Wit," I said. Then, after a pause: "But I've been doing a lot of thinking, and it's okay."

Because it was. Since leaving the Camp, I'd made peace with them having met, and in a way, it made me happy they had. *I wish you could've met her. She would've really liked you.*

How many times had I said that this week?

I'd lost count.

"Sarah talked about her for months before her visit," Wit said quietly. He chuckled. "It was like Taylor Swift was coming to town."

I half smiled. Sarah was the most devoted of Swifties.

"I spent Christmas in Vermont with my mom and stepdad," he continued in the darkness. "But I flew back to New Orleans for New Year's. Sarah and Michael invited me to dinner with them at Basin. Well, more an instruction than an invitation. I *had* to meet the famous Claire."

I took a breath, nervous to ask but needing to know. "What did you think of her?"

Wit whistled. "I thought she was extraordinary," he said. "She looked like Sarah's twin, of course, but I'm not making air quotes when I say she had a sparkling personality."

"Yes," I nodded. "That was Claire. She dazzled." She just had no idea she dazzled, what big things awaited her.

My heart sank.

Had.

Big things *had* awaited her.

I didn't think I would ever get used to that past tense.

"What did you guys talk about?" I asked.

Wit's fingers mingled with mine. "What do *you* think we talked about?"

"I don't know," I said. "Tulane?"

"No, Tulane didn't come up," Wit replied. "While I was

watching your sister *not* eat her salad, she couldn't stop talking about *you*."

My stomach dropped. "What?"

"'You need to meet my sister,'" he said. "'You would love her, Stephen. She's so many things, but really a combination of adorable and acerbic. All your jokes I only laughed at? Meredith would've had killer comebacks instead. I bet you two could go back and forth for hours.'"

I slowed my pace.

"Smart," Wit went on. "Goofy." He took a breath. "Dramatic. Midnight snacker. Loyal. Fantasy reader. Competitive. Deep sleeper. Fearless." He hooked a few fingers around mine.

The corners of my eyes stung. I hadn't felt like that girl—Claire's sister—in a very long time, not until coming back to the Vineyard and meeting Wit. My voice cracked when I spoke. "How did she know your name was Stephen?"

"She guessed Wit was a nickname for Witry," he said. "So she asked what my first name was." He paused. "Why? Does it matter that I'm named Stephen?"

I stopped in my tracks. We must've walked only a mile out of three, but it was time. "No, it doesn't," I said, untangling my fingers from his. "There's nothing between me and Stephen."

Wit didn't respond at first. "In what sense?" he eventually asked. "You and the name? Or you and me? Us?"

I sighed. "The latter."

The moon was shining bright enough that I saw Wit's brows furrow. "I don't—"

"The week's over, Wit," I said, swallowing hard. "And when the wedding ends, the other things end, too."

"Wait," he said. "Other things?"

"*Our* thing," I said, gesturing between us. "What we've been doing for the past few days, acting like..."

#HitchMeToWitry, I thought. *Acting like #HitchMeToWitry.*

"Well, why can't things continue?" he asked. "Why can't we go beyond this?"

My pulse spiked. "You imagined going beyond this?"

He was quiet, then sighed. "Not exactly."

"See?" I shook my head.

"No, no," he said quickly. "I expected this week to go one way, but then it didn't, and I got caught up in the magic—got caught up in *you*. It sounds stupid, but I never considered that time was running out. This place..." He trailed off to gaze up at the moon. "It's one of those special places where you feel like time doesn't exist. Where it will always be summer, where I'll always wake up with you."

My body began trembling. "Well, that's not how it works," I said. "It may feel that way, but it's an illusion—a fantasy. This week will end. It will."

Wit put his hands on my shoulders. "We don't have to," he said. "We can stay together."

"How?" I backed away from him. "You're going to New Zealand! You're going to the other side of the world for a whole *year*!"

"A *school* year," he corrected. "Late August to May, and we can do long distance."

Long distance.

Everyone said it was difficult, and I applauded those couples who skillfully navigated it…but me? There was a reason why Claire hadn't said "patient" when painting a picture of me to Wit. I was *not* patient. The huge time difference, waiting for scheduled FaceTimes, or if we were lucky, a visit—I would not be able to handle that. I would be *miserable.* Ben and I had planned on staying together, and look how that had turned out! He'd changed his mind before we'd even tried. Four years together, and he didn't have enough confidence in us.

"We'd be long distance anyway," Wit was saying. "Even if I was back at Tulane."

"I can't," I said. "I can't do long distance—at least not a-whole-other-hemisphere long distance. It wouldn't be enough, Wit. It wouldn't work for me."

The breeze rustled the tree branches, and I pretended I couldn't smell the skunk stench in the air. Hopefully all the dogs were inside for the night.

"Then come with me," Wit said softly. "Come to New Zealand."

I snorted. "You're kidding."

"I'm not."

A shiver ran up my spine.

"We've had so many great adventures here," he said. "Let's go on more together, so many more. Claire said you're fearless." His voice dropped to a murmur. "And I think you need this as much as I do. I think you *need* something, something differ-ent..." He trailed off. "Come with me."

I felt my throat begin to close. "I can't," I choked out. "I can't. I have to start school. I have to meet my roommate, sign up for classes, make new friends, study, walk home for dinner once a week. I can't leave. No way."

Wit didn't respond. We just stood there for a couple of minutes and then resumed walking down The Farm road. Even if the mood had plummeted, he was going to touch the Paqua obelisk. He was going to complete the dare.

And complete the dare we did. We did it in silence, but I tagged the cold stone and released a long, exhausted breath. If only we didn't have three miles back to the houses.

It was 2:00 a.m. by the time Wit walked me to the Annex's door. We awkwardly stood there for a moment, not quite sure what to do. "Good night," I said at the same time he took my hand and said, "One more day."

"What?" I asked.

"There's one more good day," he said. "The week isn't over yet. We still have the wedding tomorrow." He squeezed my hand. "Let's pretend."

Pretend.

I knew what he was suggesting. *Let's pretend that time doesn't exist. Let's pretend that this week isn't ending. Let's pretend that we will always be us—happy, sunburnt, and tangled up together.*

It would hurt. It would *really* hurt, but it would be

wonderful, too—one last perfect day with him. "All right," I whispered, squeezing his hand back. "We'll pretend."

Instead of curling up on the love seat, I walked through the sitting room and into the bunk room. The window was open, wisps of the Cabin's music and laughter spilling inside—a lullaby of sorts. I smiled to myself and then slipped under Claire's covers and closed my eyes.

SATURDAY

TWENTY

The sun woke me up, soft beams spilling in through the bunk room's blinds. I hadn't expected to sleep so well in Claire's bed, but I hadn't woken up once. *Thank you*, I thought, snuggling back into the cozy pillows and closing my eyes again before taking a sweet deep breath and pushing back my sister's white coverlet.

Today was a special day.

I fed an impatient Loki and then headed over to the Cabin, welcomed by the remains of the rehearsal dinner after-party—someone's guitar on an Adirondack chair, empty beer cans scattered around the firepit, and a few coals still glowing. The walk to Wit's room was now second nature, the screen door opening and squeaking shut behind me. "Ugh," he groaned, voice absolutely shot. It crackled like a campfire. "Michael, *no*—I'm not going on a run."

"It's not Michael." I took a flying leap onto his bed. "It's someone much, much worse!"

"Oh, is that so?" Wit laughed, and together we maneuvered

me under his covers and into his warm arms. He smelled like oranges and the Vineyard breeze but also cigar smoke.

That explained his broken voice.

"Party too hard last night?" I joked. He must've joined the shenanigans after our disaster of a driveway dare.

Another groan. "Peer pressure."

"Yeah," I said. "They say you're supposed to resist it."

Wit buried his face in my blue Hamilton College T-shirt, and I ran a hand through his hair. It was stiff from the ocean's salt. "I'm so tired," he croaked. "Things didn't wind down until 4:00 a.m. I went to bed at 2:30, but how are you supposed to sleep when the party's right outside your door?"

"You aren't," I replied, suddenly nervous for him. It was 8:00, and his first obligation of the day was in less than an hour.

Wit nodded before popping his head up to look at me. "Did you sleep well?" he asked.

"Yes," I said, smiling a little. "Yeah, I actually slept really well."

"Good." He smiled back. "That's good."

Then we just looked at each other, his heavy-lidded turquoise eyes staring into mine. I knew he wanted to kiss me, and I knew I wanted to kiss him. Because if we were going to pretend today, I was going to *pretend*. "Will you brush your teeth first?" I whispered. "Cigar breath..." I wrinkled my nose. "Yuck."

Wit pushed back his covers, and I watched as he stood there

in his boxers, stretching his wiry limbs—languidly, dramatically, totally-on-purposely.

"You're wicked," I said.

"You go wild for it," he said back and disappeared into the tiny bathroom attached to his room. Just a toilet and sink—the Cabin's only shower was out back. I heard him turn on the faucet.

"Do you have a plan?" I asked a few minutes later after several minty-fresh kisses.

"A plan?"

"Yes," I said. "A plan."

Because you needed a plan for Paqua's Assassin Showdown. Forget about having the entire Farm as your playground; the grand finale was held Hunger Games–style in a certain sector of the vast field. Spectators created the borders of the arena with their beach towels and chairs; the commissioners' were almost exact replicas of Wimbledon's tall green referee thrones. They'd been wheeled out of the barn yesterday, and each had an awning to prevent any sun-related view obstruction.

This morning, people yawned as they unfolded their chairs. Eli had even brought a pillow along, spreading out his beach towel and promptly falling asleep. "Way to support, Eli," Luli grumbled as she double-knotted her sneakers. "You'll be the first I thank when I win."

Jake and Pravika laughed. Per Aunt Christine's request, the Showdown was happening much earlier than usual so as not to interfere with the wedding itinerary. Both the bridesmaids

288 *K. L. WALTHER*

and groomsmen were having private brunches before spending the day getting ready. Well, at least the bridesmaids were. Wit had mentioned that Michael and his groomsmen had agreed to go surfing later. "It's a suit and tie," Gavin the Best Man had rationalized. "It'll take ten seconds."

"All right, everyone!" Wink's voice boomed through his commissioner megaphone. "Welcome, welcome to this summer's Assassin Showdown!"

Exhaustion aside, we mustered up cheers.

"Are all our finalists here?" Honey asked, glancing around today's playing field. Like clockwork, the number of active assassins had severely diminished in the last few days. The largest showdown I'd witnessed was twelve, the smallest three.

Either way, Claire had always made short work of everyone. I felt a tug in my heart, still disappointed that I hadn't been able to pull the trigger on Wit. If I had, maybe I'd be one of the assassins gearing up for their final assignments.

This year, there were seven contenders: Wit, Luli, Uncle Brad, Nicole Dupré, Pravika's older sister, a groomsman, and...

"Everyone but Julia!" Uncle Brad told his parents. "Although she might—"

"She might what, Brad?" Aunt Julia asked, sauntering into the ring with her water gun. "She might *what*?"

"Mommy!" Hannah and Ethan exclaimed from the sidelines.

Aunt Julia smirked. "You didn't think I was going to forfeit, did you?" A hand on her hip. "I would *never*."

Except that was *exactly* what she did. When Honey blew the whistle for the Showdown to commence, every assassin spread out and claimed their own space while Aunt Julia stood stock-still in the center of the arena. "I'm not going anywhere, Divya!" she said to Pravika's sister. "Come on over here." She sat down in the grass. "I'm all yours!"

Divya seized her chance and quickly struck.

"Wonderful!" Aunt Julia stood and surrendered her target—Luli, I knew. "Let's go, kiddies," she said to Ethan and Hannah, waving to them. "There's someone Mama and I want you to meet!"

Play got serious after that. Now with plenty of momentum, Pravika's sister was making Luli work for it, the two of them running in circles. "Seriously, Divya?" Luli shouted. "After all we've been through together? Sharing a tent for the past week?"

"Ooh!" Jake jeered from the sidelines. "What happened in the tent?"

His sister flashed him the finger and continued dodging Divya.

Meanwhile, Nicole Dupré was pursuing the groomsman as he pursued Uncle Brad—a triangle that was far too preoccupied to notice bandanna bandit Wit perch in the tree at the field's edge.

He hid there for ten minutes, revealing himself only when it became clear Divya was worn out from chasing Luli. Her ponytail swung back and forth, her breathing heavy. "Divya!"

he called out, swinging down from a branch. "Do you need water?" He held up his Gatorade bottle. "I have water."

Hands on her knees, Divya nodded.

"Oh, Divya," Pravika sighed. "You idiot."

"She's dehydrated," Jake said. "She's not thinking straight."

Pravika snorted. "I certainly hope not."

I stifled a giggle as Wit, seemingly harmless, walked up to Divya and squirted her in the stomach. "Divya!" came Honey's voice over her megaphone. "Terminated!"

"And Vincent!" Wink said. "Terminated!"

Our heads swiveled to see Nicole cheer as the groomsman fell to the ground. It was down to her, Uncle Brad, Luli, and Wit.

But you could only see the women in the arena. Wit had scrambled back up into his tree, and Uncle Brad had hidden in the tall grass.

Two of the most offensive players, I smirked to myself, *now playing defensively.*

"Brad!" my dad whisper-yelled. "You're almost out of bounds!"

"Hey!" I called down the line. "No coaching!"

Hypocrite, Claire joked, and I felt myself blush.

Luli and Nicole were both pacing to catch their breath. Wit now had Luli, while Luli had Nicole.

Go for it, I wanted to tell my friend. *She's right there—*

"Oh, shit," Eli said, all of a sudden awake. "Look." He pointed to Luli, who was picking up Wit's Gatorade bottle.

He'd abandoned it in the grass after knocking off Divya. We watched Luli chug water—the sun was beating down on us this morning. "Is this..."

"A trap?" I said and gestured to Wit's tree when Eli raised an eyebrow. You couldn't see Wit, but poking out from behind the trunk were the six purple nozzles of Claire's elaborate water gun. With three nozzles on either side, the jetpack contraption provided inconceivable range.

"No," Pravika whined. "Not Luli! Not yet!"

Jake shifted excitedly. His humiliation over Wednesday's water balloon attack was nothing compared to what was about to happen to his sister. "Pass the fucking popcorn."

One, I thought, heart speeding up, *two...*

Pause.

Three!

Six streams of water nailed Luli in the back. "Ouch!" was the collective reaction from the crowd. Luli's shirt was soaked. She whipped around, and when she spotted Wit, she chucked his water bottle at him.

"You asshole!" she shouted. "You complete ass—"

"Stand down, Luli!" Wink interrupted. "Stand down!"

She scoffed and stomped over to the sidelines.

"Cover your ears," Jake said as Honey announced Luli's termination. "She's gonna scream."

We did as told, but nothing could drown out Luli's cry of frustration.

Out on the field, Wit left Claire's jetpack on the ground and climbed up the tree. Nicole, his new target, stood there, study-ing him. "He's going to win this from a *tree*," Jake said. "I'm calling it right now. He's going to win this whole thing without leaving the tree."

"No, he's not," I said.

Jake leaned forward in his beach chair. "You wanna bet?"

I laughed. "Jake, I really don't want to rob you of your Mad Martha's tips."

"Okay, but Meredith," Eli said a few beats later, "how many weapons"—he pointed to the tree, the neon Super Soaker now dangling from a branch—"does he have up there?"

"And is that even legal?" Pravika asked. "Should I ask Wink—"

"Sit your butt down, Pravika," Luli said, joining us. It looked like the screaming had helped—she seemed calmer, and she immediately accepted the iced coffee I offered her. "You know the only rule is to stay within the arena's border."

"I believe that's all of them," I said to Eli as Wit slung the Super Soaker over his shoulder. He needed to switch from defense to offense now; there was no way Nicole was going anywhere near the tree, and Uncle Brad was slowly army crawl-ing through the tall grass.

"So how're we gonna do this, Wit?" Nicole asked her stepbrother. Even from afar, I could see her water gun shaking in her hands. It wasn't aimed; Wit wasn't her target. "You wanna run around some?"

He shrugged. "Not really."

"You're no fun."

"Suppose not."

They remained in a standoff. I glanced down the sidelines to see Michael looking absolutely distraught. His younger sister and his beloved stepbrother. Who did he want to win?

Wit raised the Super Soaker with one hand, and Nicole tried to fake him out a few times before running straight *at* him.

Just as predicted.

"Drop it," I murmured. "Drop it now."

"Holy crap," Luli said when Wit dropped the big water gun in favor of grabbing Claire's handgun from the back of his shorts. He shot his stepsister in the neck. "That was—"

"Amazing," Pravika breathed.

"Genius," Jake marveled.

"I think I'm in love with him," Eli declared.

"Think again," I muttered at the same time a roar went through the crowd and Honey announced with way too much joy in her voice, "Nicole! Terminated!"

"Oh, think again?" Eli asked. He leaned over and pinched me. "Why's that, Mer?"

Luckily, I was saved from answering; Nicole had fully tackled Wit, and they were rolling around in the grass. "Stop!" Aunt Christine and Jeannie Dupré shouted. "The wedding photos!"

And Uncle Brad, I thought. *It's just him and Wit now.*

Nicole conceded, following in Luli's footsteps and stalking off the field. "Well, it's you and me, Uncle Brad," Wit said when the father of the bride rose from the tall grass. "You and me."

"I knew it would be," my uncle said, shaking his head. "You or Mer—I knew it would be one of you." He bowed. "May the best man win."

Wit bowed, too. "May the best man win." His hands were splayed open, nothing to hide.

"Oh my god," Pravika said. "He's unarmed."

Eli latched on to my arm. "Please tell me he has another water gun hidden in his shorts."

"How would I know?" I asked.

My friends gave me a look.

"No," I told them. "He doesn't. It would only weigh him down."

Because now Wit needed to be light on his feet, taking Uncle Brad on a little run. He weaved in figure eights across the field, then abruptly pivoted and sprinted in the opposite direction. Sarah's dad fired again and again, but Wit was always gone before the spray could catch him.

"Is he going to grab the Super Soaker?" Jake wondered aloud.

"I'd do the water bottle," Luli said. "Easy to sweep up."

"What about the handgun?" Pravika suggested.

I looked down the sidelines, everyone now wide awake and leaning forward in their seats. *Soon*, I thought. *We'll be celebrating soon.*

Five minutes later, Uncle Brad was winded. It wasn't that he was out of shape, but Wit was nineteen, and my uncle was nearing sixty. Wit stopped running and turned his back to us. There was a line of sweat running down his T-shirt, and his bandanna was now down around his neck. "Hot," he commented.

"Blazing," Uncle Brad replied, wiping his brow.

Still unarmed, Wit started walking backward toward the sideline, and my uncle noticed. I watched him step forward and reposition his water gun. "No," Pravika whispered. "He's backing himself out of bounds."

"Relax," I told her.

Wit kept backing up, Uncle Brad advancing.

Slowly, smoothly.

They exchanged funny pleasantries along the way. It was a dance—a dance that concluded with Wit seemingly trapping himself in a corner.

But one directly in front of me.

"Wait, stop!" I exclaimed as Wit put a hand behind his back, fingers ready and waiting. "You're right on the border! Don't move!"

"Yes," Uncle Brad drawled like a Disney villain. "Don't move, kid."

There was a gasp when he pulled his trigger and an even louder one a heartbeat later when Wit crouched down to avoid the stream and whispered, "Now, Killer!"

I quickly grabbed the pink squirt gun from under my seat and pressed it into his hand, my insides in a knot as Wit leapt up, lunged forward, and assassinated Uncle Brad for the victory.

The crowd went wild. "Witty!" Michael appeared out of nowhere and hoisted Wit up onto his shoulders. "Witty for the win!"

Uncle Brad stood there, stunned. "But no," he said, shaking his head. "No."

"What do you mean, *no?*" Sarah asked. "Dad, come on. You lost." She kissed his cheek. "Second place is still great!"

"He broke the rules," Uncle Brad said, Wink and Honey now on the scene. Michael lowered Wit back down to the ground. "Meredith handed him the gun."

"Yes, dear," Honey said, "but there is technically no rule about 'phoning a friend.'" She smiled. "The finalists and their weapons need only stay within the border." She gestured to the spray-painted line—my dad's project yesterday afternoon.

"Mer's chair is over the line, though, Mom," Uncle Brad replied. "Just like everyone else's."

"Actually, it's not," I chimed in, "because I have a beach *lounger*, not your standard beach *chair*."

The lounger was another gem I had found in the Annex's storage shed. It was old and faded but still usable. I knew it would come in handy for something.

"The footrest is just across the line, inside the arena," I continued smoothly, even though my heart was racing a hundred miles per hour. "I hid the gun right under there."

Of course, an inspection followed. Wink bent down to see if there was the slightest of indentations in the grass from the water gun, and after getting Honey's input, he raised the megaphone to his lips. "Our champion, everyone! Stephen Witry!"

Screams erupted again. Sarah launched herself at Wit, and out of the corner of my eye, I saw Honey smile and lovingly pat her eldest child's cheek. "Someday," she said.

Once everyone had settled down, my grandparents presented Wit with this summer's Assassin gold medal (plastic, from the pharmacy in town). Identical to all the ones Claire had hung on her bedroom wall.

I just watched him. I watched him give handshakes to all the other finalists; I watched him high-five my mom and dad; I watched him hug Jeannie and his stepsiblings. Then he and his father hugged for a long time.

Eventually, it was only the two of us in the arena. He was so sweaty, but he swept me up into his arms. "Congratulations," I told him. "Eli has already proclaimed his love for you."

He put me down and grinned at me. "I couldn't have done it without you," he said. "You're the reason I won."

I batted my eyelashes. "Am I?"

"Yes." He nodded.

"Oh, come on." I waved him off. "All I did was hand you the gun."

Wit wrapped me in another hug. "Do you think she'd be happy?" he whispered. "I know she would've wanted it to be you, but still...is it okay that I won?"

"Without a doubt," I whispered back. The sun couldn't be brighter—Claire was overwhelmingly proud. "Without a doubt."

Then I broke away and tugged his bandanna before smiling and kissing him.

"And by the way," he murmured, kissing me back, "I don't want Eli." His hands went to my waist. "I want *you*."

TWENTY-ONE

I want you.

What did Wit mean by that? Was he pretending like we'd agreed? Or was he telling the truth? I couldn't decide, but it sounded awfully true.

I made my way to the Pond House—or, as Aunt Christine kept calling it, "the bridal suite." Sarah had invited me to get my hair, nails, and makeup done with her and her bridesmaids. It was only noon, but I had a plan to elegantly crash their brunch, in the mood for French toast.

More reception preparation was happening over at the Big House, the pace less leisurely than yesterday. Round tables and wicker chairs were being carried into the tent, and in keeping with Sarah's Pinterest board, there would also be a wide dance floor in the center with delicate fairy lights strung across the ceiling. There had also been pictures of various table center-pieces, and I wondered which one she had chosen.

My feet couldn't help but detour to the Big House—not to get closer to the hustle and bustle but to see if Wink was on the porch. "Meredith!" He looked up from his book. I didn't know how he could read with all the noise. "I thought you'd be on your way to the Pond House by now."

"Oh, not yet," I said, suddenly no longer in the mood for French toast. "They're probably still having brunch. I should wait a little longer."

"I don't think Sarah would mind," my grandfather said as I settled into the hammock. He took a sip of his tea. "Not in the least."

I nodded but didn't leave. Neither of us spoke for a few beats until Wink put down his mug and brought up Wit. "Very impressive," he said. "His triumph today was very impressive. That's why Honey and I have so few rules, you know—to see how creative players can get." He chuckled. "I told him that he has an open invitation to The Farm and must come back to defend his title." He looked out at the horizon. "The two of you have breathed new life into the game."

My heart dipped.

"And it's admirable," Wink continued before I could say anything—not that I had much to say. It felt like someone had stolen my voice. "I think it's admirable that he has recognized his discontent at school and is taking time to self-reflect and see if he wants to make changes." He whistled. "New Zealand is far, but it'll be an adventure. One worth taking, from the way he talks about it. Therapeutic, too, from my perspective. That's why Honey and I decided to move here full-time. No matter the season, The Farm heals you. It has curative powers."

"Yeah, it does," I heard myself say. "It really does."

But my stomach squirmed. We weren't talking about Wit anymore; we were talking about *me*. Me, and my choice to go to Hamilton this fall...an incredible college, but the college where my dad worked, and the college that was less than a mile from my house. I'd applied early decision last November, was accepted in December, and from then on hadn't thought twice about it.

Do you want *to be close to home?* I knew my grandfather was asking now. *Or do you* need *to be close to home?*

Need, I thought. At least back then—it had been less than a year since we'd lost Claire, and I remembered still feeling so crippled with grief that I couldn't imagine leaving Clinton. The idea of my parents being a phone call away instead of a walk down the hill from campus rattled me. *I'm safe* had been my reaction upon reading my acceptance letter. *I'm going to be safe.*

The bottom line: I'd applied to college in my hometown because I was scared of leaving. My sister had died on her first big adventure away from home, so I didn't want an adventure. I wanted family; I wanted *familiar*.

But now, after this week...after celebrating Claire's legacy and meeting someone who was so determined to live life to the fullest...

I was beginning to think *need* might not be my answer anymore. That thought was terrifying but one I knew I had to confront.

"Resume your reading," I said to Wink, hopping up from the hammock. "I'm going to go get myself some French toast."

⌇

Sarah and her bridesmaids were all wearing matching satin pajama sets, but Aunt Christine steered me out of their suite before they changed into their dresses. Wit was walking up the driveway as I was walking down it. The guys must've gone surfing after all; Wit had a wet suit pulled down to his waist. "What're you doing?" I asked, heart catching.

He looked...

"I'm getting my makeup done," he said and gestured to his face. His green bruise hadn't quite faded to an unnoticeable yellow. "Aunt Christine texted me to get my ass over here."

"Why does she have your number but I don't?" I blurted.

Wit cocked his head. "You want my number?"

"Of course!"

He gave it to me. I quickly tapped his details into my phone but didn't text him so that he would have mine. *Hi! It's Meredith!* sounded so ridiculous.

"Don't go in there," I said, taking a step closer and fiddling with one of his floppy wet suit sleeves. "Let your shiner shine."

Wit grinned. "It would give these wedding photos some more character." He slipped an arm around me. We turned to head away from the house together. "You know they're supposed to take *two* hours?"

"Yeah, that's what Sarah said," I replied. "Why don't you come to the Annex? I'll make you some snacks so you don't get hangry."

"You make snacks?"

"Yeah, really good ones. Have you ever heard of puppy chow?"

Wit picked me up and twirled me around. My guess was that meant *yes*.

"Hey, careful!" I giggled. "Don't ruin the hair!"

The hair was something I never would've been able to accomplish myself. Danielle the Maid of Honor had blown it out before weaving it into an effortless braid crown.

"Sorry, sorry." He put me back down on the ground and after a pause said, "The hair looks lovely."

I smiled. "Thank you."

We kept walking, and after loading him up with a Tupperware of Chex Mix covered in chocolate, peanut butter, and powdered sugar, I kicked him out to get ready.

"So here's the thing," my mom said after I modeled my dress for her: strapless and cream with shell-pink and deep blue lilies all over it. The skirt swirled when I spun, my heels were high, and I wore Claire's bridesmaid necklace. "You're going to bike to the church."

"Wait, what?" I stopped spinning around the sitting room, stopped imagining Wit spinning me around the dance floor later. "I'm going to *bike* to the church?"

"Yes," my dad said. "Christine said parking was a headache

yesterday at the rehearsal. We don't want to take many cars since that street is so narrow."

"Oh, okay." I nodded. St. Andrew's Church was nestled down North Summer Street in Edgartown, and while it was incredibly idyllic with its historic red brick and white arched windows, the church and everything around it was *tiny*. "Does that include biking up The Farm road?"

Because three miles on the sandy dirt road in semiformal attire?

I didn't think that would end so well.

"No." My dad shook his head. "Brad and I have already made several runs in the truck. A fleet of bikes is waiting near the obelisk."

"Who else is riding?" I asked.

"This is nuts," Luli said a half hour later, climbing onto her orange mountain bike. "We could be *late*. We could literally walk through the doors during the 'speak now or forever hold your peace' part."

"We *aren't* going to be late," Pravika replied. "It's only a fifteen-minute ride."

"And they're still taking pre-ceremony pictures," Eli said with a sigh.

Unfortunately, he hadn't been able to photobomb any.

"Well, should we go, then?" Jake asked, throwing a look at Luli. "If you're so worried?"

And so the five of us began biking into town with a band of children in tow. Luli and Jake had agreed to lead the way, Eli would ride in the middle, and Pravika and I would bring up the rear. She and I had both ditched our heels and put them in our bike baskets, deciding to ride barefoot. It would be fun.

The sun watched us from the cloudless blue sky, and I inhaled a deep breath of island air as we pedaled down the paved bike path. *She's getting married, Claire*, I thought. *Sarah's getting married today.*

We passed Morning Glory and its green pastures, cedar-shingled saltbox houses, secret driveways that twisted up into the hills, and eventually bumped onto Edgartown's brick sidewalks. "Careful!" Eli shouted from up ahead. "Not so close to the curb!"

"They're like the von Trapp family, Nick!" I heard someone say, and I turned to see a blond girl holding hands with a ginger-bearded boy. "Aren't they?"

I smiled to myself. That was exactly what we were like.

The parade into the small church was in full swing by the time we'd parked our bikes by the bookstore and directed everyone a few streets over to North Summer. "Okay, gang!" Eli clapped his hands. "Go find your parents!"

I found mine in a pew near the front, and they laughed when I sat down next to them. "What?" I asked nervously. "What's wrong?" I reached up to make sure my hair was still intact.

"Your shoes," my mom said. "Mer, where are your shoes?"

I glanced down to see only my bare feet.

Shit—I'd forgotten them in my bike basket. There had been so many children to guide.

"It's a tribute," I said, wriggling my toes to show off my pedicure. "Sarah goes barefoot on The Farm, so I'm going barefoot at her wedding."

My dad chuckled again. "I love you, Meredith," he said before kissing the top of my head. "You have no idea how much your mom and I love you."

⁓

Just like Sarah and Michael's wedding invitation promised, the ceremony commenced at four o'clock with a trumpet prelude and the grandparents' processional. I had to turn and snort into my dad's blazer when Wink and Honey strolled down the aisle together, my grandmother gleaming like a queen and my grandfather with a satisfied smirk on his face. "I don't know, Sarah," he'd joked after her engagement announcement. "I know you want to get married on The Farm, but I'm not sure it'll be possible without a grandparents' processional during the ceremony. It's a true sign of respect."

"He's such a show-off sometimes," my dad whispered now.

"He's the *best*," I whispered back.

"Yes," my dad agreed. "Yes, they both are."

Next came the bridal party. Danielle and Gavin were the first pair. The bridesmaid dresses were a dreamy blue-green color, and the groomsmen wore navy tuxes with light blue bow ties to match Michael's. He was excitedly clacking his chestnut shoes at the altar.

Wit and Nicole looked downright giddy when it was their turn, bouncing down the aisle instead of executing a smooth walk. "Oh, lord," I heard Jeannie say at the same time as Great-Uncle Richard asked if they were drunk. I knew they weren't. Their brother was getting married; they were *thrilled*.

And eventually, Sarah. She was beaming as she walked arm in arm with Uncle Brad, carrying a beautiful bouquet of hydrangeas. Her dress was stunning and simple, white and sleeveless with a long keyhole neckline and low back. She wore her auburn hair down, pulled back to show off her pearl-colored statement earrings. Even though she and Michael had had their "first look" back on Paqua, he was mesmerized. Sarah broke into an even brighter smile when she reached the end of the aisle. *Hi*, I saw her mouth. *Fancy meeting you here.*

She continued to shine later when Oscar Witry and a few others did readings before she and Michael exchanged sappy but so incredibly sweet vows. Of course, Sarah's was not complete without quoting Taylor Swift, a line from the classic "Lover."

And she became absolutely luminous as Michael kissed her and they walked up the aisle as newlyweds, every guest on their feet, clapping and cheering. Michael pumped a fist in victory on their way out the door.

"Hurray," I whispered, feeling Claire at my side. "She's a Dupré."

TWENTY-TWO

The reception was, without a doubt, Sarah's wedding Pinterest board come to life. My breath caught when I entered the tent, alive with fairy lights and cascading greenery. There was a wide circular dance floor, white cloth-covered tables, sandy-colored wicker chairs, and illuminated lighthouse centerpieces wreathed in blue hydrangeas. "Which table are you at?" Wit asked, holding up a smooth gray stone. STEPHEN WITRY, it said across the front in black calligraphy, giving me goose bumps. I loved his name.

"Let's see," I said, scanning the credenza for a beat before finding my stone...and when I did, mine wasn't the only name that jumped out at me.

BENJAMIN FLETCHER sat right next to MEREDITH FOX.

The wedding planner hadn't gotten the message about Ben; Aunt Christine or Sarah had probably forgotten to pass it along to her. I started laughing—really, truly laughing.

"What?" Wit asked as I giggled. "What's so funny?"

I picked up Ben's stone and handed it to him. "Here," I said. "Look at this."

Wit studied it before grumbling something, then turned and walked straight out of the tent. I imagined him hurling the stone into the dunes. Upon his return, he flashed me a grin. "Drink?"

"Please," I said, and so the two of us joined the long line for the bar. Eli, Pravika, Luli, and Jake had already been there, done that, and were now congregated by the three-tiered wedding cake sipping glasses of the blackberry lemonade punch that Honey had been talking about all week. I knew for a fact that it was delicious; after all, it was her secret recipe.

"Meredith, is that you?" I heard someone say after Wit and I had been waiting a while, and I turned to see one of Sarah's cousins who'd just flown in for the wedding. "It's been years!"

"Darcy, hi," I said, remembering her from several summers ago. She'd socialized so much on the beach that I swore her voice was still stuck in my head when I went to bed at night. "How's it going?"

And just like that, I'd unintentionally opened the gates for a catchup. I listened to Darcy and nodded along as best I could, but all I wanted was some lemonade, and my stomach had started to rumble.

Wit tactfully cut her off by introducing himself. "I'm Michael's stepbrother," he said, and after giving us an up-and-down look, Darcy smiled.

"You two are cute," she said, taking a sip of wine. "How long have you been dating?"

My gut twisted. *We aren't*, I almost told her, even though I knew it looked like the opposite. Wit had absentmindedly hooked an arm around my waist, and I was leaning into him so that my chin rested on his shoulder. His was on the top of my head. It was all so natural—so amazingly but *agonizingly* natural.

Wit straightened up a bit, but his arm stayed firmly around me. "Not long, Darcy," he said, clearing his throat. "Meredith's sister, Claire, actually tried setting us up a couple of winters ago, but we only got together this week."

"This week?" Darcy laughed. "Really?" She put her hand on my forearm. "I would've guessed at least a year!"

"Yes, really," Wit said, and I nodded. Not because we were pretending, but because my heart...

It swooped and soared the way it always did around Wit.

"I have to text you!" I exclaimed once we finally reached the bar. "I never texted you, so you don't have my number."

Wit watched the bartender fill our glasses. "You don't need to text me," he said quietly.

"What?" I accepted my drink. "You don't want to text?"

"No, I do," he said. "I do, but you don't need to send me your number." He scrubbed a hand through his hair and then sighed. "Because I already have it."

His words didn't quite compute. "You already..."

"I wasn't joking earlier," he murmured. "Claire really *did* try to set us up—she gave me your number that night before leaving the restaurant."

All of a sudden, my eyes were stinging. "But you never texted," I said, voice catching. I let him lead me away from the bar. "You never reached out."

Wit's lips quirked up. "Killer, why would I reach out?"

Because I would've adored you, I thought. *I adore you now, and I would've adored you then.*

"Everything else aside," Wit said, taking my hand, "Claire failed to mention that you had a boyfriend." He paused. "I admit that after hearing about you, I found you on Insta—"

"See!" I exclaimed, blackberry lemonade sloshing around in my glass. "You say you *don't do* Instagram, but you're really all over it!"

Wit blushed.

"Okay, you went on my profile..." I prompted. "Like a stalker..."

"I scroll," he corrected. "I don't *stalk*."

I sipped my drink. "Mm-hmm."

He sipped his. "Mm-hmm."

"So what did you think of it?" I asked.

"I thought it looked carefully curated," he answered.

"It was," I said, thinking of how ridiculously long I would spend editing photos and brainstorming captions. "Anything else?"

Wit hesitated.

"Say it," I told him. "Just say it."

He glanced into his punch, then at me. "I thought it didn't match the girl Claire couldn't stop talking about," he said. "If I'm being honest."

I felt my upper lip tremble, because I knew it was true. I was not that light pink–tinted girl posing at parties and dangling from her boyfriend's arm like an accessory. I was the girl who loved laughing with her friends in the sunlight, sleeping in a sandy bunk bed, and grinning while licking butter off the face of a beautiful boy named Stephen. That was the real me.

Wit squeezed my hand. "But that only made me want to meet you more."

I squeezed his hand back. I squeezed it back and kissed his knuckles but didn't say anything.

⁓

Michael and Sarah Dupré danced their first dance not to a Taylor Swift song but to the band's rendition of Ed Sheeran's "Hearts Don't Break Around Here." There were seventy-five people watching them, but I doubted they noticed their guests. My cousin and her husband were too wrapped up in each other, smiling and swooning and so in love.

"No way," Aunt Julia said to our table, shaking her head. Aunt Rachel and the baby were doing well, so she'd convinced Aunt Julia to come to the reception. "I love this song, but there's no way Michael picked it. He's an R&B guy."

"But also a Sheerio," Wit said. He was sitting next to me; he'd decided to alternate tables throughout the night. "He's a secret Sheerio."

"I'm sorry," my dad said, cocking his head. "A what?"

"A *Sheerio*," I replied. "For example, Sarah is a Swiftie

because she's part of the Taylor Swift fandom, so Michael's a Sheerio because he loves Ed Sheeran."

"Well, what am I?" my dad asked. "If I'm a Dave Matthews fan, what does that make me?" He pretended to puff out his chest. "You know I'm at forty-five concerts now."

"Oh, wow, Tom," Aunt Julia deadpanned. "You've never mentioned that before."

Under the table, Wit's hand went to my knee. "What's wrong?" he murmured.

I didn't take my eyes off Sarah and Michael. "How do you know something's wrong?"

"Just do."

The back of my neck warmed, and I willed myself not to let it spread to my cheeks. "Nothing's wrong," I told Wit and kissed his cheek—once, twice, three times. Across the table, my mom gave me a look. "I'm just dying to dance with you."

"You should be," he replied lazily. "I am an exceptional dancer."

"Are you now?"

"Yes," he said. "Because if you can believe it, skiing and dancing skills sort of overlap..." He trailed off as the music faded out and everyone rose to applaud the newlyweds. Wit grabbed his tux jacket from the back of his chair before returning to his assigned seat with his family. He winked. "You'll see soon enough."

Everyone loved the toasts. Danielle spoke about Sarah being the sister she'd never had, while Gavin read aloud a series of texts that Michael had sent him after first meeting Sarah. "I've saved these messages for five years," he said. "They say you can't convey tone in texting, but back then..." He shook his head. "Back then, I could tell—I could tell through all his hungover typos that *something* had shifted, something had *happened*." He raised his champagne glass. "Cheers to you, bud. Cheers to you and the nerdy hot girl in your way-too-fucking-early psych class!"

Tears streamed down both Sarah's and Michael's faces from laughing so hard. She punched him in the biceps. "How is *any* of that complimentary?" she asked. "You almost skipped class!"

"But I didn't!" he said. "And I said you were hot!"

The entire tent burst into laughter all over again, and soon dinner was served. True to form, I ignored the salad plate in front of me; instead, I pushed back my chair and found Danielle devouring hers several tables away. "That was a wonderful speech," I told her as she put down her fork and slid over in her chair to make room for me.

"Thank you," she said. "Gavin's had more flair, but for Sarah, I wanted to speak from the heart." She smiled. "Even if it was kind of all over the place."

"No, it wasn't all over the place," I said. "Not at all. I really liked the part where you talked about needing to take a semester off school and what Sarah said when you asked for advice." I swallowed hard.

Danielle took a sip from her water glass. "You're starting college next month, right?"

I nodded.

"How are you feeling about it?"

"Confused," I admitted, thinking of my conversation with Wink about whether I wanted or needed to stay near home. First *needed*, then *wanted*, now *worried*...that I'd made too hasty a decision. Was I even ready for college?

Because there's more than one path, I realized. Danielle's speech had hit it home, but Wit had pointed it out last night. "I think you *need* something," he'd said. "Something different."

Danielle tilted her head. "Do you need to talk, Meredith?"

"Yeah," I said. "I think so."

It was a relief when dinner ended and the band struck up again. Uncle Brad and Sarah's father-daughter dance ended with my uncle in an absolute puddle, and Jeannie Dupré also needed tissues during her dance with Michael. Wink leading Honey out onto the floor signaled that the rest of us could follow. I broke into a grin when Wit twirled me into his arms. "You *are* smooth!" I said once our fingers laced together and we were waltzing. A little discombobulated, but we managed.

"Yes, I am, thank you very much!" he responded and grinned back at me.

I threw back my head and laughed.

"What?" he asked. "What's so funny?"

"Your teeth," I answered. "Your teeth..."

Purple. His teeth were purple from the blackberry lemonade.

"Oh no!" Wit dropped my hand to cover his mouth. "What will Aunt Christine say?"

I rolled my eyes before he took my hand again and unexpectedly dipped me, my legs wobbling like Bambi's in my high heels. Half my hair had also fallen out of its braid crown. "She would say we're a hot mess," I told him.

"We're more than hot," Wit said. "We're *stunning.*"

A shiver ran up my spine. The tent was humid from so many bodies, but still, a shiver, because I didn't think Wit was referring to what a mess we were. "Don't." I shook my head. "You said, you promised—"

He kissed me.

Just a light brush of his berry-stained lips against mine, but he kissed me as a flash went off somewhere nearby. There were three wedding photographers moving about the tent tonight. "Do you think that was of us?" I whispered.

"How could it not be?" Wit whispered back. He already had us dancing again.

I giggled into his chest, then rested my head there for a moment. He had undone his bow tie along with the top couple buttons of his shirt. I let myself breathe in his familiar scent: oranges, sweat, sunscreen, the ocean.

Melt. I wanted to *melt.*

"No, honestly," he went on, "we are stealing the show."

Stealing the show.

Wait. A. Second.

I popped up my head. "Eli!" I shouted, looking in every

direction, hoping he wasn't in our vicinity. Because he'd been schmoozing like everyone's favorite guest all night, and I didn't want him to have photobombed Wit's and my picture. Something told me it was a truly special one, one I wanted...

Well, one I wanted more than anything.

"Eli!"

"Yeah, Mer?" I glanced over my shoulder to see Eli a dozen yards away, about to slip into a photo with Aunt Christine's side of the family. "Everything good?"

Yes, everything was good.

Wit and I danced for a while longer, and then my dad spun me around the floor, then Wink, and after that, I congratulated the groom. There was still frosting on Michael's face from the ceremonial cake cutting. "Don't even think about licking it off," he joked. "I know you and Witty are into that sort of thing, but..." He held up his hand, a silver band glinting in the light. "I'm a married man now, Meredith."

"Indeed you are," I said, looking over at Sarah. She was barefoot and whispering something to Wit, who was on his second slice of cake. "But don't assume that'll deter Honey."

My grandmother and her steadfast crush on Michael Dupré.

"Eh, I'm not worried about that," he replied and nodded toward his wife and stepbrother. Honey had just joined them. She hugged Sarah and patted Wit's cheek. "I think she now has eyes for someone else."

We watched Honey smile like a schoolgirl as she smoothed down Wit's hair.

"If you want him," Michael said, "go get him."

I waved him off. "Honey's harmless."

"No, Mer," Michael said. "I'm serious. Imagine if I hadn't gone to class five years ago." He gestured to Sarah. "I could've missed my chance. She saw me *that* day. There were two hundred people in the room, and somehow, she saw me." He shrugged. "Any other day, maybe she wouldn't have. But she saw me, she did, and now here we are. Here we *all* are." He glanced at Wit, then gave me a look. "Enough with this *pretending* nonsense. If you want him, go *get* him. Don't miss your shot."

Sarah tossed her hydrangea bouquet right before she and Michael left for their honeymoon. Wit and I laughed—not only did Nicole Dupré catch it, but Eli also launched himself into the air. "I'm at thirty photobombs," he'd told us earlier. "I've introduced myself and posed, I've sat down at tables and smiled, I've done my thing on the dance floor." He shook his head. "Believe me, I've done it *all*."

Wit and I were sipping from a stolen champagne bottle in a corner. My stomach was fizzy and warm, but I couldn't tell if it was from the champagne or from *him*. "Did you know," he was saying, "that your face is shaped like a heart?"

"No," I told him. "I didn't."

"Well, it is," he replied and lightly sketched out the shape. "Probably because you have such a big one."

I grinned. "That was not your best line."

He grinned back crookedly. "I suppose not." He raised his hand again to trace my lips. "I haven't gotten to kiss you enough tonight," he murmured in that melodious voice. "I kind of want to kiss you."

"Kind of?" I ran a hand through the blond hair at the nape of his neck, giddy when I felt goose bumps rise. "Only *kind of*?"

Wit sighed. "Okay, I desperately want to kiss you."

"Desperately?"

"Desperately."

But when he leaned close, I dipped away from him. "Not here." I nodded toward the tent's exit. "Follow me."

We snuck outside onto the Big House's porch and traded the champagne for one of the quilts Honey always kept on the hammock. I tossed it to Wit, who draped it over his shoulders while I kicked off my heels. "Where're we going?" he asked.

"You'll see," I answered, heart in my throat.

This was really it. This was our last hurrah.

Tonight's stars glimmered above us, and the moon shone so brightly that we didn't need flashlights. It was like Paqua was illuminated in a mysterious glow, mysterious in such a way that you knew the world was full of possibilities. We navigated The Farm's network of trails together, my feet silent on the sand and Wit's scuffing in his shoes. If he realized where we were going, he didn't say anything.

The tall grass swished as we got closer to the dunes, and instead of crashing against the beach, I heard the ocean waves calmly wash ashore before retreating back out to sea.

Barely a week, I thought. Barely a week ago, Wit had snuck up on me during my late-night walk. I'd threatened him with a knife, but by the end of the evening, I didn't want his knees to stop knocking against mine. His energy—his everything—was infectious.

"I wondered if we might end up here," he said once we'd found our secret nook. I took the quilt from him and spread it over the sand and matted grass. We both looked at it, ready and waiting.

Unlike our first kiss in Wit's room with all its awkwardness, we didn't hesitate—we just began. He drew me close and kissed me as I shimmied up his body, tangling my legs around his waist.

I slid off his navy tux jacket before he unzipped my dress. It fell first to my hips, then to the ground when he put me down, and we unbuttoned his shirt together. I kissed his shoulder, his collarbone, the hollow of his throat—skin tinged blue in the moonlight. "I adore you," I whispered. "Please tell me you know how much I adore you."

Instead of answering, Wit kissed me again. He kissed me long and lingering, lips leaving behind the spiral sensations I loved so much.

I think he does, I told myself before the rest happened. *I think he knows.*

Afterward, we lay wrapped up together in Honey's quilt. I had no idea what time it was, the world wonderfully hazy—so wonderfully hazy. I was nestled into Wit's warm chest, and his fingers were splayed across my shoulder blades. They felt like butterflies. "Mmm," I murmured, but he didn't say anything back for a while, not until I was drifting off to sleep.

"I know you don't like hearing this," I heard him say, "and I know I promised not to tell you, but you *are* pretty, Killer. You're pretty, beautiful, stunning, *mesmerizing*." He paused. "But that's not *all* you are. You're everything Claire said and more. Clever, funny, caring, lively, strong, brave—all of it. You are *all* of it." He kissed the top of my head. "And I do know how much you adore me," he whispered. "I just wish it was as much as I adore you."

SUNDAY

TWENTY-THREE

The sun was nowhere to be found when my parents and I packed the car the next morning, the sky gloomy with gray clouds. Leaving the Vineyard was always upsetting, and the island felt it. "Okay," my dad said once he'd slammed the Raptor's tailgate shut. "Should we start, then?"

I nodded, even though my head ached and my eyes were puffy from crying. Every summer, we did "rounds" before catching our ferry home. While my mom and dad's first stop was the Big House, I headed to Lantern House to say goodbye to Uncle Brad and Aunt Christine. "You better be in the Showdown next year," my uncle said as he hugged me. "I feel like we have unfinished business. It was pure luck that I got you when I did."

"You can count on it." I hugged him back and then thanked Aunt Christine for a beautiful wedding. "It was one of the best nights of my life," I told her, the honest truth. "Please plan mine someday."

"Oh, Mer," she said, shaking her head and smiling. "You

and your mom are going to do that." She kissed my cheek, then whispered, "But I would be happy to consult."

After I left them, I wolfed down some waffles with Ethan and Hannah in the Camp. "Swing by the hospital," Aunt Julia said. "Say goodbye to Rachel and meet the baby."

"Aunt Julia, we'll miss our boat if we meet Oliver," I joked. "You know how much I love babies." I grinned—we were already planning on stopping there on the way to the ferry. I couldn't leave without meeting my newest cousin.

I hugged Ethan and Hannah hard before heading to the Big House. "We'll send you our art projects," they said. "For you to hang on your wall at college."

My stomach stirred.

College.

"Thank you," I said. "I can't wait."

But could I?

My parents and I crossed paths on my way to the Big House. "Honey has tea all ready for you," my mom said.

"And Aunt Julia made extra waffles," I told her.

"Keep moving, ladies," my dad said, and my mom and I exchanged an eye roll. My dad was laid-back on The Farm except for the day we departed. Then he was all business, always wanting to catch the earliest ferry so we could get on the road home. Luckily, my mom had convinced him to let us sleep in a little after the wedding.

Wink and Honey were very quiet when I walked into their kitchen—the wind was too rough to sit on the porch. I sipped my Earl Grey in silence. "Yesterday was amazing," I eventually said. "I don't think I've ever seen Sarah that happy."

"Yes," my grandmother agreed. "Me too—it was a gorgeous night." She reached out and put her soft hand on top of mine. "Meredith," she said, "we don't mean to pressure you, but have you thought any more about what your grandfather said?"

What your grandfather said.

What he'd said to me, all through talking about Wit.

Need, want, worry.

Would I go to Hamilton this fall, or would I take a gap year?

I looked at Wink. "I'm thinking," I whispered. "I'm *really* thinking." A lump formed in my throat. "Will you back me up, though? Whatever I decide?"

Wink came over to the kitchen table and put his hands on my shoulders. "I am your biggest fan," he said. "I have *always* been your biggest fan. I will stand by you no matter what."

"As will I," Honey said, wrapping me in her arms. Her bracelets jingled, and I breathed in her lavender scent. "We love you, sweetie. We support you."

I squeezed my eyes shut and told them I loved them, too.

Wink pulled away first. "Now, hurry up," he said. "You've got a few more houses to hit and, according to your father, not a lot of time."

No one was awake at the Pond House, and I skipped the Cabin altogether. Only Oscar Witry and Jeannie were up and about at Moor House. Michael's mom offered to whip me up some breakfast, but I was still full from my waffles, so I shook my head and hugged her. "I know it's difficult," she murmured, rubbing my back. "But please, Miss Meredith, come to New Orleans anytime. There is so much to see, and we would love to have you."

My final stop was the Nylon Condo Complex. I unzipped Eli and Jake's tent first—they were both asleep, nowhere to be anytime soon. My friends were staying here through the summer. "I'm going to drown my sorrows at work tonight," Jake said after I woke him. "Make a sundae and eat it in honor of you...extra rainbow sprinkles." He yawned. "I'm gonna miss you, Mer."

"I'm gonna miss you, too, Jake," I said. "We'll keep in touch."

"You better mean that," Eli mumbled when I told him the same, ruffling his long hair. "And come back next summer."

"I will." I giggled. "I promise."

Because I knew I would. I didn't know what the next nine months held for me, but I knew that a year from now, I would be *here*—on the Vineyard, on The Farm, with my favorite people. Claire and her dreams of working on the island had inspired me. She would forever inspire me.

I took a deep breath before slipping into Pravika and Luli's tent. Divya was nowhere to be seen—*with a groomsman?* I wondered—but Pravika whined when I said goodbye. "No," she said, latching onto my sweatshirt sleeve. "No, not yet. It's only been a week. You can't leave us."

"But duty calls," I replied, sighing. "I must get back to

Clinton and the bagel shop. They need to re-chain me to the register." (My boss had been genuinely annoyed when I'd asked for a week off.)

From her sleeping bag, Luli snorted.

"Hate you." Pravika gave me a warm hug. "Love you."

"Love you, too," I said and then turned to Luli. Earlier, I'd told myself that I wouldn't be nervous when I said goodbye to her. I had apologized; I had done everything in my power to clear the air between us. The ball was in her court. There was no need to be nervous. "Farewell, missy," I said, a joke from when we were younger. Aunt Christine called us both *missy* whenever we got into mischief. "I'll talk to you soon, okay?"

Luli didn't respond at first; I waited, but there was no reply. Then, finally, she rolled off her air mattress and across the tent to Pravika and me. "When I send funny Snapchats," she said to me, "please answer them. You missed a lot of my best work this year."

I nodded. "I'll try to match your genius."

And then, in a blink, I was out the door. *Saying sorry just isn't like Luli*, I told myself, tears pooling in my eyes. *I already owed her an apology, and since I didn't say anything before she came at me, she doesn't think she owes me one—*

"Wait, Meredith!" I heard someone shout. "Mer, wait!"

I turned to see Luli, her dark hair a nest of bedhead, zigzagging through the tents. "What's up?" I said.

"I'm sorry!" she blurted. "I know this is way late—*too* late—but I'm sorry for being such a bitch, for what I said in the bathroom about how you dumped us for Ben and how you were doing the same with Wit and about how he was going to break your heart." She sighed. "And I'm *really* sorry for telling you to leave after you apologized. I know now...Claire was my friend, but she was your *sister*. It hurt being ignored all those months, and I know you wish you had handled it better, but she was your sister. I can't even imagine, if I were to lose Jake..." She shook her head. "I can't even imagine."

My eyes welled up again. "Thank you," I whispered. "Thank you, Luli. That means so much to me. I hope"—I let out a breath—"I hope we can be friends again."

Luli gave me a look. "Missy, we *are* friends."

I smiled. "Forever friends."

"Yes, forever." She glanced around. "Now, where's your not-so-secret lover?"

"Oh." My smile faltered. "We said goodbye already."

Last night, Wit and I had eventually gotten dressed, folded up our quilt, and silently walked back to the houses holding hands. When we'd reached the Annex's mailbox, he hugged me long and hard, my feet leaving the ground for a moment. There was no kiss, only the hug. "Bye," he murmured.

"Bye," I murmured back.

And then I'd watched him walk back to the Cabin, hands tucked in his pockets and head tilted back to gaze at the stars.

"Goodbye?!" Luli said now. "You said *goodbye* last night?"

"Yeah." I nodded. "It would've been too painful this morning—"

My friend held up her hand. "Goodbye *for now*, or goodbye *for good*?"

"For good," I whispered, stomach twisting into a knots. "The week's over, Luli. The wedding's over—"

"Meredith!" Luli was incredulous. "Are you joking?"

I shook my head.

She shook hers, too. "You're so exasperating sometimes. Everyone with eyes saw how much you two were freaking falling for each other. For god's sake, I heard you slept in his bed every night this week." She gave me a look. "Bold, by the way."

"Well, yeah," I said. "It's Wit, and we're..."

Totally tangled together.

Luli smirked. "See, that's what I'm talking about. You guys are *far* from finished."

"But he's going to New Zealand!" I exclaimed. "He's going to the other side of the world for the next *year*, and yes, he asked me to come with him, but I don't know. We've only known each other a week. I have to keep reminding myself that we've only known each other a week."

"Who cares?" Luli said. "Go with him, or stay here and date him anyway!" She laughed. "I'm sure he loves to FaceTime, and you're going to get your act together in that department."

My eyes prickled. "Luli, I don't know."

"Meredith, come on," she said. "This is your chance."

This is your chance.

I remembered Michael at the reception last night, telling

me about almost missing his chance with Sarah. *Now here we are*, he'd said. *Here we all are.*

My pulse surged. *If you want him*, I thought, *go get him.*

I hauled ass over to the Cabin only to bang into Wit's room and find that it was empty. Bed stripped, nightstand cleared, nothing in his dresser or closet. Absolutely empty. My throat thickened, trying to recall if he'd told me when he planned on leaving. His dad and the Duprés were still on The Farm, so why wasn't he?

Where are you, where are you, where are you?

"Jesus Christ," Gavin said, his screen door's hinges squeaking as I pulled it open. "What is with you people and the no-knocking thing?" He sat up in bed, and I noticed he wasn't alone.

Danielle had pulled his covers up over her shoulders.

"Wit's not in his room," I said, voice cracking.

"Well, no, he wouldn't be," Gavin replied. "He left for his ferry." He rubbed his forehead. "Heading home to Vermont, I think."

I gaped. "What?"

"He left," Danielle said, tone indicating that she wanted me to get the hell out of the room. I could understand why. "He has an early ferry. His mom is picking him up at Falmouth and driving him home to Vermont. Okay?"

"Okay." I nodded and quickly spun around to leave, both Gavin and Danielle groaning when the door slammed shut behind me. Everyone had hangovers from last night.

"Luli," I said when she answered her phone. "Meet me at the tractor barn. We're going to need the Jeep."

—————

"Why don't you just text him?" Luli shouted over the roaring wind as Wink's old Jeep raced down The Farm road. She was driving; my hands were shaking too hard to hold on to the steering wheel or shift gears.

"Because I deleted his number!" I responded. After parting ways with Wit last night, I'd collapsed into Claire's bunk and deleted his contact before crying into my sister's pillow. Even after so much back-and-forth, I'd thought cutting all ties with him would make me feel better.

Now I was regretting it.

"What about Instagram?" Luli said. "DM him!"

"It's not loading!" I said shrilly. "The app isn't loading!" I closed Instagram and checked the ferry schedule again. It was 10:15. The most recent boat had left Vineyard Haven at 10:00, but there was another leaving in twenty minutes. Hopefully, Wit was going to be on it.

I glanced at the Jeep's speedometer.

Twenty-seven miles per hour.

It felt like five.

"Hurry up," I said, my heart pounding. "Please, Luli, go faster!"

She raised an eyebrow. "Faster?"

"Yes." I nodded quickly. "*Faster.*"

I still winced a little when she stepped on the gas but less so than earlier this week. Luli was a good driver; we had driven together since before getting our licenses. Wink had taught her well, she was sober, and she had full command of the car. I knew in my bones that nothing was going to happen. Luli stuck to the speed limit on the way to Vineyard Haven, my legs bouncing up and down the entire time. Of course we kept hitting red lights.

"What are you going to say?" she asked at one.

"I don't know," I said through gritted teeth. "We just need to get there."

"What if he's already on the boat?"

"Then I'll buy a walk-on ticket—" I started before covering my face with my hands. "Fuck, my wallet's in my backpack! In the Raptor!"

"Don't worry," Luli said. "I have mine, complete with some of Jake's Mad Martha's tips."

I leaned across the Jeep's console and kissed her cheek. "Bless you!"

When we reached Vineyard Haven, the Steamship Authority was an absolute mob scene with all the cars waiting to board *The Island Home*. Kayaks strapped on top of Volvos, Range Rovers weighed down by luggage and beach chairs, bike racks hanging off massive SUVs. Even the roofless Wranglers were there, but no music pulsated from them. Everyone was mourning their departure.

"Good luck!" Luli told me as I unbuckled my seat belt and hopped down from the Jeep. Cars were being waved up the ramp now, and I did a quick scan of the walk-on line. People were making their way onto the ferry, but I didn't spot a blond-haired boy among them. *Well*, I thought, *here we go.*

I sprinted into the Steamship Authority only to find a line of people waiting to buy last-minute tickets. My stomach stirred as I waited, and when it was finally my turn, blood pumped so loudly through my ears that I couldn't speak—I just handed over a wad of dollar bills. Even that was blurred.

The walk-on zone hadn't been cordoned off yet, but I was in such a panic spiral that I worried boarding was about to end. "Wait!" I called. "Wait for me!"

The ticket taker laughed. "Just in time."

I flashed him a brief smile, then booked it up the ramp and onto the boat. If Wit wasn't on this ferry, I would wait for my parents on the other end. Luli would tell them everything.

"No, Jeffrey, not yet," a woman said as I weaved through cars. "I need to unbuckle your seat belt first!"

"You're kidding me, Becca," someone else said. "You forgot your charger at the house?"

I made it to the stairwell and tore up the steps. *Top deck*, I guessed. *If he's here, he'll be on the top deck.*

A fresh breeze swirled around me when I emerged, and

the clouds had cleared so the sun could shine, Claire working her magic. It was warm against my back. A bunch of families filled the seats, and near the railing, children stretched to look through the big binoculars.

My stomach dropped.

There he was, tall and wiry with salt-stiff hair, wearing jeans with half-tied sneakers and a familiar light blue T-shirt that read #HurrayShesADupré on the back. The fabric billowed in the breeze, and my eyes immediately welled up. I blinked the tears away, and even though I still didn't know what to say, my feet moved forward.

As I crossed the deck, a little girl tugged on Wit's shirt and pointed to the binoculars. She wanted a turn, and I watched him smile and step aside. He leaned against the railing and gazed out to sea. The ferry horn sounded.

I took a deep breath.

And then I did it.

"Hey, Stephen!" I called, and two seconds later, I was right next to him. I grinned, took his hand, and said, "Tell me more about New Zealand."

ONE YEAR LATER

EPILOGUE

The pies came out at 2:00 p.m. It was a beautiful July afternoon, the sky bright blue with white clouds that looked as puffy
as pastries. After finishing my shift at the bookstore, I checked
my phone and found a text: What time should I be there?

I rolled my eyes and replied: You've done this before! 1:50!

Just teasing, he wrote back as I hopped on my bike. Calm
down.

It was 1:53 by the time I turned off the bike path and Morning
Glory came into view—the endless acres of green fields and the
rambling cedar-shingled farmhouse surrounded by wildflowers, gardens, children, and packed picnic tables. Sweat dripped
down my back from the ride, and my pulse pounded. I hoped he
was inside already; today there would be serious competition.

But of course he wasn't.

"Michael!" I called, stomping across the gravel parking lot.
"What the hell?"

He was busy showing off his car. It was a 1973 International
Harvester Scout, the ultimate beach cruiser. "Our island car,"

he called it. He shook hands with the car's newest fans before jogging over to me. I all but dragged him up the path and into the house, where sure enough, customers circulated for groceries while cutting their eyes at the still-empty pie display. "I don't understand why *we* need to do this," he said as I positioned his football-player frame to block the inevitable stampede. "I thought one of the benefits was—"

"Only if there are leftovers," I said, tilting my head to admire my handiwork. "Which is never the case with pies."

He nodded, then raised his arms and cracked his knuckles. The bakers were putting the pies out now, the sweet smell of sugar and berries wafting over to us. Clusters of people moved in on the display shelves, predators eyeing their prey. "Do your thing," he muttered.

"And you do yours," I said before dropping down to my knees. "Excuse me!" I crawled through the customers in front of me. "Excuse me, but I think I dropped an earring! My grandmother gave it to me for my birthday. It's a family heirloom."

Michael whistled when I surfaced with a whopping four pies: blueberry, apple, peach, and of course, strawberry rhubarb. Then we meandered around the store, collecting other necessities for Wink and Honey's annual family dinner tonight. Two dozen ears of corn, fresh lettuce, massive tomatoes, bell peppers, red onions, mozzarella cheese, and zucchini bread (my dad had finished our loaf this morning).

"Can I drive home?" I asked as we joined the line for the registers.

"Sure," Michael said. "If you promise not to go at light speed."

I gave him a look. "Michael, it was five miles over the speed limit."

"Meredith, the speeding ticket said *fifteen*."

"I wasn't the one driving!"

He shrugged. "You were an accomplice."

I smiled to myself. Pravika, Jake, and I had taken Mad Martha's orders a few weeks ago and had to race home so everyone's sundaes wouldn't melt. A policeman had caught us right before we'd turned onto The Farm road. Never having been stopped by a cop, Pravika swallowed her tongue while Jake handed over his license and I got the insurance out of the glove compartment.

Wink had lectured us later.

"Look, that car is my baby," Michael said.

I snorted. "Don't let Sarah hear you say that."

"She knows what I mean..." he said, but the rest went by the wayside. We'd finally turned the corner in line, and my heart swooped.

Then soared.

"Stephen!" I shouted, and the cashier stationed behind register two looked up at me. Mop of sandy hair, shining turquoise eyes, sun-kissed skin, and that goddamn crooked grin.

Michael sighed as he headed for his stepbrother's register. "I swear I will never get used to that. Nobody—and I do mean *nobody*—except you calls him that."

"And nobody should." I laughed. My special nickname for Stephen wasn't a nickname at all.

"So this is a thing now?" he'd asked so many months ago. "I'm no longer Wit?"

"Who's Wit?" I'd responded. We were in Vermont, five days before he was leaving for New Zealand.

He'd started tickling me on his family room couch. "Fine," he said as I giggled. "*Fine.*" His fingers had sparked against my side. "But only for you, Killer."

"What are you doing in here?" I asked now, watching him scan our stuff. There wasn't a speck of dirt on his blue Morning Glory T-shirt. Usually Stephen worked outside in the fields.

"Someone called out sick," he replied, "so they needed an extra hand inside during the rush...oh, nice!" His eyes lit up. "Four pies!"

"That you could've easily set aside and brought home yourself," Michael said dryly.

"That's against the rules."

"It really shouldn't be," Michael grumbled.

I helped bag up our food, and even with Stephen's employee discount, I thought of Wink's famous saying: *It's impossible to leave Morning Glory with pies and a bill under a hundred dollars!*

"Wait," Stephen said before we left. "You forgot something."

"Nah, I have the receipt," Michael said, but I smiled and shoved my bags into his arms so I give Stephen a hug goodbye.

"You're very affectionate," he murmured after I stretched to give his cheek three quick kisses. I didn't know why, but it was always three times. Once just wasn't enough.

"Yes, I know," I said lightly, sliding an arm around his waist. "Someone once made that observation."

Michael coughed. "Not professional, Witty."

Stephen released me, then winked. "I'll be very affectionate *later*."

I winked back. "You know where to find me."

Michael did let me drive home. We loaded my bike into the back, and to show him how serious I was, I pulled my hair into a ponytail and dramatically slipped on Wink's left-behind aviator sunglasses. "Let's blow this farm stand!" I said.

He chuckled. "You are such a knucklehead."

I adjusted my Hamilton baseball cap before turning over the ignition and carefully backing out of our parking spot. I'd just finished my freshman year. When I'd caught Stephen on last summer's ferry, somehow it had all clicked. He was raring to go and ready for an adventure, but I was not. At least not yet. Going to another continent wouldn't solve my problems; I knew I needed to work through them at home, with my parents close by if I needed them. Did I *need* to stay close for college? Or did I *want* to stay close for college?

Both, I'd decided. My parents looked relieved when I

suggested we go shopping for dorm supplies, and of course, Wink and Honey stood firmly behind my decision.

I loved Hamilton. I really, really loved it. My orientation group had continued eating together long after orientation had ended, becoming a tight-knit friend group. A few of them had spent time on the Vineyard last month. "Yes, Luli!" they'd said when she and I had picked them up from the ferry, remembering her Hamilton visit in April. "So happy to see you!"

There were perks to being just up the hill from my parents, too. If I needed to do laundry, I could forgo the communal machines and walk home, and my friends loved coming to my house for a home-cooked meal every now and then. My mom was always excited to cook for a bunch of people. I'm trying a new lasagna recipe tonight, she would text me. Let me know if anyone's interested!

I had very few complaints.

Except that I missed Stephen. I missed Stephen *a lot.* "You're not going," I'd said during our final goodbye in Vermont. We were standing by the Raptor, my head buried in his shirt. "You're not going. You're coming to Clinton next weekend, preferably with maple sugar candies."

He'd laughed. "Are you going to tell yourself that for the next nine months?"

I knocked my head against his chest. "I'm going to damn well *try.*"

Long distance was even harder than I'd thought. We'd communicated every way possible, but it sometimes felt *im*possible. I'd sit in my dorm's common room until 8:00 a.m.

FaceTiming him and then cry my eyes out in the shower before leaving for breakfast. "She's in a Stephen Slump," my roommates had said on those days.

But there were Stephen Surprises, too. Without any warning, packages arrived in the mail with my name scribbled in all capitals. His handwriting had the power to stop my heart. My favorites included little souvenirs from his travels, a leather journal that always contained a new letter to me, and either a faded T-shirt or long-sleeved flannel that smelled like him: his orange shampoo, soap, sweat, and some new scent he'd picked up Down Under. I always wore the T-shirt to bed and the flannel around campus until they smelled like me, then sent them back with my own entry in the journal.

We'd ended up filling multiple notebooks—letters, drawings, stickers, song lyrics, poorly written poems. I told him I loved him for the first time in a notebook.

> I love you, Stephen. I adore you,
> but I love you even more.

"I love you, too, Killer," he'd said one night on the phone, and I grinned, knowing he'd finally gotten the notebook back. "I adore you, but I love you even more."

Nothing was better than spring break, though. Hamilton gave us two weeks off, and I'd spent them exploring Australia with him. We'd been apart seven months by that time. Stephen had laughed as I'd scrambled into his arms at the airport and tangled my hands in his hair. He hugged me tight. "You have no idea how much I've missed you climbing all over me."

Then we'd proceeded to be everyone's most annoying Instagram couple, taking pictures together around Australia and its lush landscapes. Never any captions, just #HitchMeToWitry.

Oh god... @mpdNOLA had commented on the first photo. It's back.

Hell yeah, it's back! @Sarah_Jane had replied. And better than ever!

When it was time for me to leave, neither of us would let go of the other, and I'd promised to be at the New Orleans airport when he flew back in May. Because that city was another fear I had conquered—Sarah and Michael had hosted Thanksgiving, and I'd loved it.

"Okay, good." Stephen had sagged in relief. "Ugh," he groaned. "Now I have to go back to Meredith Missings..."

Goose bumps had broken out on the back of my neck. "Wait a second," I'd said, pulling away to look at him. "What are *Meredith Missings*?"

I put the pies on the Annex's kitchen counter and then changed into a bikini I'd bought in Australia. The rest of my friends were still at work, so I packed a tote bag and headed to Secret Beach. Loki, Clarabelle, and a few other barking dogs ran across my path, tracking the scent of something.

Of course, Paqua Pond was deserted. I unrolled my towel and lathered on sunscreen before settling down and pulling a journal out of my bag. This one wasn't full of letters between Stephen and me; this one held only my handwriting. He had inspired me—if I could write letters to him, I could write letters to anyone.

Claire had treasured her collection of fountain pens, so I used only those, marking the date in deep blue ink. *Dear Claire*, I wrote.

> For some reason, today made me think of all the Paqua scavenger hunts we used to go on when we were little. Remember how Wink would create the clues? And The Farm map we drew together? I'll never forget that one summer when...

I didn't write to her every day, just when I missed her most. My therapist back home had helped me understand that no matter where Claire now read her books, she would *always* be my sister. Nothing could ever truly part us. Each letter was a memory, whatever came to mind in the moment, and I always signed them:

> Sending my love anywhere and everywhere,
>
> Mer

Afterward, I tucked the journal back into my bag and swam out to the pond's float. The worn wood planks were warm from the sun, so I stretched out and shut my eyes. It felt like I'd been asleep for only five minutes when I felt water being flicked onto my toes. I wriggled them but didn't fully wake up. Then I felt it again...and again...and *again*.

"Stephen!" I sat up, only to see that I was alone. "Nice try," I said, rolling onto my stomach to army crawl to the edge of the float. "I know you're here."

I still screamed when he broke the pond's surface, head popping up out of the water. He laughed at me, my fists raised as if ready to punch him. "Scared you," he said. "Didn't I?"

"How are you back already?" I asked.

Stephen's brow furrowed. "Work's long over," he said and glanced at the sky, at the slowly sinking sun. "Everyone's finished for the day."

Oh...so I *had* fallen asleep for longer than five minutes. My stomach began to twist, and Stephen kept a hand on my knee while treading water. "I wrote to Claire," I told him, running a few fingers through his slick hair. "Earlier—I wrote her a letter in my journal."

He nodded. "I wondered if you would, given what tonight is..." He trailed off and flipped his hand over. I took it and laced our fingers together.

We stayed silent until the sun had noticeably lowered in the sky. I raised our entwined hands and kissed his knuckles. "We better go," I said, slipping into the cool water beside him. "We're expected."

"Yeah," he said. "But first…"

I ducked underwater before he could kiss me, bubbles of laughter fluttering to the surface when he dipped under, too, and hugged me to him. Then I escaped his clutches and beat him back to shore. "Hurry!" I shouted. "If we're late, we'll have to do the dishes!"

The kitchen was crammed, so I took the baby outside. One of Honey's quilts was already spread out on the lawn, and I sat down to rock her in my arms. We smiled at each other—she was a very smiley baby. "I'm going to teach you everything," I told her. "I'm going to teach you everything there is to know about The Farm, and we'll have such fun together."

Only a minute passed before we heard her mother's voice. "Oh my god, where is she?" Sarah screeched from inside the house. Most of the windows were open to the evening breeze. "Where is Claire?"

"I believe my bride has her outside," Stephen said.

"Wit, sweetie, that's not how it works," Honey told him.

"Why not?" he asked. "Meredith is Claire's godmother, and I'm Claire's godfather—we're her godparents. It seems logical to me." A pause. "Plus, Mer's called me her *groom* once or twice."

"It was in a dream!" I shouted to him as everyone laughed. "It was one time, one dream!"

"Either way," Stephen said, "wouldn't you *love* to have me as a grandson, Honey?"

I blushed, and I could picture my grandmother blushing, too—she had such a crush on Stephen. He was living in the Big House this summer, and she cooked him breakfast every morning while merely mentioning to Wink that the coffee was ready.

"Oh, good!" Sarah joined me on the quilt and kissed her daughter's forehead. "I was wondering where you were, my little love."

The dinner table was covered in platters of delicious summertime food, surrounded by its usual mishmash of chairs. Uncle Brad and Aunt Christine boasted about their couples tubing victory that afternoon—my parents agreed to disagree—while I gave Aunt Rachel all the details about Eli's new boyfriend. Michael was holding Claire, and Sarah gazed adoringly at them, snapping pictures. And sitting high on his stool, Stephen talked to Aunt Julia about how he hoped to start an herb and vegetable garden somewhere on The Farm. "Moor House, ideally," he said. "I'm thinking that lawn is the most fertile."

Eventually, once the pies had been sliced and served with scoops of ice cream plopped on top, Wink rose from his chair, and the table quieted. "Tonight is a special night," he began, then backtracked. "Well, that's not entirely true. *Every* night with you"—he gestured around the table—"my family, is special. I cherish every beach day and every twilight tractor ride. Honey and I feel so lucky that we get to live here and watch our children grow and their children grow."

As if on cue, Claire gurgled.

Everyone chuckled. "Yes, Miss Dupré," Wink said, "and we're lucky to watch even *their* children grow." He smiled, the laugh lines around his eyes deepening. "But tonight is a special occasion," he continued, "because it marks the inauguration of a new chapter on The Farm." He nodded at Honey. "Darling, if you could..."

My grandmother disappeared into the house, and everyone gasped when she returned with a gleaming gold trophy. I reached for Stephen's hand under the table, my eyes stinging. I had already guessed what this meant, but I squinted at the elegant inscriptions as Honey passed the trophy off to my grandfather. My sister's name was inscribed over and over again, followed by Stephen's.

"The Claire Fox Cup," Wink told us, "will now be awarded to each summer's Assassin winner. I know you all appreciated those plastic medals, but this..." He trailed off and glanced down at the trophy, hand shaking a little. "Last summer, we played in memory of Claire, and from now on, we will *always* play in memory of Claire."

"Our Assassin goddess," Honey concluded. "Her legacy will live on forever."

The entire table applauded in solidarity. I squeezed Stephen's hand and then got up to hug my parents. My mom wiped away my tears and kissed my cheek.

"Oh, and one more thing," Wink said several minutes later, casually serving himself a third slice of peach pie. "Your targets will be assigned at midnight!"

———

I slipped out of bed when I knew my parents were asleep, even though I also knew I would wake them up when I left. The screen door and its rusty hinges hadn't lost their magic touch. "Not too late, Meredith," my mom called dreamily when it squeaked shut behind me.

The wind whipped as I crossed the field in my sweatshirt and pajama bottoms, and I laughed for no reason once I reached the Big House's driveway before crouching to pick up bits and pieces of crushed seashells.

Then I snuck around to the front of the house to throw them at Stephen's window. "Rapunzel, Rapunzel!" I whisper-yelled. "Get your ass down here!"

His window squeaked open. "Only if you promise to protect me!" Stephen whisper-yelled back. "Do you happen to have a *knife?*"

I giggled. Yes, my pocketknife was now at Paqua instead of hiding useless in a box at home. "Of course," I said. "Anyone who crosses our path is doomed."

Stephen laughed and climbed onto the porch's roof, effortlessly navigating it. He'd become practiced since his rooftop assassination last summer. After all, we did this every night.

Some nights we met here, others at the Annex, but every night, we went on rambling walks together. "Okay," he said once he'd shimmied down a column onto the ground. "Ready?"

I offered him my hand; he took it and twirled me into his arms so we could kiss. "Ready," I said afterward.

And we set off.

We talked about anything on these walks. We talked about everything. We talked about the future. Stephen was transferring from Tulane to University of Vermont, and he was excited to teach me to ski this winter. Meanwhile, I was excited we would be on the same coast, let alone the same *continent*.

I still insisted on my Stephen Surprises, though. I didn't care if it was just an autumn leaf or a UVM newspaper. When his packages arrived, when I saw his handwriting...

Well, it made me melt and my whole day better.

"Okay," he'd agreed, "just as long as I get my Meredith Missiles in return."

Tonight, we discussed Assassin. "Look at them!" Uncle Brad had accused at dinner, seeing us whispering to each other. "They're already plotting!"

"Actually, we're not," Stephen replied. "I was telling Mer how lovely she looks tonight."

It took everything for me not to laugh.

We'd so been plotting.

"Who do you have?" I asked now.

"Who do *you* have?" he answered.

I whispered a name in his ear.

He whispered a name back and then, "Should we make a new pact?"

"No." I shook my head. "You know we already have one." I climbed up his warm body and wrapped my legs around his waist, slinging my arms around his neck to run a hand through his hair. "Because I adore you, Stephen," I murmured. "I adore you, but I love you even more."

"As much as I love you, Killer?" he asked, grinning at me in the moonlight, his smile so crooked and perfect.

I didn't answer. I just kissed him, and then he just kissed me.

After sneaking out of Stephen's room early the next morning, I visited the old oak tree at the edge of the Annex's lawn and ran my fingers over Claire's notches in the trunk while imagining the inscriptions on her trophy. "I'm going to win," I whispered once I reached the final mark. "This year, I'm going to win."

ACKNOWLEDGMENTS

Again my top billing, again in bright lights: Eva Scalzo, my fantastic agent. You know I had to close the door to one world and its incredibly special characters in order to travel to this new one—thank you for understanding how difficult that was for me. Yet here we are, and I couldn't be happier. Thank you for possessing the unique ability to help me stitch together a story when all I do is shout random phrases over the phone: *Martha's Vineyard! Taylor Swift! Wedding! Sisters! Assassin! Timothée Chalamet! Notting Hill ending!*

What witchcraft is that?

Thank you for thinking I'm a delight, and please know that the feeling is mutual.

To my editor, Annie Berger: I believe I made a similar pitch to you? Perhaps it was a bit more specific? *Set over one week! A wedding on Martha's Vineyard! But also a competitive game of Assassin! A charming and quirky family! And a super cute romance!*

Either way, thank you for rolling with the concept and

letting me write the summer book of my dreams. All I want right now is to grab a copy, go to the beach, and read until the sun sets. I couldn't have done it without your support and guidance.

The team at Sourcebooks! I want to give major shout-outs to Cassie Gutman, Jackie Douglass, Ashlyn Keil, Alison Cherry, Nicole Hower, Michelle Mayhall, and to my amazing cover artist, Monique Aimee. Every inch of this book is a beauty to behold.

Martha's Vineyard: you enchant me. Our love affair began before I could walk, and I know it will last a lifetime. I especially am in awe of the Flynn family for working tirelessly to preserve such a slice of paradise and opening it up to me every summer. Paqua Farm did not simply pop into my head. I am so lucky to know what the obelisk really says.

To the Summer Squad of 2011—oh, what a week. We celebrated my sweet sixteen in custom and colorful T-shirts, Hayden boogied on the beach, and Scott shot Jen from the rooftop. Fun was had by everyone!

I also couldn't have written this book without weddings on the mind. Trip and Cindy Stowell, College Boy and Miss Machette, Hayden and Danielle Schenker, and of course, Jerry and Jennifer Walther. It took a fusion of four to create Sarah and Michael's special day.

Belated congratulations to you all, by the way.

Erica Brandbergh, I loved our laptop club and lattes. Thank you for keeping me in check during my drafting phase. "Are you writing?" you would ask (when you were supposed to be writing, too), to which I would sheepishly respond, "No, but I'm working on the Spotify playlist."

I am once again so appreciative of my beta readers: Delaney Schenker, Mikayla Woodley, Madeline Fouts, and Kelly Townsend. "This is the ultimate crack read!" might be one of the best compliments I've ever received, and Sarah DePietro, you have no idea how much your flummoxed silence and wild hand gestures fill my heart.

Much love to the NOLA crew! Josh, for being you. Kasi, for answering all my gumbo questions. And Katie, for letting me steal your beautiful son's name. If I am not already down there, I promise I'm coming soon.

At the homestead, thank you to the Brandberghs, Schenkers, and Webbers for letting me write at your kitchen or dining room tables when I got tired of writing at my own. Stacy, is it *geez* or *jeez*? More Sweetarts, please, Suzanne! Uh, Kathleen, which cat is which?

And MDS, where to begin? In a fifth-grade classroom, perhaps? With you wearing a green zip-up hoodie and striped boho skirt (#fashion), explaining to our teacher that you were supposed to be in *humanities*, not *social studies* like the rest of us? I could write you words upon words, but what it boils down to is this: thank you. Thank you, Madison, for writing Meredith's story with me. For carefully considering every brainstorm, for reading each chapter the morning after it was finished, for pumping me up whenever I lost steam. You are my favorite creative consultant, you are a freaking genius, you are my best friend. XO, K.

I am so grateful for everyone in the Walther family's orbit. This past year has been a universally difficult one, but thank you for all the love and support you have shown my family and me during our own trying time. Whether it was cooking us dinner or taking care of our dogs or hosting me for a night or two, thank you for your kindness and generosity.

The Webber clan: the Foxes would be nothing without you. Bits and pieces of our big family are weaved into these characters, and I wouldn't have it any other way. Thank you to Ross Webber most of all. I am not a grandfather, but writing Wink came so naturally because you are mine..

To Mom, H, and E: I hate the expression *Thank you for putting up with me.* But really...thank you for putting up with me. I had a one-track mind while drafting this book, and that didn't make me very easy to live with. I wasn't engaged in every conversation, my temper was extremely short, and for that I am sorry. Please know that I love you, I am here for you, and that I believe we will get through this. We are strong.

And finally, Dad. You knew this book was coming, but I wish you could've held it in your hands. I wish you could've flipped to the dedication page, nodded in that subtle way of yours, and said something sly like, "Two for two."

"No need to get greedy," I would've said back.

You have no idea how much I wish we could've had that moment, no idea how much I *miss* you. Twenty-four summers.

We had twenty-four Vineyard summers, and they were magical ones, ones I will treasure forever. I will treasure *you* forever, my wonderful, brave, loving father. While I might not be able to hear your laugh anymore or feel you shake my shoulders, I know you are still with me. We'll always walk The Farm's trails together.

ABOUT THE AUTHOR

K. L. Walther was born and raised in the rolling hills of Bucks County, Pennsylvania, surrounded by family, dogs, and books. Her childhood was spent traveling the northeastern seaboard to play ice hockey. She attended a boarding school in New Jersey and went on to earn a BA in English from the University of Virginia. She is happiest on the beach with a book, cheering for the New York Rangers, or enjoying a romcom while digging into a big bowl of popcorn and M&M's. Find her on Twitter @kl_walther or visit her online at klwalther.com.

#getbooklit

Your hub for the hottest young adult books!

Visit us online and sign up for our
newsletter at FIREreads.com

 @sourcebooksfire

 sourcebooksfire

 firereads.tumblr.com